Contents May Have Shifted

ALSO BY PAM HOUSTON

Sight Hound

A Little More About Me

Waltzing the Cat

Cowboys Are My Weakness

Contents May Have Shifted

A Novel

PAM HOUSTON

W. W. Norton & Company

NEW YORK · LONDON

For information about permission to reproduce selections from this book,
write to Permissions, W. W. Norton & Company, Inc.,
500 Fifth Avenue, New York, NY 10110

For information about special discounts for bulk purchases, please contact
W. W. Norton Special Sales at specialsales@wwnorton.com or 800-233-4830

Manufacturing by RR Donnelley, Harrisonburg, VA
Book design by Chris Welch
Production manager: Anna Oler

Library of Congress Cataloging-in-Publication Data

Houston, Pam.
Contents may have shifted : a novel / Pam Houston. — 1st ed.
p. cm.
ISBN 978-0-393-08265-4
1. Life change events—Fiction. 2. Travel—Fiction.
3. Self-acceptance—Fiction. 4. Domestic fiction. I. Title.
PS3558.O8725C66 2012
813'.54—dc23
2011042403

W. W. Norton & Company, Inc.
500 Fifth Avenue, New York, N.Y. 10110
www.wwnorton.com

W. W. Norton & Company Ltd.
Castle House, 75/76 Wells Street, London W1T 3QT

2 3 4 5 6 7 8 9 0

For Carol Houck Smith,
who loved books, and the places they took her

I turn everywhere,

I see shapes by which
a holiness declares itself more
and more, as if to be noticed

were all it wants of me.

—Carl Phillips, from *Armed, Luminous*

Theologians . . .
They don't know nothing,
About my soul.

—Jeff Tweedy, Mikael Jorgensen,
and Chris Girard, from *Theologians*

Contents May Have Shifted

UA #368

WE ARE TWO HOURS out of Sydney when the pilot's voice comes over the PA system. "Ladies and gentlemen," he begins, "I'm sorry to tell you this, but our instruments up here are indicating fuel system failure. We're on the phone with central in Chicago—they are advising us—and we've contacted Sydney air traffic to let them know we're headed back. You can probably tell we're making a big turn right now, and we're going to get you on the ground just as quickly as we can."

I pull my headphones out of the seat pocket to listen to the tower communications. I hear the words "747-400 heavy" right before the channel goes dead.

All around me people are turning back to their conversations and their magazines, rolling their eyes and shaking their heads like, *Oh those crazy airlines.* I listen for a shift in the tone of conversation and do not hear one. I ring my call button. Am I the only person on board who has experienced fuel pump failure in a car?

"The problem isn't that we don't have enough fuel," the handsome-in-a-rangy, greyhoundesque-way flight attendant says, "the problem is we've got too much. Our max landing weight is 630,000 pounds and we're probably over that by 200,000. We've got two giant overwing fuel tanks, and the captain can't tell which tank the fuel is coming from. If it's all coming from one side it won't take long before we have a serious balance problem."

"Not to mention if it stops altogether," I say.

"Right," he says.

I tell him I'm feeling a little panicked, and when I'm feeling a little panicked information usually helps.

"When we get close to Sydney we'll circle once to dump fuel," he says. "Then I'm betting he'll put us in crash position."

I know how to get into crash position. I have been in crash position an inordinate number of times.

We roar back to Sydney like a bat out of hell. The next time the pilot's voice comes over the speaker there is less apology, more bravado. "Ladies and gentlemen, this is your captain speaking. We are getting ready to land this airplane about 170,000 pounds heavier and about 60 miles per hour faster than regulations allow. The Sydney 240 A runway is the longest in the world, and we are about to use every square foot of it. In a few minutes the flight attendants will demonstrate modified crash position . . ."

I watch my friend the greyhound cross his arms over his head and brace against the imaginary seat in front of him. When the demonstration is over he stops in the aisle next to me.

"There's a good chance we're going to blow a tire," he says. "It might be uncomfortable for a few minutes, but generally speaking, when a tire blows, nobody dies," and then he is off.

We are getting close enough to the ground now to feel how unnaturally fast we are going.

"I thought we were going to dump fuel," I say, to no one.

"Not the bankrupt airline," says the Aussie next to me who is supposed to be going to his sister's wedding in San Francisco. "Do you have any idea how much 60,000 gallons of jet fuel costs? Not to mention the EPA fines. That's the Great Fucking Barrier Reef out there."

Not to mention, I think, if they pick the wrong wing to dump the fuel from we are all of a sudden upside down.

Never has a plane felt so heavy and sounded so loud. We hit the runway hard, and unimaginably fast, but we don't bounce and we don't swerve, and we come to a complete stop beyond the white lines, beyond the navigation lights, just before the blacktop turns to dirt. A cheer goes up inside the cabin. This time the captain's voice is softer.

"Ladies and gentlemen," he says, "Welcome back to Sydney. Your patience and cooperation is greatly appreciated. As you might imagine, our brakes are a bit overheated at the moment. We will sit out here for something just under an hour to let them cool, and then a technician will come out and inspect them, to see if they have enough grab left to stop us at our designated gate. At that point you'll disembark and you'll be directed to buses that will take you to a hotel for the evening. We'll get a good night's sleep and try this thing again tomorrow."

When we get off the plane in the golden light of late afernoon, the terminal is deserted. All the grates are pulled down over all the snack bars and newsstands and duty-free shops. There is no one to greet us at customs or passport control and we breeze right through like it's the end of the world and there are no more countries. Once we are on the bus, a lone customs official boards and puts a big red stamp in our passports that says DID NOT DEPART, which gives me pause.

If we never left Sydney, then who were the people on the plane they were so sure was going to explode on impact with the ground that they evacuated the entire terminal? Who were the people they had already assumed would be reduced to fuel dust and ash?

1. Georgetown, Great Exuma

Two o'clock on a Sunday afternoon in the Chat 'N' Chill bar on Stocking Island. KB, the Bahamian who owns the place, is looking for an argument and can't find one. Mandela versus Buthelezi, University of Chicago versus Harvard, chanterelles versus portobellos. Even Mushroom John, who brought his wife Sandy down here from their tuber farm in Pennsylvania for their twenty-fifth wedding anniversary, says the rule is, *To each his own.*

Down the beach Junior is making the best conch salad on the island, conch so fresh it is still wiggling when he puts it down in front of us. I drink two Goombay Smashes to Ethan's five Kalik beers and after some critical mass of mosquito bites we tumble outside to hit the blue, blue water. I told Ethan there is no blue like Exuma blue before we came and now he says, "It's so pretty, it's corny."

They call this archipelago the friendly islands—365 Exumas, one, they like to say, for every day of the year—and it's true, even the teenage boys with their skullcaps and their hooded eyes feel compelled to say hello when they pass us on the street. At the Peace & Plenty hotel Kaliks cost three dollars, but there is a reggae band at Eddie's Edgewater club on Fridays, and if you go to the kitchen door and smile politely, old Mrs. Beatrice Goodnight will sell you fried chicken, and peas and rice wrapped in the Sunday paper with salt.

For ten years, ending ten years ago, I came here with my friend Henry. We would sail his boat, whose name was *Parmenides*, down from Fort Lauderdale in November and spend the dangerous weeks between Thanksgiving and New Year's drinking rum, eating grouper, listening to "Son of a Son of a Sailor," sleeping in the open cockpit, and watching the Christmas lights called the Pleiades spin across the midnight sky. Henry is the only man I've known in my life that I knew how to love well, and as luck would have it, we were never lovers. I was the only woman in his life who knew that when he said, *Do you want to go to Paris? Do you want to go to Cuba? Do you want to take the mast off* Parmenides *and take her through the canals of Burgundy?* the answer was always *yes*.

Henry always paid for everything, which makes it seem only right that I pay for everything on this trip. Ethan has a PhD in poli sci and vacillating political ambitions. He lost a tight race for county commissioner on the Green Party ticket when he was barely out of grad school and now practices civil disobedience semiprofessionally, which, he often reminds me, is not the most lucrative use of his degree but yields many other rewards. I talked him into squeezing this trip in between a Rumsfeld resignation rally and a remembrance vigil for the miners in West Virginia.

Every Sunday at the Chat 'N' Chill, KB roasts a pig. Ethan

and I can smell it where we're floating, you can smell it all over the island when the wind is onshore. A stingray floats across the white sand below our floating bodies, and a little school of sergeant majors mistake the yellow in my bathing suit for one of their own. The floating is so effortless, the sun so soft and warm, I'm almost asleep when Junior hollers that the conch fritters are ready, and we swim to shore and eat them, roll them around in the red sauce that has just the right amount of kick to it, get in one more swim before it's time to eat the pig.

2. Davis, California

Early morning on the greenbelt. Walking with Sadie, while Helen leaps between furrowed, fallow fields. Everyone we know calls Sadie Helen and Helen Sadie, which is strange, since Sadie is a thirty-five-year-old woman, and Helen is a German short-haired pointer, but when you see the way they look at each other, you begin to understand.

Sadie has her sister's name—Annabelle—tattooed across her bicep. Last month, Annabelle tried to kill herself; succeeded, temporarily, was gone, in almost every way that counts, for more than two whole days. Then she came back from the dead.

Last night I heard a mockingbird imitating a car alarm in a jacaranda tree. This morning, a white heron teases Helen with a touch-and-go pattern along the creek.

I remember the day last fall when the grad students and I walked on Limatour Beach after the storm and watched the pelicans. The storm had brought out all the animals, tule elk, fallow deer, and three coyotes who ran and leapt and did the kinds of things coyotes do in Native American sand paintings, while we watched, openmouthed, from the side of the road. We saw so much wildlife that day Noah finally asked if I'd sent a guy ahead of us to push animals out of boxes. We were each locked inside our individual sorrows, didn't know each other well enough to share, but we agreed, out loud, that like moose, pelicans were surely put on earth to act as suicide preventers, agreed we'd never kill ourselves within the sight of one.

3. Ozona, Texas

Nine o'clock on a Thursday night, the bar full of Halliburton guys in their red all-in-one suits, roughnecks in from the oil fields for preseason football, hunting stories, and beer. It is just dumb luck that I've worn my camo miniskirt, and I take the best seat in the house for watching the Patriots beat up on the Redskins, until the bartender comes over and tells us we've entered a private club.

Ethan rises to leave. He recognizes enemy territory, knows that environmentalists and Halliburton guys shouldn't drink together, especially not in Texas.

"In that case," I say, "I'll take two memberships and two double shots of Patron Silver and a Coca-Cola back."

We can mark this down as my last fearless moment, because even though I've already seen the photo of the sad-eyed Romanian in Ethan's glove compartment, I haven't really let her sink in. She's married to a high-ranking political official. Every time Ethan goes over there to visit her someone comes up to him in a trench coat and says, "You know the price of a man in Bucharest is one hundred dollars U.S."

I tell Ethan with a straight face that the Romanian's essential unavailability denies me all my magical qualities, then I ask him for money for the jukebox. He gives me three dollars and I play every antiwar song I can find wedged in between Clint Black and the If You Don't Believe in Freedom We'll Kick Your Fuckin' Ass Quintet: "Who'll Stop the Rain," and "Imagine" and "War," *Good God, y'all, what is it good for, absolutely nothing, say it again.*

By the third round of Silver we've won the bartender over, we can tell because the tequila starts coming in tumblers.

Ethan says, "You might be the first woman to ever drink in this bar," and I say, "You might be the first conscientious objector." Later, in the parking lot of the Best Western, I pick up both our heavy suitcases and make a beeline for the stairs.

Ethan says, "No! Pam, no!" which makes me lift the bags higher and run for it, and when I get to the top I laugh so hard I pee.

4. Juneau, Alaska

They said we wouldn't see any orcas. They said the humpbacks were in and when the humpbacks were in you didn't see the orcas, because the orcas are predators and the humpbacks are prey.

It's been a long day. We've been all the way up Tracy Arm to the glaciers and everyone but the captain and I are sleeping when word comes over the radio: Orcas in Shearwater Cove.

By the time we get there there's nothing stirring. A couple of lazy humpbacks out in the main channel a sure sign that the orcas are gone. The captain is worried about the hour, worried about the fuel he's got left, worried about his daughter, who's got magenta hair and a T-shirt that says *THIS is what a feminist looks like*, who is back from somewhere like Reed College working on his boat this summer, selling sodas to the tourists through a permanent scowl.

There's a fin flash on the far side of the channel, distant but unmistakable. Orca. Male.

The captain says, "That's four miles across this channel, minimum."

I show him the silver charm around my neck, remind him that it's my last day in Alaska, promise to swim for shore if we run out of gas.

"Don't lose that fin," he says, turning the bow into the sunset, but I couldn't lose it if I tried, the water of Stephen's Passage backlit, a million diamonds rushing toward me in the sun, and one black fin, impossibly tall, absurdly geometric, the accompanying blast of whale breath above it, superimposed onto the patterns of light.

Spotting whales at sea is not so different from spotting deer in the woods. For hours you see nothing, and then you see one, and suddenly you realize you are surrounded. This pod has twenty-five, by my best counting, the one male, who keeps his distance, and twenty-four females, all of them running steadily west.

We get out in front and the captain shuts down the engines. Every time the big male's fin turns itself up and over and back down under the surface of the water, I can't help myself, I gasp. We are directly in the path of one of the females. Every time she surfaces we can hear her breathing, every time she surfaces I can see the spot of white at her heart. Twenty years ago, on my first trip to Alaska, I bought a string of white-heart trade beads, and for this trip I tore the house apart to find them.

In three more dives she'll be under the boat. I touch the beads at my neck and try to guess which side of the boat will get me the closest. The others are stirring, crowding the port side, watching her approach. I choose starboard. She dives one last time and I start counting, at five she rises right under my hand. The breath from her blowhole is cold on my face. If I dared I could reach down and touch her on her white spot. Someone behind me screams, maybe the captain's daughter, but the whale is already diving, already resurfacing a few yards farther on.

I listen to the sweep of her fin, the puff of her breathing until she disappears into the disappearing diamonds. When the male's big fin is the only thing visible—a speck on the horizon, we turn the boat north and head for home.

5. Good Hope, Jamaica

The sun is high above the Cockpit Country, and Jude and I are getting stoned at the pool. I am way too old to smoke pot, but Jude isn't and he convinces me, you wouldn't go to Italy and not drink the coffee, you don't go to Jamaica without smoking the weed. And he's right. This pot is so potent that every time the sun reemerges from behind the cotton-ball clouds I think a cartoon character I've invented called Big Mr. Sunshine is caressing my arms with baby-powdered hands.

Jude's brother died in a car accident when Jude was eighteen.

Four months later Jude was the one to walk in on the body of his mother. Four months later his father went to jail. For the five years after that Jude played Division I hockey, turned his entire focus toward dodging the pucks that were continually flying at his head. Then his goalie knees gave out and the next logical thing was to try to become a writer.

Good Hope is a papaya plantation that for a few weeks each year turns itself over to the making of art. Last night the ceramicists pulled an all-nighter to fire up the big wooden kiln and the writers decided to stay up with them. It was quite a party, writers throwing pots, potters writing pantoums, the big clay figures glowing crimson inside the house-sized kiln like bodies, the oncologist from Santa Fe unable to resist a recitation of "The Cremation of Sam McGee."

Jude's been on a tear around the world this year: Iceland, Finland, Amsterdam, Jamaica. After this he is supposed to go see his brother's grave for the first time since his family blew up—his expression—and even to talk about it makes him shake in his chair.

"You don't have to do that if you aren't ready," I tell him. "Your brother is with you every second; it doesn't make any difference to him whether or not you stand at his grave."

I am thinking, as I say this, about Henry, about how every time I drive over Kenosha Pass late at night on the way from the Denver airport to Creede, he seems to want to have a conversation, which makes no sense whatsoever because when he was alive he was an urban guy and a warm-weather fan to boot.

The sun moves out of the clouds again, turning the flowers a purple I thought existed only in coral reefs and crayons. "You're right," Jude says, "thank you," though we don't fool each other for a second, and that's how we know we are friends.

6. Creede, Colorado

The first snow fell on the peaks today. An edgy wind brought clouds that looked like thunderheads, but when they cleared, just before sunset, everything above 11,000 feet was blanketed, not in white, but in chrome.

I have only recently come back to this place of ice-colored stars strewn across ink-dark sky, where frost on the wooden walkway is likely every night of the year—and heavy tonight—where I scare up a barn owl traveling the short hundred yards between my door and my car, and his wingbeat is the loudest sound for ten square miles. The owl stops me in my tracks, makes me take a breath of the cold night air, and when I do I think, *I am breathing in the stars.*

Yesterday I walked with six of the best women I know up above Spring Creek Pass to the 12,000-foot flattop called Jarosa Mesa. Cinder, Mackenzie, Willow, Hailey, Nora, and Practical Karen. Our ages span twenty years, thirty-four to fifty-four, and what we have in common is a love of the world so fierce it makes us edgy.

The aspens near the pass are holding their breath this week, hints of yellow and crimson, the meadow grasses high after August's monsoon. We talk about Myanmar, Cuba, New Orleans. We talk about stepchildren, wind pants, Italian food, sex. We snack on the season's first clementines and raspberry Fig Newmans. To the west of the mesa the 14ers lay themselves before us, a multicolored kingdom of stone: Handies Peak, Sunshine Peak, Redstone Peak, the Wetterhorn, and Uncompaghre.

Ethan is in Tampa this balmy midnight, sitting on his temporary front porch surrounded by chirping lizards, writing a speech against offshore drilling by the glow of a string of Christmas lights, the paper curling at the edges, his hand damp where he holds the pen.

If I die tonight it will be with every single thing unfinished (like, I suppose, any other night), and yet, what a gift to die on the verge of tears. I have spent my life trying to understand the way this rock and this ache go together, why a granite peak is more dramatic half dressed in clouds (like a woman), why sunlight under fog is better than the sum of its parts, why my best days and my worst days are always the same days, why (often) leaving seems like the only solution to the predicament of loving (each other) the world.

It's hard to know whether the bigger problem is space or time. The forty-three years I didn't get to miss Ethan, the unlimited rent-a-car miles between Tampa and anywhere he could really see the stars. All the way across the I-40 last month, the sky kept making him offers: thunderclouds over Flagstaff, a double rainbow near Tucumcari, and Mars, the closest to the Earth in fifty thousand years, burning candy-apple red and following the moon from Albuquerque to Gallup, while we went the other way—the *wrong* way, any given star would tell you—hurtling west to east.

7. Vancouver, British Columbia

The bi-polar halibut fisherman from Kodiak with ocean eyes and biceps like something right out of Michelangelo. He's spent ten years in Joburg, ten years in Bangkok, ten years back and forth between Kodiak and B.C. As a result, his mouth does crazy things to the letter *o*, the letter *h*, and anything with a lot of *r*'s in it.

He tells me he doesn't like to throw around words like *CIA* and *Special Forces*. He tells me we've been put on earth to crack each other open, and then to stick around long enough to watch the thing that, having been cracked open, suddenly shines. He says he knows there is only a thin wall between himself and all that shining, but sometimes he forgets how thin the wall is, because somebody came along when he wasn't looking, and painted the damn thing black. He tells me he has tried three different times, but he just can't stick with the lithium. Even when he talks about not wanting to use his powers for world domination, even when he uses the phrase "dark arts," he looks like a little boy who wants more than anything to catch a fish.

When I tell my friend Fenton the human about him, Fenton hears *Kodiak*, hears *fisherman*, hears *bi* and *polar*, without the hyphen, and asks if maybe we can share him. When I remind Fenton about Ethan, he reminds me about the Romanian in the glove compartment. "Love gets bigger after forty," Fenton tells me. "After forty, love says, 'Come one, come all.' "

8. Laramie, Wyoming

In the summer, the trains come through town more than once an hour, and Ethan and I, locked all night in the bookstore like a fantasy left over from clumsy childhood, pulling books off whatever shelves we want to and reading to each other—poems first, and then settling into stories—on the old purple couch.

We came down from Walden, *Moose Capital of Colorado.* I was sure we would find some marker on the fence where Matthew Shepard had been tied.

Later, when we have turned out all the lights in the bookstore and thrown the mattress on the floor in the back room, the cowboy band across the street tries to play "Free Bird" as an encore, and I watch his face above me change color with the flashing light. He takes my hand and makes me feel the place we come together.

Holy, he says, not believing in God.

9. Oakland, California

Drinking espresso with Cinder at a two-top outside Blue Bottle Coffee, waiting for the phone to ring. Cinder had her needle biopsy last Thursday, is expecting results today. She is the same age now her mother was, when she was first diagnosed with breast cancer. After the news, good or bad, we are going to the spa for Watsu, where a large and beautiful woman named Amanda will float us around a pool one at a time, twist us and turn us, all the time supporting us, pull us tight against her shoulder, her arms snug under our butts, and rock us into something like sleep.

In the car on the way home, after the first Watsu, Cinder said, "So did that kind of freak you out when she held you like a baby?' and we laughed so hard she had to pull to the side of the road. Now we can't get enough of Amanda and the way she holds us like a baby. Both of our mothers have been dead a long time.

The only good thing about finding the Romanian in the glove compartment was looking forward to telling Cinder that in the ensuing argument I had referenced my own magical qualities.

When I told Cinder that after sex in the missionary position (the Romanian won't let Ethan do anything her husband doesn't do), the Romanian ran around the hotel room saying *I'm a motel whore, I'm a motel whore,* Cinder started calling him the stupid fucking politico who won't get out of his own stupid fucking way. "SFP," Cinder said, "like sunscreen, after forty-five it's all the same."

Beyond the empty lot and the abortion clinic, the seagulls are cracking jokes over the silvery surface of Oakland's Inner Harbor. I say, "What was the best piece of advice your mother ever gave you?" Cinder thinks a minute, and reddens. "It was when Matthew and I had our first big fight," she says, "Valentine's Day, 1994. I didn't think we were going to make it. I called her out of desperation. 'Honey,' she said, 'can I just ask you one question. You know when you are having your period? Are you giving Matthew enough blow jobs during those times?'"

Cinder's cell phone rings and we both stare at it a minute before she answers. I start counting inside my head, and when I get to seven, relief breaks across Cinder's face like sunshine. I realize with some surprise that I am paralyzed with gratitude. If this building were on fire, I could not use my legs to move away.

10. Gulfport, Mississippi

Ethan and I walk out on the pier to watch the pelicans dive. On the way back we pass a young man in a wheel chair. He is smoking a cigarette, taking long pulls off a bottle inside a paper bag. He is sunken in on himself in the particular way of the dying, but has a look of such despair on his face I know that in that way, at least, he is still very much alive. Ethan doesn't notice his ball cap, brown corduroy, the word *worthy* embroidered in cursive, in gold.

When Henry's colon cancer came back the second time, the end came very fast, and he wouldn't let his wife or his sons call me until after he was dead and buried. When his youngest son finally called a week after the funeral, he told me Henry decided I'd had enough death in my life already, and he didn't want to serve me up any more.

Now in Gulfport, it takes Ethan and me ten minutes to gather the courage to go back up the pier and talk to the young man in the wheelchair. From a hundred yards away, he watches us in our deliberations. Ethan and I can never decide anything, where to go to dinner, whether or not to stay together, what to do about the Romanian in the glove compartment. By the time we go to him, ask in quiet, nervous voices if there is anything we can do for him, he feels equally sorry for us.

11. Madison, Wisconsin

Saturday morning. Middle of October. Good strong coffee from Michelangelo's. Last night Ethan sang "You Can Close Your Eyes" to my voice mail, and I did, and for the first time this week, slept for six hours straight.

This morning on State Street a little blond girl—maybe three—threw the kind of temper tantrum we'd all like to throw, long and loud, and almost entirely artificial. "Jessica," her mother said, in a perfectly reasonable tone, "I'm going to have to ask you for your complete cooperation . . ."

Fenton the human called to say he has come up with the perfect book for us to write together, *Pam and Fenton's Tales of Failed Love and Romance,* chapter one, mine, called "I Can't Believe I Slept with a Politician," followed by chapter two, his, "I Can't Believe I Slept with a Priest."

Everything I know about Wisconsin can fit in one paragraph. It is the home of the Butter Burger. It is the state where, on the day his father died, Brett Favre had the game of his life.

On Thursday I gave my class this assignment: Write your own suicide note. There was half a beat where they all looked at me, and then each other. "No problem," Noah said. "I'll just go to my computer and call one up."

12. Tampa, Florida

Eight o'clock on a Friday night and downtown is rolled up tight. Half a block from the old Tampa Theatre, lights, voices, and the slow roll of reggae spilling out into the street. Ethan and I have been having a hard time finding fun in Tampa, and the Jamaicans at the Jerk Hut seem to be having some. It has the feel of a private party, and no one else there is white, but the bouncer says five-bucks-a-person cover, twelve for a bucket of Red Stripes, you can get yourself some food in the back.

We fill a plate with jerk chicken and fried bananas, open two beers and settle in on the perimeter. The band is talented, everyone in the place knows the words and sings along, and even though Ethan keeps trying to bend the lyrics political, all the lines I catch are about love and sex and girls.

Ethan is not a dancer, but the beat is irresistible, so I compromise, as others do, by swaying in my chair. When we are not ignored entirely, we are looked at with pleasant curiosity.

Earlier that day, I was trying to buy some grouper somewhere other than a supermarket, and the woman at the Born Again Produce Stand sent me to the Fresh Fish Market in the projects. "It's crazy," she said, "water, water everywhere, but that's the only one there is."

The Fresh Fish Market was in a strip mall. Next door at the Joyful Noise Holiness Tabernacle of Jesus Christ, beautiful teenage girls in white and purple robes holding hymnals were lining up to go inside. There was only one grouper fillet left and the woman behind me in line said she wanted to arm wrestle me for it, before she broke into a smile so wide it showered the dingy market walls with light. "Sister got lost on the way to the Publix," she said.

Back at the Jerk Hut, the band is on break and Ethan says, "We might be the only white people to ever drink in this bar." And I say, "And you might be the only conscientious objector."

I'm beginning to understand that when we want to kill ourselves, it is not because we are lonely, but because we are trying to break up with the world before the world breaks up with us.

When the band comes back, a waitress named Shaila with beaded dreadlocks and bright green pumps takes both my hands and pulls me to the dance floor. She says, "We are going to get *everybody* dancing tonight." Two songs later she says, "I'm going back to get the mister," and I know Ethan won't be able to resist her invitation. She brings him to me on the dance floor, and two songs later Shaila gets her wish, every single person—even the bouncer, even the kitchen ladies, are dancing—joyful—to the beat.

#N577WA

I AM FLYING OUT of the Little Delta drainage, tucked illegally
into the luggage area of George White's converted Super Cub.
Converted, that is, to haul gear instead of a passenger. It is not
that my presence puts us in danger, George assures me, I am well
within the aircraft's specs, weighing, as I do, significantly less than
a boned-out moose or caribou. But there is no seat for me, not to
mention a belt, so my instructions are to make myself look like a
duffel bag when we land in Fairbanks, and wait for the all-clear
from George before I untangle my limbs and crawl over his seat
to the door.

George is one of many pilots who found their way to Alaska
more or less straight from Vietnam. I once saw him break a nine-
year-old boy's arm at the dinner table right after the boy, in an
attempt to get his mother's attention, put the tines of his fork
through the back of her hand. I have also watched him dig through
buckets of rusted nuts and bolts to find the one ancient screw that

will restart a seemingly defunct airplane engine. He likes to push both the light and the equipment, landing on airstrips made of nothing but river rock between steep canyon walls deep into the Alaskan twilight.

George uses a great deal of duct tape. He has gone down three times because of some combination of weather and equipment failure, and he has walked away each time, once for seventy-five miles before he hit the nearest road.

His brother, who I flew with out on the coast from Dry Bay to Yakutat—the clouds forcing us so low that we could feel the spray from the breakers on the bottom of the aircraft, so low that we could watch the brown bears chasing each other off the wild strawberry patches on the beaches—had not been so lucky. His death slowed down George's adrenaline-seeking tendencies not one iota.

Normally George flies me in and out of the backcountry in the Maule, his newest and safest plane, the only one licensed, in fact, for commercial passengers, but today the Maule is down, and so I am in the back of the ancient but trusty Cub, my knees up around my ears, as the wheels leave the rocky runway.

It is only about a forty-five-minute flight back to Fairbanks, where, in winter, pilots have to call ahead and ask the luggage handlers to chase moose off the runway. But this is September, and the tundra is red and golden below us, giving way, as we head down valley, to dense forest, an occasional moose standing in a little tarn carved out long ago by the glaciers. We have seen five big bulls since we became airborne.

We are about halfway to Fairbanks when the engine sputters and quits, and George's hand jerks up to the tank control, and then his shoulders slump, and he says, "Shit," and I say, "What," and he says, "What do you think? We're out of gas."

What scares me more than anything is the violence with which he jerked his hand.

For ten or twenty seconds we ride in the very particular silence of a small plane gradually losing altitude and then George says, "Do you remember, like in the last few minutes, any place we could maybe put this thing down? A lake, a dirt road, even a river?"

What I remember from the last few minutes are a few tiny glacial tarns and a million frost-heaved spruce trees, pointing drunkenly in every direction. "I don't," I say.

"Here," he says, shoving the open aviation chart over the seatback toward me, "we are somewhere around in here," he indicates vaguely with his finger. "See if you can see anything up ahead, even a cut for a power line . . . sometimes those are wide enough."

I try to make sense of the map fast, try to ignore the fact that the treetops are getting closer. "It looks like there is some kind of dwelling to the north," I say, "with a little road coming into it," and he says, "How far?" and I say, "Four or five miles," and he says, "I don't think we can make that."

I know plenty about the need to be airborne, and plenty about how raising the degree of difficulty sweetens the pot. I understand why Alaska and why fly-in-only Alaska and why even that isn't far out enough. I know what it's like to feel calmer—better—face to face with a female grizz at dusk on a caribou trail than when I'm contemplating, say, a year, or a month, or even a week in the significant comforts of my very own house. I know all about the anatomy of restlessness and the crossover point of adrenaline addiction, but I'm not quite ready to be accessory to George's own personal death wish, even so.

"Can't hurt to try," I say.

By my best guess we are now less than 2,000 feet above the treetops.

"Well," he says, "there is *one* other thing we could do," and I say, "What's that?" and he says, "Switch to the reserve fuel tank."

And with that he raises his hand to the little lever, switches it to the left, points the nose slightly downward, and the single engine sputters back to life.

13. Bumthang Valley, Kingdom of Bhutan

Christmas Eve. Darkness falls quickly and early, and when it does, the temperature drops sixty degrees. Before sunset Ethan and I stood on our balcony overlooking the Bumthang River watching the thousands of white prayer flags that line the river's course, that stand all over town in battalions of forty to four hundred, that move in the wind like something alive.

In December, all the colors of Jakar are muted: browns, grays, and silvers, the river an icy line of mercury that runs through the middle of town. Now the stars are emerging, Orion and the Pleiades straight overhead—Christmas guests who always come on time, even here, where no attention gets paid to Christian holidays—and Sirius, the dog star, the brightest solitaire in the Himalayan night.

We put on layers of fleece, hats, neck gators, boots, and gloves and walk a couple miles up the road to the monastery. The monks are bustling around in their saffron robes, goose-fleshed elbows flapping in the cold, many of them barefoot against the icy stones of the courtyard. Many of the younger monks are here only because their families cannot afford to feed them. A boy no more than six toting a giant bucket of water grins at me as he walks past.

Karma asks the Master for permission to enter and we take our seats in the back row. Ethan is too stiff to cross his legs monk-style so he holds his knees like little peaks in front of him. The monks begin chanting, drums and gongs, the songs half hymnal, half college fight song (to engage, and then intimidate the evil spirits, Karma will tell us later).

The Master makes the rounds, walking the rows between the boys, gently waking the ones who have nodded off, lost in a half-trance of his own. He is balding, fortyish, with a pleasant and somewhat apologetic countenance. If he lived in the States you'd peg him as a junior high school basketball coach, or the only decent salesman on a car lot, the one you feel so lucky to have snagged. I picture him, momentarily, in a Craftsman in West Denver, a plump sweet-faced wife and two toddlers in the yard. I picture Ethan in a saffron robe, devoted to the brotherhood, having sworn what these monks have sworn, never to be touched by a woman.

Concurrent with the Romanian in the glove compartment, it turns out, is a Costa Rican who picked Ethan up in a bar by asking, "Do you have the heart to go with those eyes?" Eventually revealed to be a line from a Dutch Top 40 pop song, it still got the Costa Rican—whose name is Fatimah—some slice of the last four years with Ethan, excepting the times he's in Bucharest, avoiding his lover's husband and his posse of trench coats, and the time he spends with me.

Women have a surprisingly hard time getting over Ethan. The woman he broke up with sixteen years ago still keeps a room for him in her house. Once when he tried to call things off with Fatimah she made him promise he'd never bring another woman into her whole *country*. Even his high school girlfriend (Class of '73) recently won *Redbook*'s "Rekindle Your Old Flame" contest by writing an essay about why he should fly across the country on the magazine's bill to see her, to have drinks and then dinner, and see what might be left after thirty years.

I asked him how many people entered the contest.

"Thousands," he said, humbly. "Actually, tens of thousands, I recall, the editor said."

14. Horseveldt Camp, Wrangell Mountains, Alaska

Early morning in the cook cabin. Outfitter Frank sits in the dim glow of a kerosene lamp with a cup of coffee on the table next to him, *The Collected Poems of Mary Oliver* in his hand. The day I arrived, he introduced me to the horses.

"I call this one Faggot," he said, watching for my reaction. "Because he's got beautiful gaits."

Later that day, after we had dismounted to walk our horses up a steep stretch of trail to a meadow and were getting ready to remount, Frank indicated a huge mound of the humped-up bunch grass that alternates with muskeg to make up the Alaskan tundra.

"Come on over, Pam," he said. "There's a niggerhead here with your name on it."

Frank is a man who cares deeply for his animals and a man who cares deeply for the land. He bought Horseveldt three years ago from another hunting guide, and he's got dreams of expanding the hunting operation, and also of keeping history alive. The lowest and greenest spot in the St. Elias ecosystem, Horseveldt has been a place where hunters, trappers, prospectors, and settlers have wintered their horses for more than a hundred years.

The horse I have been assigned is named Flint.

"Spirited," Wrangler Luke called him.

"Sometimes he sees boogers," Frank said.

Flint is the smallest horse at Horseveldt, and next to the ten others, big Morgan geldings with dinner-plate feet, I wonder how he holds his own. Frank brought Flint and two of his Arab-quarter horse cousins in two summers ago, and when winter came the Morgans took off over a ridge and left the three Arabs to fend for themselves against the twenty-foot drifts and the ice storms and the bears. Only Flint made it through that first winter, and Frank says he's a whole lot spookier now.

"You would be too," he said, "if you saw your two best friends turn into a pile of bones while you sat there waiting to see if you'd ever get another meal or be one."

It's hard for me to imagine how Flint gets by, even in summer, his tiny Arab feet poking deep suctiony holes into the tundra while the Morgans set their big flat paddles down on top. Flint goes belly deep into some of the bogs with me on top of him, and one day, when we have to cross a swift and icy river, I cling to his neck while he tries to find spaces between the rounded boulders to put his little feet. I can feel the water rise over the tops of my boots, over the tops of my knees, and then we are going over sideways into the heart-stopping cold. We get washed a couple hundred yards downstream before he finds his footing and drags himself—me clinging with one hand to the saddle, the other to his tail, flutter-kicking for all I am worth, into an eddy.

Before I left the town of McCarthy to take the four-seater plane into Horseveldt, I called Ethan and asked if he wanted me to come home from Alaska two days early to make the drive with him from Sacramento to Tampa and he said, *Absolutely not.*

After Flint and I don't drown in the river I make a list, on the back of the tag that is against the law to remove from my sleeping bag, of all the people I'm pretty sure would be happy to have my company on a drive from Sacramento to Tampa and come up with twenty-four.

Now, in the quiet of the predawn, Outfitter Frank says, "Have you read these poems about her father?" and I say that I have. He says, "Don't they just want to break your heart?"

Part of me wants to tell Frank that Mary Oliver is gay. Part of me wants to ask Frank about his own father, or tell him about mine. Instead I back out the door into the mist-soaked morning, leaving him with his coffee and the poetry. I can hear the hobbled Morgans hopping along in the river gravel, making their way toward camp.

15. Ichetucknee Springs, Florida

Easter Sunday, our butts stuck down in inner tubes, floating seven miles of crystal-clear spring-fed waters, under live oaks, between mangroves. How this place has survived the concretization of Florida is beyond my understanding, but here we are, floating, the only other people in our line of sight a dad and his son in a sit-on-top kayak.

Giant turtles sun themselves on fallen logs, their shells a mosaic of oranges and greens. They lift one back foot at a time and stretch it as far out of their shells and into the sunlight as it will go. A banded kingfisher darts from tree to tree in front of us.

Ethan likes floating more than anything. In the bathtub, in Exuma, and here, in the inner tube, the hours of another holiday ticking safely away. Ethan and I don't have a relative left alive between us, which makes holidays easy, except when it makes them impossible. Easter at Ichetucknee is a no-brainer. No rabbit, no chocolate, no Christ on a Cross.

Last night, in the hotel room in Gainesville, Ethan, still asleep, raised his hand and said *Bingo!* He woke himself up just enough to tell me he'd dreamed he won the bingo game at the gay fundraiser, that the guy next to him only needed one more number for the longest time, but Ethan had filled his card first.

Ethan has the sweetest dreams of anyone I have ever known, which I would like to think is the sign of a clear conscience. One night, in Lubbock, he said, from sleep, "You pretend to be an elephant, and I'll pretend to be an elephant."

Another night he woke me to tell me he had had a terrible

nightmare. He had gone to the Pyramids, he said, and they wouldn't let him in.

16. Negro Bill Canyon, Utah

Change of season in the desert after a good wet winter. The piñions are full of gray berries, the claret cup is brilliant red, the paintbrush, globe mallow, and skyrocket gilia are all full and bright. In the late afternoon, the light softens, and the rugged, grass- and cacti-covered hillside looks as inviting as a clover field.

Such great pleasure setting up my old VE-24. The snap of the shock-corded poles, the feel of slickrock under my boots. Lizards doing push-ups in the sand.

I've brought Ethan's pictures here with me. In one he's wearing my Avalanche jersey and in the other my Broncos sweatshirt, as if I can make him a Coloradoan by some kind of voodoo. Also, a book of Katherine Mansfield's stories, all servants and garden parties, strange pairing with these orange canyon walls.

Only yesterday, Willow and Nora and I woke up in Calistoga at 6 a.m. and hit the mineral pool, which is Olympic-size and gives off great clouds of steam into the early, chilly air. We swam laps and floated until the pool felt too warm and more than a little clammy, and then we put on our white robes and stood in front of the funhouse mirror, which gave us short short legs and elongated torsos, and hands like dwarves or Thai dancers, depending on where we held them in the frame.

One plane flight, a seven-hour van ride, and six miles of

backpacking later—because this is how *I* roll—my therm-a-rest is self-inflating in the tent and the writing students from the Women's Wilderness Institute are scattered across the slickrock in their bright fuzzy clothes like pieces of ribbon candy.

The U.S. Government changed the name of this canyon *to* Negro Bill in 1967, over the protests of the locals, stopping at least one tick short of a real fix. Bill Granstaff grazed sheep and cattle here from 1877 to 1881, when he was run out of the area for selling whiskey to the Indians. In the eighties a change to African-American Bill's Canyon proved too heavy to fly, and in the nineties a simpler Bill's Canyon got voted down on the grounds that it denied Bill his heritage, which makes the recent suggestion of Brother Bill Canyon seem like a winner all the way around.

Danika, the yoga instructor, is the only one of us who has been willing to say the name of the canyon out loud, and she says "Nay-gro," giving the old moonshine maker a decidedly Spanish flare. I'm the teacher of record here, but Danika hasn't stopped talking since we shouldered our backpacks, and for the rest of this day that suits me fine.

At the last English department potluck, an eighteenth-century expert named Yolanda said, "I find it really disturbing, that you think of me as a human being." Yolanda is tall, dark, and thin, utterly lovely. "It's okay if my students think of me as a human being, but I don't want my colleagues to think of me that way, especially not my senior colleagues."

"How should we think of you?" I asked her.

"Gray matter," she said, as if it were obvious, "gray matter producing text."

"I know what you are afraid of," Ethan said, our last night in Wyoming. "You are afraid that I will sleep through all the good parts."

Once when I drove all night to San Diego just to see him he said, "I'm not displeased that you are here." Another time when he said, "My feelings about you are in no way ambivalent," I tried to put the very best spin on it possible.

It is always the skinny girls who want to peel off their clothes and go swimming. It is called Morning Glory Arch, but the canyon below it is covered with poison ivy.

The sun goes behind the wall of Negro Bill Canyon, and for the first time today the yoga instructor lowers her voice.

17. Santa Cruz Province, Argentina

Estancia La Oriental is a slice of paradise, set down neatly on the shore of Lago Belgrano, at the edge of a huge, green, bird-filled horse-heaven of a meadow behind rows of Lombardi poplars, planted fifty rows deep in a dedicated attempt to block the wind.

This morning, after breakfast, I follow Areillo on horseback up to Lago Volcán, straight up a green moraine littered with hummocks, then across a broad flat swath of the Continental Divide, like God's giant roadway, smooth rock with patches of moss, the peaks getting more and more backlit all the way to Chile. We walk along the beach of the lake, the turquoise of glacier water spun up in wind-created waves coming right at us like giant plates of sea glass. Making a circle above the lake are five condors. They are huge and playful, a little like our vultures, but like everything in Patagonia, much bigger, with wing feathers several feet long.

When I ask Areillo if he has always been a gaucho he says *yes*, and when I ask him why he likes it he says, *Es vida linda.*

In the 1900s Patagonia was an ocean of grass, ten fists high as far as the eye could see, but thousands of Europeans came in the twenties, and more in the forties. There were five fists, then two fists. Areillo's generation is the last of the gauchos because now there is not even one fist left. "First the grass ran out," he says, "eventually the women left. Now we eat what is left of the sheep and drink a lot of Kool-Aid."

I am here to do a story on the gauchos, who, as far as I can tell, put American cowboys to shame. They sleep out in the wild on only their sheepskins, bring no food or water but forage for both, and they gallop, barefoot and stirrupless, all day, sometimes barely taking a break. A gaucho can find his way, Areillo tells me, by the Southern Cross at night, and by the direction of the wind in the day. That's how consistently it blows. Hot wind is always from the north, dusty winds are from the west, high winds are from the east, and cold winds are from the south.

Areillo names the three things that are sacred to a gaucho in order: his horse, which is his freedom from the earth, his *facón*, which is his companion and protector in a fight, and his *chiná*, or woman, who seems to fall squarely into the honorable mention category.

"In Spanish, when you get engaged," he says, grinning, "the word is *compromiso*. Before you are *solitario*, after you are *compromiso*." Being here without Ethan, I guess, means I am lonely, but not compromised.

Areillo tells me that when he is training a colt, he will stroke him for hours each day for two months before he does anything else, and when the colt gets sweaty he will dry him off with his own shirt so the colt will grow to like the smell.

On the way back down the mountain we take a shortcut that leaves us with a difficult river crossing, so Areillo sends me across on his horse, Blanco, first, and I send Blanco back across the raging water to Areillo with a single slap on his butt.

The full moon rises in the blue blue sky over the blue-gray mountains, and Areillo tries to teach me all the colors of the Criollo horses by singing a little song: "Blanco, Bayo, Gateado, Cebrino," he sings, "Rosillo, Overo, Pagare, Tostado."

18. Stone Harbor, New Jersey

Cinder and I arrive on the island close to midnight and all we see are *No Vacancy* signs. We would have been here sooner if we hadn't stopped in Seaside Heights, the town my Aunt Martha took me to for a week each summer from when I was two till I was seventeen.

Seaside hadn't changed much, maybe gotten a little seedier, but there is still Khor Brothers' Frozen Custard and Jimmy's Cheesesteak Hoagies on the boardwalk, which was what we were ordering when the lady who took our money told us about the Springsteen cover band that was playing, starting at 7, at the end of Funtown Pier.

On the way down from Boston I had told Cinder all about Art Stock's Playpen in Wildwood Crest, in 1978, and the band called

Backstreets that played there Wednesday nights. How I used to get off from my job as a beach inspector in Stone Harbor and hit the Wendy's in North Wildwood where the other beach inspectors and I learned to balance carrots and cucumber slices just so around the edge of the paper bowl to make a small salad ($1.49) hold as much as a large salad ($4.99). Then we'd head down to the Crest and pay the $1.00 ladies' cover charge and dance to Springsteen covers, and only Springsteen covers, till they threw us out at 4:45 a.m.

Cinder and I got close enough to the end of the pier to hear the first fifteen notes of "Thunder Road," to see the passel of groupies—mostly young men—holding their twinkling lighters above the glistening twilit sea, and I got goose bumps all over. This band calls themselves B-Streets, but even after Cinder said, "I guess they had to change their name after the rise to power of the Backstreet Boys," it still took a few minutes for me to register that these were the very same six guys—a little older, but still sounding damn good—whose show I danced to in 1978.

But as a result of all of that fun, only one entirely generic motel a couple of blocks off the beach in Stone Harbor says *Vacancy*, so we pull into the parking lot. In the tiny lobby the owners have set up what can only be described as a shrine to George W. Bush. A photo of him, above a photo of him and Laura, with little red, white, and blue sparkle sticks poking out from behind them, and a red, white, and blue candle, on a red, white, and blue doily, and behind all of it a giant American flag.

"Where are we? Thailand?" I say, and the manager looks at me sharply.

"I only have one room. It has one bed," he says, sizing up Cinder and me for the obvious reason. "You can have it for two hundred dollars."

Back at the car I say to Cinder, "Do we want to give two hundred dollars to sleep in one bed at the George Bush Motel?"

"If it is the only way we are going to get horizontal tonight," she says, "I think we do."

The room, it turns out, is not really a room at all, but a space wedged underneath the stairs and next to the laundry room they have converted into a room for high-season nights just like this, and suckers just like us. There are no windows, and the bed smells like roach poison and dryer exhaust.

"Early Abu Ghraib," Cinder says.

There are little signs crammed with words posted all over the room. One says, *This is a nonsmoking room. If the manager finds evidence that you have smoked your credit card will be charged $250.* Another says, *Anyone who takes room towels to the pool will be charged $50 per towel.* Another says, *No guests allowed. Anyone entertaining guests in their room will be charged $50 per guest even if the guest does not stay overnight.* Another says, *Checkout time is 11 a.m. If you are not out of your room by 11 a.m., we reserve the right to remove your things and you will be charged $50 for every fifteen-minute period past 11 a.m. until you vacate the premises entirely.*

When I first found out Henry had decided to die without me I was pretty mad, but too numbed out to trust it. By the time I trusted it, it had already given way to the missing, which we all know is both better and worse. A decade later Henry feels like a really good dream I was awakened in the middle of, but no matter how many times I try to go back to sleep I can't get back there. On the night Bill Clinton was elected Henry said, "It will be so refreshing to have somebody in the White House who can actually get it up."

19. Davis, California

Jude and I are having our weekly meal together, this time at Zen Toro Sushi. We order a roll called *palette of fire,* and it is the hottest thing I have ever tasted anywhere in the world, including Chengdu, China; including that time I was teaching in Minneapolis and had such a bad head cold I could hardly see out of my eyes, and I dragged myself across the street from the hip hotel which was built inside an old flour mill to Sawatdee Thai and told the waitress, "Please make it as hot as you possibly can."

Each piece of the *palette of pain* comes with a slice of jalapeño on top, and after barely living through the first bite, I remove the jalapeño from the second slice before I give it a try. It seems to make no difference whatsoever, and hot tears spring again to my eyes.

I look across the table at Jude, who is also suffering. The water, of course, only makes it worse; there is no chance we will taste anything we put in our mouths from here on in.

"I can't eat anymore," I say. "I'm worried about doing myself permanent damage."

That night in Minneapolis, delirious with fever, I ate every bite of what was served to me, the kind of hot that hurts so much you can't actually stop eating but have to keep shoveling in bite after bite just to stay a few seconds ahead of the pain.

I had been to the Walker Museum that afternoon, and in the

basement there was an exhibit that featured a table set for a large family's Sunday dinner, and off in the corner a book of Braille, under glass—unreadable—and an extremely androgynous voice reading what I thought was Latin over loudspeakers in stereo sound. Every five minutes it snowed flour onto the table from several small holes along a pipe in the ceiling, which was, over the course of the exhibit, creating a giant mountain range of flour running the length of the table. I had found the exhibit profound and unnerving and incomprehensible—my fever was already starting to spike—and that night, whenever someone spoke to me, including the Thai waitress, the words kind of fell apart around their Latinate roots in midair and I couldn't make sense of anything.

When I tell Jude, who has just eaten another piece of the *roll of death*, that Ethan said he missed the country of Costa Rica with a ferocity he had never felt for anything before, not even a woman, but that he couldn't ever take me to his place there no matter how long we stayed together because it was, after all, Fatimah's town, Jude says, "San Ramón is a town full of spoiled-brat trustafarians from places like Pittsburgh. If it's Fatimah's town, she sure shares it with a lot of dolts."

Jude eats five of the six remaining pieces of the *ream job roll,* though he's in considerable pain the whole time. When he gets to the last bite I pick up my rejected jalapeño slice and place it on top of the slice that is already on there. He puts the whole thing in his mouth and chews, smiling. He says, "You know once you put it on there, I didn't really have any choice."

20. Albuquerque, New Mexico

Dolores, the lady whose job it is to take me from the airport to the hotel, can't understand why they've put me in the Marriott. "It's on the wrong side of town for all of your events," she says, "and besides, nobody important ever stays there." I remind her that by any objective definition, I am not anybody important either. Ethan and I stayed at that Marriott on our drive across the country, so it has sentimental value for me.

As we turn onto the access road that leads to the hotel we see a hundred motorcycle cops, twenty-five mounted policemen, forty cruisers, three fire engines, and two tanks. A guy in an expensive suit steps into the road in front of Dolores's car. His tie is flapping in the desert wind and he actually appears to be speaking into something attached to the edge of his lapel.

"I'm sorry, ma'am," he says to Dolores, "but if you want to go any farther, your car will have to be swept."

"Swept?" she says.

"By the dogs," he says, and sure enough, to our right there is a small parking lot where German shepherds are leaping into and out of Honda Accords, Chrysler SUVs, Ford pickups.

"I can get out here and walk," I say.

"Are you staying at the hotel?" the man asks.

"I'm trying to check in," I say.

"What is your room number?" he asks.

"Trick question," I say. "Right?"

A motorcycle cop revs up to the window as I wedge my rolling carry-on out of Dolores's backseat. There is some kind of comic gleam in his eye when he says, "You can tell all your friends you stayed at the same hotel as the president."

"The president of what?" I say, and he just winks.

The man in the suit asks his lapel if they should take possession of my suitcase.

In the lobby there are a lot of clean-cut young people in suits standing around waiting for something to happen. The women at the front desk all have smirks plastered onto their faces.

"All the hotels in the world," a woman whose name tag reads *Montavia* says to me, "and he had to walk into mine."

When the security guard gets finished laying all my silky underwear out on the card table next to the elevator and I am thanking God and whatever oversight has caused me to leave my rabbit-pearl vibrator at home, he says, "You're clear, ma'am," which I understand is my signal to repack my bag.

I am in room 801, on the corner, overlooking all the activity. The motorcycle cops taking pictures of each other with their camera phones, the mounted police taking turns picking up horseshit, and eventually, a line of ten limousines emerge from some hidden underbelly of the building and speed away. About half the motorcycle cops follow the limos and the other half stay behind. On each of the three overpasses in my line of sight, a sharpshooter stands at the ready, his long-range rifle pointed at the highway.

I call Ethan's answering machine and leave him this riddle. "It is completely amazing who is staying at my hotel with me. But I am not excited at all."

When we were in Lubbock last month, Ethan came out of the hotel room bathroom naked and tried to get my attention by slapping his butt repeatedly, hard and loud. I was busy answering email and didn't look up, and eventually he felt so ridiculous he had to stop.

"He is so sick, Pam," Janine said last week, at acupuncture, "and you are so very nearly well."

The next morning at the Marriott, a huge African-American man with kind eyes delivers my oatmeal and says, "Well, dear, I can tell you this much. Your oatmeal is perfectly safe."

21. New Orleans, Louisiana

The first place Devon takes me when I get off the plane is Drago's, for oysters, because that is the first place we went when I came to visit the year before. "Wow, look at that," I say, when we pull up in front, because the giant sign over the restaurant has been blown out from the center. All that remains is the top of the big black *D* and part of what looks like the apostrophe.

Devon looks at me blankly, a PTSD glint in her eye that says, *I hadn't particularly noticed,* or *That is so inconsequential it doesn't even register,* or *There are absolutely no conditions under which I will ever feel safe again.*

What she *says* is, "You know Drago's was one of the few places that never closed its doors. They fired up their propane heaters and started cooking. They served more than forty thousand meals to the volunteers, all of it free for the taking."

After lunch she takes me to see her new paintings, huge canvases with big words scrawled across them in pencil, painted over and over in shades of white until there is only the slightest hint of what they might have said. In one painting, a final wash of bright yellow begins in the upper left-hand corner and falls diagonally almost all the way across the canvas, as if Devon has hurled a bucket of paint at it, leaving only the ghost of the words *leave or stay* and a question mark, exposed at the bottom right.

She drives me through the West End in Orleans Parrish. Every house has a big X on the front in black, or fluorescent orange, or sometimes green, giving the National Guardsman who inspected the house when the water began to recede four divided spaces to record his findings. In the left-hand space there is a multi-digit number identifying his unit. In the top of the X is the date— often as late as a month after the levee broke—that the guardsmen finally got to the house and went inside. In the bottom of the X there is another number, usually zero, though sometimes 2 or 3, or once, on the outside of a public library, 5. This is the number of bodies that were found. The right space is reserved for additional information: *Two tabby cats found DOA in bathroom*, or *one dog found alive, taken to SPCA*. On another, all in big block letters, NO REPTILE FOUND.

Whenever I am in New Orleans, I think of the story "No Place For You, My Love," which makes me think of me and Henry, always in some car with the top down driving and driving to the end of somewhere, though Henry and I liked each other a whole lot more than that couple in the story did.

Every telephone pole in the city bears advertisements: WE DEMOLISH HOUSES. Another with one word, GUTTING, and a phone number below. Near the breach in the levee speedboats and sailboats up to forty feet in length are tossed around a parking lot like kid's toys, some of them still upside down. There is a house that looks like it was made of Play-Doh, then stepped on by a giant. Someone has hung a banner from what is left of the porch: *FEMA paid $10,321 for this house*. At the end of a block where all of the houses' insides seemed to be piled up on the outside is a big white door propped up sideways against a twisted newspaper dispenser, LAME CAT MISSING scrawled in huge black letters across the six-foot door.

22. Santa Cruz Province, Argentina

La Delfina is a place right out of a Katherine Mansfield story, an English formal garden ringed all around by the ubiquitous Lombardi poplars—beautiful and green on the inside, dry flat wasted land on the outside—lace curtains on the clapboard windows, a dog in the yard chained to nothing, a windmill pulling up the water that keeps it all intact.

Today, the gardens at La Delfina contain white peonies stained with red, peach, and pink roses, purple tulips, silvery lupine, strawberries, rhubarb, peas, lettuce, potatoes, carrots, broccoli, apples, and pears, and Tatjana prepares a lunch for me using a little of everything, that is as delicious a meal as I have had in my life.

Ethan always says the fruit in America doesn't have any taste, even the organics. He says once you have eaten a Costa Rican mango, an American mango tastes like shit.

In 1913, there was a meeting of the governors of the three southernmost provinces of Argentina—Santa Cruz, Chubut, and Tierra del Fuego—to discuss, seriously, if they could pull off a mass Patagonian emigration without involving women at all, but it was decided that women were necessary for sewing, ironing, and washing. That is when they started taking women out of

European and British prisons and sending them to Patagonia—
women like the bandit Elana Greenhill, who, when forty men
tried to capture her, single-handedly kidnapped two of them,
held them for ransom, and made them spend three days tied up
in their underwear.

Tatjana came to La Delfina from Yugoslavia more than half a
century ago. Now, because of overgrazing, most of her land can't
produce. Tatjana and Luis, her Chilean caretaker, live here all
winter together, no phone, no mailbox. They make jams and jellies
and sell them in town to help make ends meet. Tatjana is trying
to get a loan to buy a few cows.

Luis tries to keep Tatjana's spirits up by working hard to make
beautiful things for her, but he's letting her down, he says, because
all the roses in the world can't make this better. She's letting him
down, she says, because there are no cows for him to work anymore, and he was born to live the beautiful life of the gaucho. If
she has to sell the place or dies, she says, "he'll be with a bag on
the side of the road." Luis has tears in his eyes when he asks me
if I know anyone who can help them. He says he can no longer
remember how young or old he is.

23. Denver, Colorado

A short list, in chronological order, of suicides I have known:

1. My father's friend, let's call him Charles, who ate rat poison and
   then threw himself in front of a train. What my father could
   never get over was the fact that Charles was a millionaire, as

though rich guys, by definition, ought to be exempt from psychic pain.

2. The girl in the first writing class I ever taught whose boyfriend left her in a campground in the desert. She walked for fifteen miles to the nearest highway, hitched to Grand Junction, borrowed the cash for a bus ticket to Denver, walked ten blocks from the bus station to their apartment, turned the key in the lock, and hung herself from the rafters. Following her death, I heard that the boy who really loved her, who had been watching her canaries for her while she went to the desert with the other boy, wrapped the small birds in cellophane and shot them with a BB gun so he would not have to hear the flapping of their wings.

3. My mother, more or less unintentionally, with a combination of vodka, Vioxx, and anorexia-induced pulmonary stress.

4. The writer Michael Dorris.

5. My dentist Grayson, who shot himself through the heart in the Denver airport parking lot, with a note pinned to his shirt that said *Please call my wife*.

At our first therapy session in over a year Patrick said, "Pam! Don't you get it? If Ethan spends every minute he's eating your mango, longing for the old mango, he doesn't have any brain space to worry about losing the mango he's got right now."

24. Bumthang Valley, Kingdom of Bhutan

When we show back up at the monastery on what is our Christmas morning (just another Wednesday to the monks) with forty blankets and forty pairs of shoes, the Master looks mostly bemused. We stand quietly while Karma explains the piles of gear in front of him, his ancient Dzonka so peppered with absorbed English words we can almost understand everything he says.

"In Pam and Ethan's country today is Christmas. If they were at home they would make food for the poor. They were so happy to be allowed to hear the evening prayers. A token of their gratitude. They noticed that the smallest boys seemed a little cold."

The Master's reaction to it all is a crash course in Buddhism for Dummies, a tilt of the head, the slightest frown between his eyebrows, a thoughtful series of nods and grunts. *In a nonattached universe,* his face seems to say, *the arrival of forty blankets and eighty shoes is neither good news nor bad news, but simply the thing that makes yesterday different from today.*

Last winter, in Chicago, I accidentally found myself at the first *playdate* of my life. I was supposed to meet my journalist friend Patricia for lunch, but when I called her from the restaurant she said she had forgotten she was hosting the kids that day and invited me to come on up. *Up* was to a thirty-seventh-floor penthouse on the edge of Lake Michigan, 5,000 square feet, all glass, chrome, and angles, the floor crawling with toddlers who were being tailed by Serbian nannies who were overseen by the mothers who drank Diet Coke on the couch. Two of nine babies had Down's syndrome. Every mother was or had been a major player: architect, litigator, politician, chef.

"Do you have children, Pam?" asked the architect responsible for two art museums and a symphony hall. It was hard to look anywhere except out at the sun-splashed surface of the lake.

"I have twenty graduate students," I said, "and a very childlike boyfriend."

"That," said the architect, "sounds like a very well-thought-out plan."

"It may have been," I said.

"What brought this group together," said the lawyer, "the thing we all have in common, is that we love our children very very much, and if we had to do it over again, we wouldn't."

Here in Bhutan, the Master calls out some words in Dzonka, the kitchen jumps to life and we are served tea and biscuits. One boy at a time comes in and bows to us, is allowed to select either a blanket or a pair of shoes. It takes an hour for each boy either to get the right shoe size or to change around with another boy for a blanket. Ethan weeps quietly through the entire thing.

When all is said and done four boys still need bigger sizes, but we have made the shop lady in town promise she will exchange them. Our last view of the young monks is of the whole gaggle of them descending the hillside into town behind their Master, testing their new shoes on the rocky outcrops, their robes billowing behind them in the wind.

#N814DW

C LIMBING OFF THE TARMAC up into the bright red and
orange four-seater owned by Wrangell Mountain Air. There
are just enough clouds, I know, of the big white puffy variety,
to create shadows that will make these most spectacular of all
mountains even more spectacular.

I have had the good fortune to circle Denali in a small plane,
to fly into and out of the Himalayas, riding in the cockpit both
directions, but these mountains, the Wrangells and the Chugach
and the St. Elias, rising from sea level all the way to the peak of
Mount St. Elias at 18,008 feet in ten short miles—glacier after
glacier after mountain after mountain—make them, in my opinion, the most dramatic in all the world.

This plane will take me to the other side of the Wrangells,
north of the Chugach, close to the Yukon border, by anybody's
measuring stick, one of the world's most remote locations.

There I will ride reluctant horses through boggy tundra, listen to eager hunting guides play the washtub and the spoons around the fire, keep my eyes and ears peeled for brown bears, and try to teach six Alaskan women, and one man from Nova Scotia, how to write.

William—from Halifax—and I drove the long road from Chitna into McCarthy together. He is tall, handsome, moderately literary, towheaded, and still very much hung up on his ex-wife. Something about the way our conversation turned us inevitably back to her six or seven thousand times in three hours has thrown me deep into abject loneliness, which lately has been a pretty short trip.

When I left on this monthlong adventure, Ethan gave me a Mike Schmidt baseball card, and dangling poet earrings, black on black. Now the woman who lives in his cell phone says, "Ethan is not available," with just a hint of impatience in her voice.

I am up front, next to the pilot, Halifax William behind me, a woman from Juneau next to him, our three packs taking up every inch of space in the tail. The pilot turns the plane in a tight circle, we accelerate and lift off, and before he has even pulled in the flaps the first glacier is in front of us, huge and dirty and violent with stretch marks, plunging out of the cloud cover and into the shimmering sun.

Instantly I feel that old surge come back, that seizing of my own life on my own terms. It is such a physical thing, like the time I had my forearm shattered and the nurse came in every four hours on the dot to give me a shot of morphine—*that's* how physical—and I look down at the glacier and the ice-ridged peaks that go on forever behind it and say, *Remember this remember this remember this* the next time you think it's over, because some man, or some hope, or some life takes away instead of gives. Remember this and get on an airplane, a small one if possible, because it always works.

25. Ban Xang Hai, Laos

My guide Xai and I are standing in the warm mist of a Mekong River morning in the village of Ban Xang Hai, Laos, watching an unusually tall Laotian tend his boiling vats of *Lao-Lao*, the rice-wine moonshine that has put his village on the map. Monkeys scream in the trees above us, and a gentle-faced woman stands nearby holding a glass I fear is meant for me.

It is slightly after 8 a.m. and in America, that would be a good enough reason to decline politely, but here in Laos, where decorum is far more rigorous—and complicated—than it is in America, I'm pretty sure there isn't going to be a way out of drinking the pickled Mekong water that is about to come from the steaming, rusted fifty-gallon drum.

I reassure myself that no self-respecting amoeba could possibly live in 80-proof hooch, and quickly down the glass of "white" I am offered. Which gets me another glass, and then a glass of red, which I realize the second it goes down my throat without searing my tonsils, isn't nearly as strong as the white. I am seized with regret, flooded by premonitions of feverish vomiting in a Laotian health care facility.

I do what any sophisticated world traveler would do and stuff an entire antibacterial wipe into my mouth, and during the tour of the brightly painted temple, suck every drop of juice out of it I can, and swallow.

Outside the temple a beautiful woman is making ferns and bougainvillea and daisy petals out of colored paper. I buy a small bouquet from her and ask if I can take her picture. She says something to Xai and he translates, "She says she should take your picture because you are the beautiful one," and I can tell by the tone in his voice that he thinks she is mistaken.

Xai is the most formal guide I have ever had in Asia, which is saying a great deal. He had been a monk for three months at eighteen, then he became one again for one day last year when his mother died, so he could carry her body, he says, to the other side. His English is impeccable, except that he says *electric city* when he means electricity, and *comfort table* when he means comfortable, and anyone can see why he would think that was correct. At least twice a day he says, "If I am not speaking right you will please graduate me," but I rarely do.

I'm pretty sure I have managed to eat the antibacterial wipe clandestinely until we are back on the boat heading down river to the magical city of Luang Prabang and Xai says, "Have I told you yet how the Buddha died?"

When I say no, he says, "He was invited to the house of a friend for dinner and they were serving pok."

"Pok?" I say.

"Pok! Pok!" he says, mildly impatient with me as usual, and he makes an oinking noise in his throat.

"Aha!" I say, and Xai smiles.

"He knew the pok was bad," Xai says, "knew, even, that it would kill him, but he ate it anyway because it was most important not to offend his hosts."

"I guess that's the difference," I almost say, "between Buddha and me," but on the off chance that Xai has paid me a compliment, I smile out at the muddy river and nod.

26. Davis, California

When I go to close my Hotmail inbox there is another Hotmail inbox behind it, which I assume is some kind of computing glitch, before I open what seems to be an unopened email that has just come through for me. As I read it, my brain slowly orients itself to the fact that the second Hotmail account belongs to Ethan, who asked to use my office earlier in the day.

Attached to the email I have just opened is an email Ethan sent that morning in which he claims to be sitting in SFO airport, getting ready to fly to Colorado to see me, while at the very next gate, he writes, a flight is boarding passengers bound for Costa Rica. *I am so overcome with longing*, he writes, *I want to leap up from my chair, bound across the aisle, throw myself on the gate agent's mercy, and beg for a seat on the San Jose–bound plane.*

Among the curious things about the email, are (1) *Ethan hasn't been within fifty miles of SFO in months*, and (2) *He can't be going to see me in Colorado because I am here, in Davis, with him*, and (3) *Like most large airports, SFO has a dedicated international terminal, and any plane going to San Jose would surely leave from it.* Also curious is that he wrote the email, not to Fatimah , as one might expect, but to yet another woman, this one in Cleveland, whom, he said, he missed with a profundity he had not felt before, even for the country of Costa Rica.

A quick check into the Sent box on Ethan's account revealed that he had also, that morning, written to Fatimah saying he didn't know when he could next see her because in an effort to keep him away from her, I had helped him to secure a yearlong lectureship in "Introduction to Political Thought" at CU Boulder. And while it is true that I had, at his request, secured him a position, it had been only ten weeks long, and in California, and had been finished now for more than a month. To the Romanian he had written that he was flying today, yet again to Denver, but it would be worth it this time because the mayor of Denver was throwing a party to honor his recent fund-raising work toward a high school for the children of illegal immigrants.

I closed his email account and picked up the phone.

"The mayor of Denver?" I said, and he said nothing at all.

After several seconds of silence I said, "It's really no wonder that some days I can't tell the difference between my father and George W. Bush."

We had plans to eat with Fenton the human that night in Berkeley and we kept them. Where Fenton found a *Someone Went to Bucharest and All I Got Was This Lousy T-shirt* T-shirt on such short notice I will never know. I sent the mashed potatoes back because they were cold, but they came back even colder. When our waitress asked if my name was Pam I thought it was because I'd given her my credit card, but then I remembered we'd all paid in cash. She said, "I thought so. My boyfriend has, like, a shrine to you."

"Really?" I said.

She said his name was Peter Sawyer, and I thought *Peter Sawyer . . . Peter Sawyer . . .* and I knew the news wasn't good but I couldn't remember in exactly what way.

"You guys lived together for like two years?" she said, correctly reading the amnesia on my face, and I nodded, *yes of course,* and she said, "He left you with a note." And then it all came swirling back, me putting the bag of groceries down on the counter, reading the words, *I really* did *love you, Peter.*

Fenton leaned over and said, "Maybe this is the night the shrine gets dismantled," and kissed my hand, and that reminded me of the time when he and I were eating with Jay at Zuni and I was saying how my best friend from New Jersey had published a book, and Fenton picked up a crayon while I was talking and wrote on the paper tablecloth, *I thought I was your best friend.*

27. Aspen, Colorado

Duncan is three, tall, and healthy. Doctors still aren't sure why it took him a year and a half to sit up. Driving up-valley between Basalt and Snowmass on his way to day care, his dad asks him whether he thinks God is a man or a woman. Duncan looks out the window for a minute, watching his hand ride on the air currents that rush past the car.

Duncan's parents have gotten used to the way he thinks about a question before he answers it; they no longer panic that he's gone deaf or mute or so far into his head he might never come back. I am sitting sideways in the back of the Club Cab, catching a ride with them as far as the ski area, but both boys seem to have forgotten I am here.

"God is spirit," Duncan says, turning his bright blue matter-of-fact eyes on his dad, who can barely stand to look away, back to the road that curves and curves through the canyon, "but woman . . ." he says, pulling his small arm back inside the cab of the truck and tracing a wide arc from driver's window to passenger's window, indicating the canyon walls, the bowl of sky and the entire wide valley in front of them, "woman . . . is everything."

28. Muong Sing, Laos

Lat speaks English with an Australian accent, because he used to work for a petroleum company a thousand miles into the bush from Adelaide. He says *eh* and *mate* and *good fun* so often it is like he is only kidding. Every time we return to the Land Cruiser he nods approvingly and says, "You are big potato."

Our driver's name is Peng. He is Chinese and narcoleptic. He'll try anything to stay awake, flicking his thumbs hard to either side, pulling hunks of hair out of his scalp, even sucking on lemons, but nothing works, and there are holes in the road big enough to swallow the Toyota right up.

When we finally get to Muong Sing, Lat says, "This region? It is not rich in money but it is very rich in sticky rice."

I have learned all about sticky rice in the last two weeks and like best to eat it with fresh mango slices at the end of a meal, even though my paranoid guidebook tells me not to eat the mangoes because of cholera. The book also describes dengue fever and malaria and hepatitis A in ways that make me think I am coming down with them all every second, so I have promised myself not to look at the guidebook for a while.

Lat says there used to be sixty-eight minorities in Laos, but last year they did a survey and now there are only forty-seven.

"Where did they go?" I ask him, and he says he doesn't know.

He can name twenty-four of the tribes without even trying: Aheu, Alak, Arem, Bo, Bru, Chut, Dai, Halang Doan, Hmong Daw, Hmong Njua, Hung, Ir, Jeh, Jeng, Katang, Katu, Khang, Khlor, Khmu, Kuy, Lahu, Lamet, Phutai, and Phatet Lao.

In an opium den in the center of a Khmu village, the father smokes and so does the eldest son, and all the little kids have the same big eyes as children of alcoholics back home.

Lat tells me a story about how the director of his company was working with some Khmu on a project, and they offered him food and he looked down at it and it turned into a snake and after that he was sick for weeks. Then he tells me a story about how a bunch of Danish social workers came over to try to tell the villagers how to use condoms, and they used their thumbs in the demonstration, and when the social workers came back to see if they'd successfully lowered the pregnancy rate they learned that after they left the villagers were putting the condoms right back on their thumbs before they had sex.

Now, speaking *as* the Danish social worker, Lat says, "No, mate, you put your condom on your cock before you fuck your wife!" and I can tell by the way Lat says it and the look on his face that he has no idea what he is saying to me, that these are just translated words like any others, and I keep my face perfectly neutral and then realize that probably every tourist he has told this story to has kept their face perfectly neutral and that is probably one way wars get started, people keeping their faces perfectly neutral when it would be kinder and braver not to.

In an Iko village there is a Keith Richards look-alike—but Laotian, and Keith Richards from 1974, before he started to look like a Latvian grandmother—who tries to sell us a bag of opium for ten bucks. Then an old woman gets mad at me for taking her photo. When Lat gives her 100 kip she gestures in a manner that says all 100 kip is good for is wiping her ass. I take another picture from the back and she chases us with a gourd full of water down the street.

29. Davis, California

I walk into the house to the smell of beets cooking. We have been officially broken up for exactly one month but Ethan has shown no signs of moving out.

I have never seen Ethan lift a finger in any kitchen, even his own, but tonight there are three of my best pans on the stove, aromatically steaming.

"What are you doing?" I ask.

"I want you to have a good Valentine's Day," he says, beaming. "Look, I have made all of your favorite foods."

I wonder briefly what act of mercy has allowed me not to notice, until this moment, that today is Valentine's Day. Dinner assembles itself in my mind based on what is on the counter: beet and arugula salad, lobster risotto, vanilla milkshakes for dessert with red licorice straws.

"Does this mean," I say, "that you are reconsidering the breakup?"

"Not at all," he says, still smiling, "I am living in your house. I know how tricky holidays can be for you. I am just trying to be considerate."

The third time I told Ethan that I was not, after all, willing to be one of a stable full of women, he sighed and said, "No Romanian is worth this . . ."

"He actually said those words," Cinder asked later, "*No Romanian is worth this?*"

But trying to convince Ethan to give up the Romanian was a little like insisting a crackhead cut down on his polyunsaturated fats.

Earlier today, at acupuncture, Janine said, "The best way to think of Ethan's energy is like mistletoe. We have all these nice kissy associations with mistletoe, and even out in nature it doesn't look that bad, but give it enough time and it will kill the tree."

She said, "What I want you to do tonight when Ethan comes through the door is just gather all his energy up and hold it right out to him. Attach a beer or a book or something to it to make it more attractive. What kinds of things does he like?"

"Money?" I said. And we both cracked up.

It is the next morning, walking Fenton the dog, when I notice I am so tired I can hardly put one foot in front of the other. For a second I think I might faint, and I try to use my voice-activated dialing system, and then the woman who lives in *my* cell phone says, "Did you say, Ethan cell?" with some whole new tone in her voice.

I picture the men from the City of Davis who finally came last winter, too late, I thought, to cut the mistletoe out of the big oak in front of my cottage, cut the tree, in the process, almost back to nothing, but then how in the spring the tree leafed out just fine, a little spindly-limbed maybe, but healthy just the same.

In therapy last month, Patrick said: "The average rat will push a lever between ten and fifteen times in hopes of getting a pellet, but if you give me three days with that rat and a bunch of intermittent reinforcement, I can teach the same rat to push for a pellet two hundred and twenty-five times."

I put the phone back in my pocket and just like that the heaviness runs off me like water, and I whistle for Fenton the dog and pick up my step.

30. Atigun Pass, Alaska

The photographers are out in spite of the weather, so it is just me and Joe, the mule handler, huddled in the soggy VE-24. I am doing basically every single thing the tags on both my Svea stove sack and my tent tell me not to do, trying to dry out the inside of the tent with an open-flame white gas stove while holding it in my hands, and Joe is telling Mathilda stories.

It rained the whole way up the Dalton Highway to Cold Foot, rained the whole two-day walk into base camp along the Chandalar Shelf. By day six we all had our feet in plastic bags, mold growing between our toes, and not one piece of dry clothing among us.

Only Mathilda seems unfazed by the constant rain that beats down on her. Joe has brought no food for her and I watch out the tent door as she stands near the rising riverbank with her front legs hobbled and long ears twitching, pulling tiny willow shoots out of the ground and eating them all the way down to their roots.

Joe is one of those guys Alaska is full of, doe-eyed and methodical, with both the loyalty and the logic of a Labrador retriever. The kind of guy who would give you his car—permanently—if you asked for it in just the right way.

The little stove is making a happy humming sound in the tent, drying a little circle in the oversaturated ceiling. We are both wearing thick damp long johns, everything else too soaked to bring inside. Then the hum turns into a rumble and the rumble turns into a roar, and I can tell by the look on Joe's face that he is hearing it too.

Our waterlogged brains kick into gear simultaneously and we leap for the tent door just in time to see a huge wall of mud descending upon us. It is more than a football field wide and three feet deep at its tongue, maybe deeper higher up. It is roughly the consistency of cookie dough, carrying rocks as big as Volkswagens in its flow.

"Holy shit," Joe yells. "Grab your boots and make a run for it." And we do, stumbling with our laces untied along the leading edge of the mud toward the lateral moraine—the hundred-foot-high ridge of humped-up earth and rock the glacier left behind along the edge of the valley.

We reach the moraine out of breath but just ahead of the mud, having managed to grab only our ponchos. We turn to watch as the mud engulfs our tent, our packs, what is left of our kitchen supplies, and three spare tripods; watch as it carries them, with a kind of absolute authority, to the river. It is there our eyes fall upon Mathilda, now almost belly deep in mud, still with the same Zen expression on her face she always wears.

"I gotta get my mule!" Joe says, and that is all, before he leaps down into the thick mud which is hitting him at hip level, and he drags his legs, one at a time, back across the valley toward Mathilda. The mud, I can see, is getting deeper, and moving faster now, hitting Joe mid chest a couple of times and throwing Mathilda off balance, and she starts braying, softly but plaintively, from the river's edge.

Time slows down the way it always does when death is lurking behind the next bad decision, and I watch Joe take what seems like forever to climb up on one of the now-in-motion car-sized rocks, and then jump from it to another, and another after that. Every so often he misjudges the movement of the rock and either misses entirely, slips off right after he lands, or stands helplessly while the rock he has chosen sinks into the mud underneath him, leaving him sputtering and spitting up from the muck, his form barely recognizable as that of a human being.

A long five minutes later, Jo reaches Mathilda, who has by now all but fallen on her side. The mud is still flowing, though more slowly, the clouds have lifted a little off the mountain, and I can see the giant slump block the slide has left behind.

Joe wraps one arm around Mathilda's lowered neck, wields his hunting knife, and dives like a frogman down between her front legs. He emerges seconds later with the severed hobbles, takes an instant to grin at me through the rain, and then throws himself up on Mathilda's back and speaks into her ear for a moment. There is another moment when the whole mud sculpture—man, horse, knife, and dangling hobbles—leans dangerously over the river. In the next moment Mathilda rights herself, and walks slowly, one sure hoof at a time, toward me through the mud.

31. Mount Shasta, California

Carmen gives me valor in a bottle. She says her mother has a special word for men like Ethan and I think it's going to be something magical and Latin but the word turns out to be *freeloader*. And even though we have only just met, we drive up as far as the snow will allow us and shout what we want in a man at the mountain. My list has stuff like (1) *Loves many things,* and (3) *Wants to have fun,* and (7) *Generous with time/money/spirit,* and Carmen's starts with (1) *Compassion,* and ends with (10) *Self-love that is not self-absorption.*

While we are at it we shout things we want besides a man, and I say *a teaching job in Colorado, less back pain,* and *a trip to Antarctica* and she says *a walk-in closet, a half-ton pickup,* and *a babysitter I can trust.*

Later at a bar full of guys in Carhartts with "Saturate Before Using" on the stereo, we meet up with two women who have both just returned from Burning Man. Ava, who wants to be beautiful and to stop eating fruit, calls Burning Man the worst four days of her life. It made her heart hurt, she says, all those people looking to fill a bottomless need. Sasha says it was the four most important days of her life, though both Carmen and I find her descriptions of the festival far more terrifying than Ava's. Then we go home and watch the Dixie Chicks movie twice, all the way through without stopping.

I check my voice mail and Cinder has left a little song on it that goes, "How do you solve a problem like Fatimah?" and Nora has left a message that says, "I think Ethan missed out on a few of the simple things, like mercy," and Practical Karen has left one that says, "Swear to God, if he isn't out of there by the end of spring break I'm driving up and we're going to the Target and getting a whole bunch of those big blue plastic containers and all his shit's going out on the curb," and I know they're all trying to help me, but seriously, after four solid hours of *Shut Up and Sing*, Ethan couldn't reengage my attention if he brought Harrison Ford home for a threesome.

At Crystal Lake the next morning, under the shadow of that giant white she-mountain, it is just a little too easy to tell Ava why she ought to stop dating the alcoholic. On the peak the wind is blowing up frozen clouds in the shape of Armageddon, though it is still as a church where we are standing, and warm.

I say, "I don't know, I'm just feeling so . . ."

"Say it," Carmen says, "Say it! Powerful."

I had been trying to decide between *directionless* and *untethered*.

"Powerful," I say, just as the wind reaches the surface of the lake.

32. Alsek Bay, Alaska

Day twelve of a fifteen-day trip down the Tatshenshini and Alsek Rivers. It has been 36 degrees and raining sideways since day three. On days one and two the sun was out and we sped along the silvery water that braided and rebraided itself so quickly and often it was almost like a video game trying to pick the right channel. Ten days later, to say we are wet and cold is the type of understatement that can get you killed on an extended outdoor adventure in hostile conditions, so I don't.

Phil is coping with his discomfort (and Nancy's relentless enthusiasm) by insisting we eat meals precisely on the following schedule: breakfast at seven, lunch not a minute after twelve, dinner at six. There are at least forty pounds of rice on this raft, oceans of instant mashed potatoes, and gallons of tuna and peanut butter, but Phil feels certain we are going to starve to death out here, and no amount of taking his hand and showing him the piles of food, or how far we have come, how few miles we have left to go, will convince him otherwise.

Last night we camped on the long peninsula where the Tatshenshini River empties into Alsek Bay, which is not technically a bay, but a lake, ten miles in diameter, currentless and full of icebergs ranging in size from something we could stick in our Mojitos (if we had some), to the Sydney Opera House or the Denver International Airport, and that is only the part of the iceberg we can see. Two-thirds of the twenty-mile circumference of the lakeshore is buried under actively calving glaciers that pour from between the tall, craggy, cloud-swathed mountains, and the explosions when chunks the size of apartment buildings break off and hit the water sound like war all around us, though we are the only three people for hundreds of miles.

We shared the peninsula with a very large brown bear, close cousin to the grizz, but coastal, which in the local vernacular only means *fewer plants and more meat*. Not a single day of this trip has passed, in fact, when we haven't encountered at least one brown bear, and on some days we have seen as many as five. There have been bears eating wild strawberries on the riverbanks as the current sweeps us past, bears running along the tundra, keeping pace with us to get a better look. On four separate occasions unspeakably huge boars have wandered past our camp to see what we were having for dinner, and the first thing we look for each morning are the size 15 triple-D paw prints that encircle our tents.

We fear for the cooler that we leave on the boat each night. We fear for the boat itself, should the bear decide to use his eight-inch claws to climb aboard. We fear for our lives enough to set up our kitchen tent a hundred yards from our sleeping tent, even though it means getting soaked to the bone every time we have to move between the two; enough to change our clothes before bed if we have spilled the slightest drop of lentil stew on them; enough to move camp entirely one night in the pitch dark and a driving horizontal freezing rain when we discovered we had set up within fifty yards of a fresh caribou carcass.

Give the bear the opportunity to make the right decision, has always been my philosophy, and so far it has worked, which is handy, because each time a bear has walked into camp just as we are about to sit down to a pot of something hot and good-smelling, and everybody's eyes say, *Now where'd we put that gun?* the answer each time has been according to Murphy's law of river rafting: Whatever you need is always in the bottom of the *other* boat box. Any one of those bears could have eaten two of us in the time it took the third one to dig the gun out. Which is why I didn't want to bring a gun in the first place. But I did, because Phil asked me to.

What's really going on here is that Nancy's father was some big outdoorsman, and Phil is, on his best day, a good sport. The fact that he is one of America's top leukemia specialists is more or less lost on Nancy because Phil doesn't want to shoot skeet or climb Everest. It was Nancy who hired me to run this trip, and now Phil's every third thought is, *Please God don't let me die out here,* and because that is at least my every tenth thought, no matter where I am, I bought a Remington 30-06 shotgun and buried it under Nissin Top Ramen and toilet paper.

Today we are taking turns rowing across the still water of Alsek Lake, because rowing is the only way to stay a few degrees above hypothermic. Between ice, sky, and lake, every color of silver is represented here. The look on Phil's face tells me he is willing all the icebergs within a hundred-yard radius not to roll over and crush us like grapes, while Nancy keeps insisting I row right up next to them so she can hop from boat to iceberg and pose for Phil's camera.

Three days from now, when we get to the ironically named Dry Bay and receive word that the weather has grounded all flights out of Haines until four days hence at the earliest, Phil will get on the two-way radio and start begging any pilot within a thousand miles to brave the weather and come get us. He will say we are out of food, though it won't be even close to true, and on top of all we have left, the local fisherman will have brought us four glistening Dolly Varden at least three pounds apiece, and a six-pack of Olympic to go with them.

Phil will finally talk a pilot from Yakutat into coming down the coast for us, and after he and Nancy leave on the first flight, a young brown bear, newly abandoned by his mother, will come to the wall tent, and we will play an ill-advised game of peek-a-boo, until I hear the pilot circling above us, returning from Yakutat for me and the gear.

33. Phonsavan, Laos

Lat takes me to Phonsavan, the Plain of Jars, the site of the Secret War, years of unreported bombings that followed the U.S. withdrawal from Vietnam. We dropped so much Agent Orange onto the Plain of Jars that what ought to be lush farmland has not yet even begun to recover, and the plain is pocked with bomb craters as far as the eye can see.

In Phonsavan, the cornerstones of the buildings are made from U.S. bomb casings. When you check into a hotel there, your key is attached to a small disabled grenade. In Vientiane, Lat showed me a pot—as big as a bathtub—that 200 Pathet Lao families cooked in as they hid from the bombers in a cave. The pot cracked right down the middle when U.S. jets fired rockets straight into the cave and killed all of the occupants, and now sits in front of the National Museum, "to remember" Lat said, quietly, as we stood in front of it.

"So, do the Laotians hate Americans?" I had asked this question many times during my weeks in Laos and had been responded to kindly in every case. They understood, Xai said in Luang Prabang, that I was a child at the time of the bombings, how could they possibly hate me? And even the bombers, said the owner of Tam Nat Lao, were acting on the orders of someone above them. Could they hate a man who was told to follow orders or die? When I asked Lat the same question he shook his head, pursed his lips. "You don't understand," he said. "We are Buddhists. For us, this life, it is nothing."

When he drops me at my hotel in Phonsavan, Lat tells me not to let anybody in after the lights go off (the whole town is on a generator that is turned off between 10 p.m. and 6 a.m.). I don't bother pointing out that my "room" is made out of bomb casings and palm fronds and that anyone who wants in can simply lift up a wall.

A local guide named Mr. Souvannaphouma takes me hiking out onto the plain the next morning. On a five-mile walk we pass seven thirty-year-old unexploded ordinances. He tells me they still do eighty amputations a week there, most of them the limbs of children. People from Europe, he says, mostly Danes and Swedes, send people to Laos to help clean it up. Americans have sent some money, he's heard, but no personnel.

"So do the Laotians hate Americans?" I ask Mr. Souvannaphouma.

"Of course we do," he says, his brown eyes steady on mine. "How might it be possible that we would not?"

34. Seattle, Washington

At the Boeing factory we stand on a catwalk, disassembled giants as far as the eye can see, while the guide tells us the story of the time a camera fell out of some tourist's pocket and did $250,000 worth of damage to a 747's wing.

"It's all about tooling and jigs," the guide says, a sentence I love the sound of even if I have no idea what it means. She has already made me put my pad and paper away—for security reasons—so I am trying to emblazon the figures she gives us onto my memory: this building is as big as 75 NFL football fields, 911 NBA basketball courts, this building is bigger than Disneyland itself. There are three million parts in a 777. The engine of a 747 is larger than a VW Bug. On the Quantas Aboriginal Art plane there are two thousand pounds of paint weight alone.

Earlier that afternoon, at the SAM sculpture garden, watching the neon *Love & Loss* ampersand turn and turn above the silvery water of Elliott Bay, I told Mackenzie I'd finally got Ethan out of my house and she told me about her new boyfriend.

"Well, the two best things about him," she said, "is that he calls up to read me Alice Munroe over the phone, and he knows how to use a trapeze."

"You mean, like during sex?" I say.

"Anytime," she says, shrugging.

One of the best things about hanging out with Mackenzie is that it's okay to be sad. Today she's sadder than me, but last year, when we met on the Oregon coast, and it rained sideways for three whole days, we were both so sad we became convinced that the hip coffee shop with the Thich Nhat Hanh bumper stickers was serving us decaf instead of regular, either on purpose or by mistake.

Directly below us is the brand-new 787, missing the back half of its body and tail. One can be ours for $168 million, the guide informs us, but even if we slapped the money down right now we couldn't have one till 2015. The first eight will be strictly for testing, Air Nippon gets number 9. There are 684 currently on order, but number 685 is up for grabs.

The tour guide is getting a big kick out of herself. She says she doesn't get paid very much to give these tours, but don't tell Boeing that she would do them for free just to get out of the house and away from her retired husband. Yeah, we say, ha ha I'll bet.

Boeing has twenty-seven thousand employees, she tells us, and thirty-nine test pilots. Of the thirty-nine, five are women. I can't tell by her voice whether she thinks this is too many or too few but her tone is laced with some opinion. She tells us that when a plane is ready to be towed out of the hangar, they always do it at three in the morning, when the spectacle is less likely to cause a car accident because of gawkers on the road. It is perfectly clear how she feels about the gawkers.

We watch electronic arms carry fiberglass, jiggle levers, tighten screws. Given that Boeing is the largest employer in Washington State, there are an alarmingly few human beings in the giant building.

When the shamans in the Brazilian rainforests drink ayahuasca the plants and animals talk to them, and they go back to the village to sing the songs that tell the story of what the animals have told them. Then the weaver women weave their songs into patterns in the fabric, and the singers know how to read the cloth, so they return to the jungle with the cloth and sing the animals' own songs back to them.

Mackenzie leans so far over the railing her long long hair almost touches the tail of the Dreamliner. She says, "It's just like building a whale."

35. Salida, Colorado

Marshall Pass, hiking with Samuel Carter, an almost-blind almost-date on a warm spring day. He tells me about his ex-wife, who set the world record for the number of female parachutists jumping in tandem. When he says, twenty-four, thirty-six, forty-two, I think measurements, picture Barbie in reverse, but he's talking about women, lots of women, leaping out of an airplane, joining hands, and making concentric circles in the sky.

Fenton the dog scares up a fawn and it starts screaming like a tortured baby for its mother, but all's well that ends well, as doe and fawn go hurtling down the mountain together and Fenton runs back to us to make sure we are duly impressed.

After the hike, as we walk around Salida, people are extra extra friendly. In Creede, on the rare occasion a black man comes to town, people usually think he is a member of the Denver Broncos, even if he is five foot three and 125 pounds.

Samuel and I go to dinner at a sweet place with lace curtains—we've been talking for hours—when all of sudden I worry that too many of the stories I'm telling involve African-Americans. First there is getting to meet Toni Morrison, because I tell that story to anyone I want to like me, and I *was* just at the Aspen Music Fest, where Wynton Marsalis came with his whole twenty-one-piece jazz band from Lincoln Center in their smart black suits, along with twelve drummers from Ghana in traditional robes with their talking drums—the great big ones they have to climb ladders to play, the ones you feel reverberating in your breastbone. And when Wynton stood there creating the fusion—you didn't even have to think about it—you could just feel the whole history of music in your body, and how could you not want to talk about that? Then there was also Habib Kote, telling stories with his sweet guitar, inviting us all to Timbuktu, and his translator from Cameroon with his bookish glasses. And Joan Armatrading, late night, playing the old songs, the sound of her voice and what it did inside me making me think that maybe I'm not as open to love with my whole heart these days as I once was, and how maybe that's a good thing and maybe it's not. Telling those stories also makes a certain kind of sense. But then we move on to fantasy football, and who comes up but Randy Moss (my perennial problem player) and Shawn Alexander (who has won me two Super Bowls), and Samuel can only be thinking, *Doesn't this chick even see other white people out in the world?*

36. Luang Prabang, Laos

In Luang Prabang, the holiest city in Laos, pastel temples rise out of Mekong River mist, children carry fresh bouquets of frangipani blossoms, and women get up at dawn every morning to stand on street corners and spoon rice into the begging bowls of monks clad in robes of maroon and saffron, who walk the streets in a tradition of generosity centuries old. Here, dawn happens at the same time every morning, we are that close to the equator. Life clusters around the temples and the river, where there is always someone bathing, washing clothes, or tending the tiny gardens that spring up from every bank.

Xai and I climb wooden stairs to temple after temple and stand before giant golden Buddhas who are reclining, sitting, standing, some of them so tall we only come to their knees. Monks of all ages tend the altars, bringing oranges, incense, silver chalices of water and wine. They tell me to write down something I wish for and leave the scrap of paper among the offerings. I start with *stop hunger* and *make peace,* but in the next temple Xai says, *something for yourself,* as if he's been reading over my shoulder, so I write, *speak French fluently,* and in the next temple *more dogs and friends, less work,* and in the last one, *For god's sake, Pam, spread it around!*

Once, on the Big Island of Hawai'i I got to watch the Earth get made. Not just me, hundreds of people. Kilauea was erupting in such a user-friendly way you could get right up next to a new lava flow with only a mile's walking, with no fear of getting acid rain in your hair.

I had seen the flowing lava from a distance one time before, seen it pour into the Pacific sending up enormous clouds of spit and steam, but standing right next to it, even straddling little rivulets of it as it found its way through tiny gullies formed in the drying black glass of the prior day's lava, made the whole thing so intimate it took my breath away.

There was a van full of geology students from some Midwestern state lunging around the new lava like gorillas, wielding pickaxes and scooping big metal fingers full of the blackening goo, and I thought about all of the stories I had heard about Pele tossing—for example—a front-end loader into the sea, driver and all, if she did not approve of the location of a construction project, and I imagined these future geologists of America getting home to Kansas with their samples, and their hair falling out, and their dicks falling off.

In the Tam Nat Lao (Three Elephants) restaurant in Luang

Prabang, tourists sit side by side with locals and the humid air seems to be infused with a mist of goodwill. Shy-eyed servers bring chicken curry, banana pancakes, grilled goldfish, dried deer meat, stuffed peppers, noodle soup, meatballs made with fish, spring rolls, stir-fried vegetables, green chili paste.

In the late afternoon, a young monk in a silken saffron robe crosses a courtyard paved with ancient cobblestones, steps into a ray of sunlight and ignites, as if for a moment he has the sun inside him, as if he is the light of the world.

KB #121

THE FIRST TIME I went to the Kingdom of Bhutan, Druk Air, their official airline, only owned two airplanes. They were both British Airways 146-100 STOL Regionals, jets famous for their tight turns and short landing and takeoff specs. Understandable, since the only commercial airport in the kingdom is at the bottom of a torturous 1,200-foot canyon, and even in the STOL it seemed like the pilot would have to shave off a few trees before he got down.

The pilot's name was Captain George, and he was originally from Yonkers, in Bhutan for ten years to oversee the training of six Bhutanese pilots who would eventually make him obsolete. Captain George was a jolly sort, a Jets fan, and a lifelong Democrat. In explaining why he couldn't seem to move on to whatever his next assignment might be, he said, "Bhutan is the only place I have ever lived where you are walking down the street and all of a sudden you are holding hands with ten children."

I was the only Westerner headed to Bhutan the day I flew with Captain George—the country had barely opened to tourists—so he invited me to sit in the cockpit. Everest, K2, Chomolhari, Kanchenjunga—the entire Tibetan Plateau rose like a city of giant frozen temples before my eyes.

Now, more than a decade later, the king is stepping down, the Amman Corporation is building boutique hotels all over the country, Captain George is long gone, and the Bhutanese have traded in their safe little jets for people-movers. The first Airbus A319 arrived on October 19, 2004, the date chosen because it was an auspicious day in the Buddhist calendar.

The Bhutanese sitting next to Ethan and me, back in row 19, looks like he might cry as he talks about his country's upcoming (in the next auspicious year, 2008) transfer to democracy. "Our king has been like a father to us all," he says, and his face reminds me of the face of the two-year-old grizzly adolescent I ran into in Dry Bay, Alaska, who had just been kicked out of the den by his mother and needed company in the worst way. "It is not as though democracy has made the people of *your* country so happy," he says, and what can we say about that?

The Airbus lands in the canyon bottom unproblematically. Have they cut down the giant pine trees? I wonder. Moved a couple of canyon walls in the name of free enterprise?

The men who come out to greet the plane are wearing the red, black, and gold wraparound fabric called a *gho*, the national dress that has only recently stopped being mandatory, but once we get inside the terminal, the first three teenagers I see are all wearing DK knockoffs.

In customs, an official wearing a navy blue *gho* and a jaunty gold tam beckons to Ethan, asks, "Are you carrying any secrets?" and I watch with pleasure as Ethan startles.

"I beg your pardon?" he says, polite, but wary.

"Secrets! Are you carrying any secrets?" the official says, this time with some impatience.

You can't even imagine . . . I want to say to the uniformed man, even though I know that what he is really saying is *cigarettes,* having just answered the question myself.

37. Tsedang, Tibet

The Tibetan sun, a lot like the Colorado sun, only more so, is streaming in the car window. Rectangular flags of primary colors are flapping in the wind. It was dark when we left Chengdu and dark most of the way to Tibet, but thirty minutes before we landed, it got light enough to see peaks, hundreds of them, and hundreds of snow-covered ridges, blue and white and receding toward forever, shrouded with morning fog. Off in the distance, head and shoulders above the others: Everest, K2, Chomolhari, Kanchenjunga, the rooftops of the world.

Then the plane stretched out and landed in the big brown valley of the Yarlung Tsangpo, which in India becomes the Brahmaputra, the highest river on earth. Hailey and I stepped out onto the tarmac in the middle of the valley, lined by brown foothills, blond dunes forming at their base, the river braiding and braiding and just the tips of the mountains catching the sun's first light.

Now we have driven a hundred kilometers downriver, past villages made of mud huts with yak dung drying on the walls for fuel because Mao *harvested* all the trees, snow-covered mountains peeking every so often through the foothills, an old woman working on her loom in a courtyard, stacks of golden hay against gray mud in the long winter light.

Denzing is driving with a small smile on his face, and Tsering keeps waiting for Hailey and me to collapse from the altitude, and we keep telling him we live at altitude. I say, "I'm so happy to be here!" and Tsering says, "I hope so and I think so."

I always say I can spot an only child of alcoholics across the room, and sometimes people want me to do it as a party trick, and that is how I met Hailey at a magazine launch in an apartment full of strangers five years ago. The editors were aghast because not one word had passed between us, but I saw it in the determined way she sliced the celery and carrots, the seriousness with which she stirred up the dip.

When we get to Tsedang, Tsering says we have to rest in the massive empty and frigid former Holiday Inn for two hours, and we say we aren't tired, and he says we have to rest anyway because he didn't get permission from the police for us to go out and walk around. The police here are called the PSB, though Hailey and I will persist in calling them the PBS. Everyone including Tsering is afraid of them, and he is right to be afraid. If you are Tibetan you can get thrown in jail for fifty years for saying or doing almost anything, and if you are a guide you can get thrown in jail for something the tourists you are paid to look after say or do.

A Chinese woman in the lobby of the frigid hotel says, "You like massage?" and the next thing I know I am laid out in an extremely cold room getting bent and twisted and thumped on by a tiny woman in a bright orange parka with the hood up, dyed orange fur all around her face, and she is snapping my fingers and toes so hard it is making me scream, which has no effect on her behavior whatsoever.

The slipcovers in our hotel room say over and over, *Who's a good luck to you,* in a repeated pattern, which reminds me of the sign in Chengdu that said, *Get on in the park!* Tsering says, *How you say,* about six times in every sentence, and then just plows right on, which reminds me of a friend of my father's named Jack Here, who we used to call *Here-Here,* who let the phrase *On it there* pepper his sentences the way some people might use *like* or *um.*

After our rest we visit Yumbu Lakang, the oldest known dwelling in Tibet, 1,300 years old. When I walk into the inner sanctuary all the smells, sounds, and feelings of Bhutan come back, the yak butter candles, the big happy-faced golden Buddhas, the sunlight pouring in on the primary colors of the thangkas, the prayer wheels spinning with the heat of the candles, and I think, *If these prayer rooms were my prayer rooms, I'd hardly do anything but pray.*

We come back to the hotel room an hour before dinner, and I fall into that baby sleep like I did on my first trip to Bhutan, in the Valley of the Black-Necked Cranes. We'd been traveling all day, a long day, and were going to be sleeping in someone's house. There were no hotels in Bhutan then, no electricity in the whole sacred valley. It was getting dark, and there were hundreds of giant pines out the window, but spaced apart so that you could tell you were in a valley. It was so peaceful, and we were in a traditional room with painted crossbeams: yellow, orange, red, blue, green; everyone was drinking tea and smiling at each other and I just put my head right down on the hard hand-painted wooden bench I was sitting on and went to sleep.

Hailey got so excited earlier today when we saw the Tibetan black-necked cranes that Tsering said, "When we get to the nunnery, Denzing says he will put wings on and fly for you and you can take a picture."

"Oh," Hailey said, "our driver flew away, it was very beautiful, but now we don't know what to do."

38. Taos, New Mexico

Listening to Joy play her saxophone, read her new poems, wishing there was something in my heritage that made my belief system more like hers.

Later, at the Sagebrush Inn, around a fake fireplace, she tells the story of buying her angelfish. How she decided, after her old dog finally died, that she felt too guilty when she traveled, a fish being the right amount of pet to hold down the fort while she led her gypsy life.

It was only the second time she brought her suitcases out from under the bed that Joy noticed that the angel's fins—she had named her Darla by then—were drooping. Then she noticed other behaviors, the PMS that led Darla to slam her head against the glass repeatedly (there would always be a little string of eggs in the water the next day), the way Darla would pout when Joy returned from a trip, hanging in the back corner of the tank for days until she decided Joy could be forgiven.

Joy brought Darla a mate but she ate him the first day. Joy went to a pet psychic, sat quietly in the back until it was her turn, clutching the tiny snapshot of Darla while others held gleaming 8-by-10's of golden retrievers and prizewinning Thoroughbreds.

"Your fish really likes being pretty," the psychic said, "you should tell her she is pretty every day. She is very happy right now," the psychic said, "I see her surrounded by white clouds of happiness," and Joy gasped because just that morning, for the first time, she had released a baggie of brine shrimp into the tank, and left Darla darting among billowing pillows of white.

In the lobby of the Sagebrush Inn, a woman who is teaching a class called "Writing for Social Change" is complaining bitterly to the management about her room out of one side of her mouth while talking on her cell phone out of the other.

I had lived with increasingly unignorable back pain for ten full years before I finally fessed up to myself and went for an MRI. When I got the report back it was filled with alarming words like *severe end-stage degenerative disk disease* and *multiple spinal lesions* so I called my doctor to ask her a few questions and she said, "We are used to our patients being a little more educated than this," and I said I'd be happy to talk to her anytime about *Moby-Dick* or *The Canterbury Tales*.

She sent me to a surgeon who looked at my chart and said, "Seems like we ought to operate. 'S'not that likely to work."

When I told him I was thinking of trying acupuncture, he looked up from his chart and said, "You think the Chinese know more about backs than we do?"

I said I wasn't sure but they had been carrying bags of rice around on theirs for a couple of centuries. The surgeon flipped my chart closed and put his hand on the door, said, "Call me when you become incontinent."

In Pueblo, Colorado, there is a burnt-out shopping mall a few blocks from downtown that says, *The Center of Everything*. I took a picture of myself underneath it by balancing my camera on the hood of my car.

Last night at the Harwood Museum I walked around the Agnes Martin room saying the names of her paintings over and over so that I would not have to hear that night's live performer, a few months shy of his seventieth birthday, read poems about masturbating into a tomato and tweezing black hairs out of the shaft of his dick.

The paintings are simple, horizontal bands of varying width, a whiter white and a bluer white taking turns. *Lovely Life, Perfect Day, Ordinary Happiness.*

39. Breckenridge, Colorado

Watching *High School Musical* in the home theater with Ruby, Will, and Kara.

Before dinner, when Ruby asked Kara to taste her pasta sauce, Kara, fifteen, put about a milliliter of it on the tip of her tongue and shrugged, said, "It's not your best work."

Now she's got her head on my lap, and I've got my legs stretched out across Ruby, while the horrible girl in the movie, whose name is Sharpay, gets exactly what is coming to her, while the sweet girl with the doe eyes and the good singing voice gets the lead role in the play.

Ruby took a writing class from me when she was single and

Kara was two, and even though it was only a one-day class we had the good sense to recognize we were meant to become some sideways version of family. Ruby threw my fortieth birthday party, where we made up a game called *Six Degrees of Helen Reddy* where one person starts a song and everybody sings it until another person pulls a word out from that song and starts another song, and in that way "I Don't Know How to Love Him" can turn into "Ain't No Sunshine" can turn into "Touch Me in the Morning" can turn into "Dock of the Bay" can turn into "Changes" can turn into "It's Too Late," and so on for hours until the game ends with a not-as-campy-as-you-might-imagine version of "I Am Woman." When Kara turned twelve I gave her the choice between London, Paris, Alaska, and Hawai'i and she picked Alaska because she knew that was the place I most wanted her to see.

It's hard to believe it's been a decade since Ruby and Kara came out to visit me in Bolinas to gear up for Ruby's impending divorce from the husband that fell between Kara's real father, who now lives in Sydney, and Will. Kara was five, and what she liked best about California was the cinnamon rolls at the bakery, and Amy's frozen macaroni and cheese.

I had been in Bolinas for six months at the time, trying to recover my own balance after Peter Sawyer left me with the note. I was renting a funky old house that used to belong to a sea captain, and it was sliding down the hill into Bolinas Bay. There was only one bedroom, a dining room table that sat twenty, and no television. We took Kara to the Exploratorium, to the Aquarium, on every kiddie ride at Pier 39 in the hopes she would fall into bed right after dinner.

The night before Ruby and Kara went home to Colorado, we were sitting around the kitchen table, all three of us eating out of a family-size microwaveable Amy's with forks.

Ruby said, "Kara, can you think of something we managed to do without all week and we didn't even really miss it?"

Kara squinted up her eyes, "Daddy?" she said, cracking Ruby and me up.

A few months ago Kara, playing Adelaide in *Guys and Dolls*, the junior high version, belted out the song about post-nasal drip and boys who won't commit like the only professional among so many amateurs, and Ruby and I exchanged a look that said, *We've given her everything we can, but on the subject of men she is totally fucked.*

Now Sharpay frowns as the cute boy asks the doe-eyed girl to the formal and Will rolls his eyes and Ruby opens a roll of unbaked cookie dough and Kara sits up in front of me, says, "Will you braid my hair?"

40. Playa El Triumpho, Mexico

The pelican's body lies in a little nest of desiccating feathers, wings outstretched in the position of crucifixion, in the compromised position of a dive. Our guide Rori says a lot of the young pelicans die early, they hit the water at the wrong angle, and break their supple necks. Ethan said the Tampa pelicans weren't the diving kind, but I saw them do it. Maybe it was the red tide and the hurricanes, the stink from all the dead fish and rotting sea turtles that turned their world upside down and finally made them hungry or confused enough to try.

This morning the other guide, Josh, told us frigate birds are intimidators, that they'll use their swallow tails to swoop down on the pelicans and scare them so much they'll regurgitate their food. Then the frigates will plunge again and snatch the food right out of the sky.

Yesterday, at Ensenada Blanca we met a dog whose real name was Capitán, but someone on a previous trip had named him Noam Chomsky which Josh had misheard as Noah, and by the time Rori tried to correct him, everyone had started calling him Norm. He was a stocky white dog, somewhere between a boxer and a pit bull with a nasty flea rash on his belly and big brown bedroom eyes.

It was the shiny gold shirt that gave the guy away, and the red kerchief at his neck like it was 1976 and he was headed for the disco. The dog had been in all of our laps by then, had already chased the sting-rays out of our paths when we crossed the shallow water carrying our kayaks out for flip drills. He had offered his belly up for each of us to rub.

The borracho was standing near the kayaks, swaying slightly. He'd been there for fifteen minutes watching us load our dry bags: twelve kayaks, eleven women, one man; you could almost hear his brain doing the math. If he made a move to come closer, I missed it, though I was keeping a pretty close eye. Whatever happened, Capitán decided he'd had enough. Not an aggressive bone in that dog's body, any of us would have said, but he went after Mr. Gold Shirt, three warning barks and then a lunge, biting his hand, drawing blood, the man too drunk or too stymied to run.

Here on Playa El Triunpho, a twenty-mile paddle down the

roadless coast south of Loreto, there are no drunks and no dogs to protect us from them. There is nobody here but the dead pelican and us. Rori says, "You can share my sand-free zone if you want," so I stretch out next to her, Orion right overhead, his shoulders, knees, and belt aligned perfectly with mine.

We talk about men and poetry for hours while Orion chases the Pleiades over the canyon wall, Canis Major right on his heel, while Leo rises out the Sea of Cortez, his mane dripping water. We make a list—five each—of what Rori calls our dreams and dragons. My first three dreams: (1) *Cross the forbidden border from Mongolia into Tannu Tuva*, and (2) *Be more generous*, and (3) *Find out if I still know how to navigate by the stars.* I take a deep breath for the first time since Loreto, and realize that the real reason I have come on this trip is to meet Rori and to see the constellations, just this clearly, in just these positions, in this dark equatorial sky.

Rori falls asleep, and on the back of the instruction sheet to my water purifier, I make a list of possible reasons why I don't seem to be missing Ethan one-tenth as much as I expected that includes things like: (5) *Figuring out a new passion like sea kayaking,* and (9) *I don't want to get old feeling like I'm not good enough.* Then I make a last will and testament on the bread-colored inside of an empty cereal box, in which I give the ranch to Fenton the human and my books and CDs to Cinder and all my future royalties to Kara, who no way will need the money, so I cross all of the names out and decide it's not a very fortuitous time to die.

I wake up just before first light and Scorpio, more brilliant than I have ever seen him, has taken Orion's place above me, and Venus is our morning star.

41. Benicia, California

On the bridge over the river between Vallejo and Mare Island, I see something that at first I think are balls of colored paper, but on closer inspection turn out to be three tiny ducklings getting whisked along by the car-created wind; swept off their feet, really, between the concrete median and the single lane of nonstop traffic.

To stop and help them would cause, at best, a ten-mile traffic jam, and at worst, an accident, and even if I decided to take the risk, to be sworn at, run over, bashed from behind, in what way might I help the ducklings that would not incite them to try to get away from me, running under the wheels of the cars that would inevitably try to get around me, plummeting to their death over the side of the bridge, or flapping over the median into the oncoming traffic.

I try to tell myself that eventually, when night comes, the traffic will slow, and those ducklings, if they are very smart and stay tight to the rail, if they are not dead under the wheels of a car, or dehydrated to the point where their little duckling brains aren't functioning, will figure out how to get back from the top of the bridge to the marshland below, and maybe even back to their neglectful mother duck. Far more likely, in the next thirty seconds they will err in the other direction and get sucked up into the engine of a semi.

I know beyond knowing that the memory of these three ducklings and my failure to save them will not fade. I fight down a momentary rage at whoever invented the word *duckling* in the first place. The word *duckling* belongs to a world in which smiling policemen drive out to the Mare Island bridge and set up barricades, stopping traffic in both directions, a world in which those who have to wait fifteen minutes behind the barricades are glad to do it, glad to have a story to tell when they get home about the successful return of the ducklings to the marsh.

Over the years my memory of those three scurrying creatures will become oddly cartoonish, Hughie, Dewey, and Louie, wearing little sailor suits, running just ahead of the tires, then veering warily together off the concrete median. I won't ask myself how I might be using this portion of brain space if I were not feeling sad and ineffectual in regard to the ducklings. I will be certain, only, that this is not the world in which the word *duckling* belongs.

42. Tsedang, Tibet

The next morning Hailey and I wake up and the room is even colder than it was the night before so we get completely dressed without getting out of bed. Tsering is standing in the lobby wearing a woolen Scooby-Doo cap unironically. He says, "Good morning, my new friends. And how are you today?"

We drive in the cold and silent dark to something Tsering calls a ferry terminal (though there is no building) and board a flat-top piece of wood with a motor for a twenty-minute ride across the Yalung Tsangpo to Tibet's first monastery, Sayme.

The great teacher Padmasambhava, the founder of the Nyingma school of Mahayana, the oldest school of Tibetan Buddhism, founded Sayme in 779 AD. Lunch is yak meat with chili paste and boiled eggs in a sunny courtyard, and after lunch we walk around everything clockwise about a million times.

We're trying to learn one Buddha from another, but it is slow-going, especially since I only understand four out of five of Tsering's words, and Hailey understands about half of those. Tsering keeps apologizing for his poor English, which is hilarious, really, because he's only using it to recount seventeen centuries of Tibetan history, and it took all day yesterday for Hailey and me to learn hello (tashi delek) and thank you (t'oo je che). Whenever he gets ready to launch into the history of, say, the Gelugpa school of Mahayana, or the complete biographies of the first seven Dali Lamas, he says, "Now I will give you a brief introduce to . . ."

There is no way his tongue can get around the vowels in "Hailey," so Hailey is fine with being Harry for now.

Last night I talked Hailey into having a foot massage back at our hotel and the highlight was when the orange-hooded masseuse asked Hailey how old her baby was. Hailey said, "No baby," and the masseuse said, "You?" and I said, "No baby." The masseuse said, "Husband?" and we said, "No," and she was incredulous.

The masseuses didn't really speak English so I did a ten-minute charades routine where I acted out our imaginary husbands saying, "Clean the house! Fix my dinner! What do you mean you want to go to Tibet! You have to stay home and take care of me!" The masseuses laughed and gave us raisins and we gave them blue nail polish, and everyone left all happy in that exalted, cultural-exchange kind of way.

After Sayme, we get loaded onto a tiny bus with about a

hundred pilgrims for the short trip from the monastery back to the ferry and I wind up shoved up against this fabulous-looking nomad with a gold furry cap, a giant knife hanging from his belt, and the best laugh lines ever, and I'm thinking despite what Tsering says about the government, there's no way an entire race of people don't flirt.

The bus stops and everybody runs for the ferry and all one hundred of us pile on. About ten different Tibetans dust off places for Hailey and me to sit and the next thing I know the crinkly-eyed nomad with the furry hat is right next to me, and all these fabulous girls with turquoise in their hair are giggling and pointing to Hailey's camera. She takes their photo, and I give them the banana that came with my hotel lunch and then I bow to the crinkly-eyed nomad and give him the apple, and the whole boatload of Tibetans laugh and clap. I keep my eye on Tsering to make sure I'm not doing anything that might send him to jail but he is mostly laughing along with us. No deportations, no recrimination, no PBS involvement of any kind.

43. Davis, California

In my dream, there's this actor, sort of like Ricardo Montalban, but younger and with darker hair—kind of Ricardo Montalban meets David Byrne—and he is a therapist and I'm going inside an enormous house to see him. He says the therapy he's recommending for me is very effective, but also very intensive, as well as expensive, and I will have to come back every day until we are done.

He is wearing a robe of camouflage colored silk, a pattern of leaves and branches, and after making sure I don't have questions, he lies down on the floor, self-combusts, and disappears. There is only a thin line of smoke for me to follow, and it leads me from room to room. In the first room there is a translucent wall, and people are reaching their hands through holes in the wall, but the thick plastic distorts their features. They are reaching out their hands to me saying, *I love you, I love you,* and I am not sure what to do so I give them a little wave.

Next there is a Serenity Room where the people are curled on the floor sleeping like dogs, and a Confidence Room where they are doing things with their bodies that display confidence like puffing out their chests, and striding around purposefully.

That's the gist of it. I go into a room, and the people demonstrate the good thing I am supposed to get from being in that room, and once I figure out the name of the room, it is like solving a puzzle and that trait has been incorporated into my being.

At some point, though, I lose the whiff of smoke I am following, and when I start to look for it again I wind up back in the office with Ricardo.

I say to him, "That was amazing," and he says, "Well, you got to quite a few rooms. You missed quite a few too, but there are other days for that."

I say, "Who are all those people in the rooms?"

"Ah, the actors," he says. "It's crazy, the only line that's longer than the one at my front door is the one at my back door, and you know, I don't even pay them. I pay my assistants and my secretaries, of course, but not the actors. They just do it for love."

44. Pueblo, Colorado

"Don't have kids!" the woman says, as I am lowering my backpack to the floor in the middle of her living room, ten seconds after I've walked in the door. My eyes adjust from the bright August afternoon to the gloomy insides of the low-slung B and B and I take in the woman, take in the room. She is squat, shapeless, dressed in a pink sweat suit with a cartoon character on the front screaming censored obscenities from a thought bubble.

Then I notice the little statues, the same ten-inch-tall, baldish, bone-colored child in hundreds of poses, skipping, picking flowers, pushing a wheelbarrow, on its knees, eyes closed, hands devoutly folded in prayer. They cover every flat surface in the living room, end tables, coffee tables, every square inch of the floor-to-ceiling shelves.

"What are they?" I ask the husband, who seemed normal enough when he shook my hand in the driveway, when he threw the ball for his German shepherd in the yard.

"They're called Precious Moments," he says. "Violet's a collector. We have over three thousand of them, but only room to display eleven hundred at a time. The rest we keep in a vault under the house."

"I've never seen anything like it," I say.

Violet levels her wooden spoon at me and I can smell the sweet sticky batter that will be tomorrow's cream-cheese-stuffed strawberry blintz breakfast.

"I mean it," she says. "Don't even consider kids, if you value your life."

"I won't," I say. "I haven't. I didn't."

"I'm going to show this pretty lady her room," the husband says, and reaches for the backpack that is still between my feet.

"So I'm sitting right here and the phone rings," Violet says. "It's my son's girlfriend, Alice." She leans across the counter toward me; spoon first, as if offering me a taste. "They live down in Trinidad. Alice's in a wheelchair, you know, and he helps her out."

The cartoon character on the woman's shirt, I can see now, is the Tasmanian Devil, and it is Daffy Duck who is exclaiming about the devil's despicability from a beak that has been twisted around to the back of his head.

"So Alice says to me, 'Are you sitting down?'" Violet says, "and I says, 'Tell me one thing, and one thing only. *Is my son dead?*'"

On the shelf above Violet's head, one precious moment statue is watering a bed of tulips, another is baking cookies, another is being trailed by a tiny family of geese.

"Alice says, 'No,'" Violet says, "'but when I tell you what I am about to tell you, you'll wish he was.'"

Violet pauses for dramatic effect. Her husband lets my pack sink back to the carpet.

"'Tiffany's knocked up,' Alice says to me." Here Violet winces, and for one split second I'm allowed to see behind all her bluster, all her little cities of defense. "Tiffany is Alice's teenage daughter," Violet says. "She's all knocked up, and guess who'd be the father?"

"Violet," the husband says, "you're exaggerating."

"How's that?" Violet says, narrowing her eyes at him, and I have to agree that paternity is a tough thing to exaggerate. The husband picks up my pack and we head down the hall, leaving Violet staring into her mixing bowl.

The next day, in town, the librarian will ask me where I am staying and when I tell her she will say, "Did they tell you what else is in that vault under the house? An arsenal. Automatic weapons, grenades, some people say enough to blow up the whole damn town."

45. Lhasa, Tibet

Today we visit the Jokhang Monastery, the most sacred one in Tibet, and since it is the fifteenth of the month—not our month, but theirs—thousands of pilgrims are here, prostrating and praying and pushing their way in. It is a little like the Who concert (not that I was at the Who concert) except everyone is saying *Om mani padme hum* while they are ramming into each other.

They're carrying yak butter lamps and prayer wheels and the monks are having a good time shoving everyone into one chapel door and hauling them out the other—I mean the full-body kind of shoving—the whole place alive and filled with candlelight and bodies wanting health, long life, enlightenment—the floor of the monastery slick with ghee—pilgrims throwing themselves on the ground with little hand protectors, short cropped gray-haired women who all look like Pema Chodron and nomads with their hair tied up in red and black cords like curtain pulls, babies in snowsuits and nuns who have wings like a Bavarian cuckoo clock, leather-clad merchants and schoolgirls in uniform, people who have come—some of them—from hundreds of miles away and prostrated on their journey—Tsering said—every third step, everyone chanting and shoving and staring at me and Hailey, and us staring right back.

There are monks writing people's names with golden ink for luck, there is a lama with a Walkman, a nomad with a cell phone, and a monk all in burgundy robes with a hat the exact same color as the robes, with a Nike swoosh that does not say—but implies—the Washington Redskins. There are firecrackers and little kids saying *Hello!* to us constantly. And us saying *Tashi delek!* back. There are pilgrims who stare and stare at Hailey's camera but then say, "No! No!" when she puts it to her eye, so she takes it down and then they say, "Okay, now!"

When we get outside, Tsering turns us loose, saying, "Today you may walk anywhere you wish," so we take the long way round to Potala Square where the red-and-black-headbanded nomads are selling sides of yak to anyone who can carry one away. We see half-yaks balanced across four people's heads, hanging out of the back of a *tuk-tuk*, suspended impossibly across the handlebars of a bicycle, we even see a side of yak in the open trunk of a Lincoln Town Car.

The next day we return with Tsering to the Potala Palace, mother of all monasteries, four million square feet with walls sixteen feet thick, the only one Mao found too beautiful to smash.

How many statues of how many Buddhas? There are a thousand in one room alone. We enter a chamber that has all of the lessons of compassion on one side, all of the lessons of emptiness on the other. I say, "In America, we have a hard time understanding emptiness," and Tsering says, "In Tibet too, only the highest teachers understand emptiness. The common people, no."

In another room we see statues of Green Tara and White Tara—two of the very few girl-gods around here—sprung from a teardrop that fell out of the Buddha of Compassion's eye.

We see a statue of that Buddha, carved from sandalwood, but according to Tsering, no one did the carving. Which reminds me of the Tiger's Nest in Bhutan that nobody built, which I guess, if you think about it, is the kind of thing most religions are full of.

Tsering says, "If you come to Lhasa without seeing the Potala, you don't come to Lhasa, and if you come to the Potala without seeing this statue, you haven't seen the Potala." In the room of the Potala that holds the Mandala of the Wheel of Time, Tsering says, "The Wheel of Time is where the Buddha resides."

I say, "Actually?" and Tsering rolls his eyes, points to his temple, and says, "Imagination."

We go onto the roof to see the Dalai Lama's apartment, which is called the Eastern Sunshine Apartment, and we hear pigeons flying with whistles in their tails. There are beggars outside the temple and when we come out of the gate they say, "Hello. Money."

46. Newport, Oregon

Goody Cable has just finished living the alphabet, two weeks per letter, for a whole calendar year. "You know," she says, as if I might, "it started out at the coffee shop. We served apple tarts during the *a* weeks, blueberry tarts during the *b*'s. I started to ask my employees to see if they could answer the phone using only words that began with whatever letter. Before I knew it, it had bled over into everything."

I'm staying in the Herman Melville Room, while offshore hundreds of gray whales make their way to California. We are up in the attic doing a jigsaw puzzle, which may be the single fastest way one OCD person reveals herself to another. Things have gotten a bit competitive and here at the three-hour mark it's clear we are going to take it all the way down to the final piece.

"During the *d*'s I took a dulcimer lesson," Goody goes on, "during the *f*'s I went fishing. Now that it is over, I'm not exactly sure what to do with myself."

"What did you do during the *q*'s?" I ask.

"Well, I tried quilting, but I didn't like it very much. So then I asked a lot of questions, and after that I practiced being very very quiet."

Last night, at the fancy hotel in Portland, I dreamed that Ethan was putting lotion on the bodies of two dark-skinned girls, in the space between the belly button and the pubic bone, but the lotion was too white and it didn't sink in. Then Hillary Clinton, who in the dream was married to Mark Strand, was telling me not to take Ethan's proclivities personally, to try to see them as an opportunity instead.

"Living with a man like Ethan simply means redefining loyalty," Hillary said, "which is not the worst thing in the world when you consider how many faithful couples never have sex."

Mark was nodding sagely in his chair, aging, I noticed, in a way that was not unlike Fenton the dog, especially around the temples. I went to tell Ethan what Hillary said, but when I got there he had left without me, left my two suitcases near the door.

One time in real life, after we'd broken up but before he'd moved out, I asked Ethan if he felt like kicking in something for the electric bill, and he said "No." After a minute's consideration he added, "Pam, men in third-world countries treat women so badly, those women actually think I'm treating them well."

47. Limatour Beach, Marin County, California

Rori and I head out to the sweeping crescent of Limatour Beach at dawn—frost on the windshield—driving over the last remnants of the coastal range, past a herd of albino fallow deer.

The Farallon Islands are as crystal clear as jewels in the cold morning, the clearest I have seen them. Fenton the dog chases pelicans and Rori takes a dip because she's missing Mexico, and also because she's a total rock star.

At acupuncture last Wednesday, Janine said, "You are in a time of your life when you need some serious mothering, but mothering in the largest sense," and I said, "You mean like the ocean?" and she said, "Exactly," and that's why we're here. My conversations with Janine often go like that. It's not just that I don't know where the things she says come from, I don't know where what I say comes from either.

Another time she said, "By the way, there are a bunch of Native Americans hanging around your navel. They want you to think about origins."

Once the sky opens like a mouth and invites you inside it, everything starts to feel like a riddle. On the I-25 between Albuquerque and Santa Fe, after midnight, the billboards read like runes. *Psychic Mary / Great at Parties* comes first, with her blue eye shadow and a red turban and a psychotic twinkle in her eye that makes one fear the kind of party she'd be great at. Next is the *A ULT DEO* sign, the burnt-out letters turning a porn shop into a Latin prayer. *Finally!* reads the next one, *Holly Holms versus Bobbi Jo Saunders, June 13th at the Isleta Casino.* Both women look tough for the camera in their boxing gloves and bunny garb.

One time on the Big Island, I got to swim next to a giant sea turtle and after I wore myself out trying to keep up with him I sat on the sand and waited for that moment when your skin stops feeling sticky and starts feeling clean, and that voice that talks to me sometimes, not like schizophrenia—but really, how would I know—said, *It's about time you learned how to pray.*

Back on Limatour, Rori is shaking off water like a dog and I think of a different day, on North Beach when a real dog walked up to us, some kind of dachshund, wearing a sign that covered almost all of his back that said, *Hi, my name is Baker, and I am enjoying myself on the beach while my dad surfs. If you want to you can throw a rock for me, but please don't let me run in front of cars in the parking lot.*

I remember the colors of Mackenzie's kite, backlit against a gray sky, the shimmer on the water, the curling blue waves, the lighthouse flashing its single beam in the distance.

Today on Limatour I am watching for spouts, thinking about how the size of a blue whale's tongue is the same size as the largest current land animal, the African elephant; how a blue whale's heart weighs a thousand pounds and is the size of a Volkswagen; how you could put a small child down its blowhole, if you wanted to; how one scientist bet another that he could walk through a dead blue whale's aorta, and then he did.

48. Gyantse, Tibet

Here are the names of the passes we'll go over: Kamba La, Karo La, and Simi La; past Yamdrok Yumtso and Nojin Kangtsang; 670 kilometers in total, from Lhasa to Gyantse to Shigatse and back. Here are the three photos I'll regret not taking: the *Om mani padme hum* burned into the hillside, the smiling pilgrim monk holding up a tea thermos in the window, the guy wearing what looked like an entire fox on his head.

In the villages, herds of dazzling dark-eyed kids run up to us and stick out their tongues.

Patrick says the fact that I only think babies are cute if they live in a third-world country is evidence of deep-seated self-hatred.

"There was one bad king of Tibet," Tsering says. "He had horns and a black tongue. So when children approach elders they touch their head to show they don't have horns, and they stick out their tongue to show it isn't black."

On the drive to Tashilhumpo we talk about the Panchen Lama, but Tsering says we won't talk about this *at* Tashilhumpo, because it was there his friend got sent to jail because one of his American clients started handing out pictures of the Dalai Lama.

I say, "We feel very lucky to have you as a guide," and he says, "Well, I am lucky to have the two of you too, because with you I can talk about everything."

In Gyantse, at the Grand Chorten, Hailey feels sick, so Tsering and I climb up the vertical stairs in pitch blackness without her. We sit together inside the tower, inside those giant eyes, waiting for the monk with the key and access to the light switch, talking in the dark about wanting to see and do everything in the world. While we are up there, Hailey gets propositioned by a Tibetan in an Arlo Guthrie sweatshirt.

"Yeah," she says, once we are all safely back in the vehicle, "I came all the way to Tibet just to give you head."

On the way to Shigatse, Tsering says, "I think now we will look for a place to make our picnic," and we stop just below the top of a pass along the side of the road. There probably isn't a bathroom for a hundred kilometers in any direction so I wander away from the group and when I come back Hailey says, "How did that go?" and I say, "All things considered—thirty-mile-per-hour winds, below zero temperatures, and right off the sheer side of a thousand-foot cliff—pretty well."

Tsering says if we want to find a good man we have to ask the Shakyamuni Buddha. He points to a monastery high on the ridgeline and says a crow stole a lama's hat and where he put it down was where they decided to build the monastery, and I say, "It would have been more convenient if the crow had put it down on the valley floor."

"But that is not what happened," Tsering says, all earnestness.

I say, "Americans say stupid things all the time, but a lot of us mean well."

It is our third to last day in Tibet and even though I have begun lusting after things like a Caesar salad and toilet paper, I am trying not think about how it will be not to see Denzing's face in the morning, that one beautiful laugh line that curls up around his eyebrow, how it will be not to have Tsering waiting in the lobby saying, "Good morning. And how are you today?"

At the last acupuncture before Tibet, Janine said, "I'm seeing an octopus with very thin tendrils that come from behind and wrap around to your solar plexus, below your rib cage and around your navel. With your permission I'll remove those."

Back in Lhasa we give Tsering and Denzing our hiking boots and all of our fuzzy outdoor clothes and Tsering says, "I will be reminded of the two of you when I wear your clothes. Pam, looking over one shoulder, and Harry, looking over the other.

QV #905

I AM LOOKING OUT the rounded rectangle of the plane window, at the right-hand tire at the bottom of two triangular struts that descend diagonally from the wing. Laos Air likes these planes with the high wings, I know, because they don't need much space to take off or land. On the tire I am looking at there is a giant X of duct tape, which on closer examination I see is actually a patch on top of a patch, an older X of duct tape beneath it.

"Look at that," I say, to the Laotian beside me. We have already established that he speaks English. In fact, a few minutes ago he told me our flight to Phonsavan is seven hours late because the drug lords up in Chaing Rai needed to borrow the plane. He said it with the type of smile on his face he might have worn if he were telling me his grandmother had baked him some cookies. Now he nods his head at the tire in a similar kind of affirmation. He is well-dressed and studious-looking, a thick book in his lap, possibly a government official.

"That," he says, "is no problem."

"It looks like a problem," I say.

"No, no," he says. "The correct way to land this plane is the left side first, then the nose, then the right side. One, two, three," he says, making his hand into a little airplane. "No problem with that one there."

Yesterday, in the relative safety of the teahouse, Xai said, "Lao Aviation has a new director now. The old director is in . . ." He paused for a minute, trying, I assumed, to remember the English word. "Jail?" I offered, but the answer was Bangkok.

On Laos Air, none of the tray tables stay attached to the back of the seats, and few of the seats stay in a forward locked position. Somewhat more disturbingly, the cabin is not sealed, so soon after takeoff, when we hit some perfect combination of altitude and dew point, clouds of steam come rolling down from the overhead bins and fill the cabin.

This is the point when the Westerners always scream, because to the untrained eye, the steam looks a lot like smoke, but this is my third flight on Laos Air, which makes me an old hand. Today when the steam starts billowing in, a blond woman in her sixties—German, I think—two rows in front of me, grabs the flight attendant's arm in alarm.

"Air-conditioning," the flight attendant says, as she must every single flight, without so much as cracking a smile.

"The Chinese have the contract to service these planes," says the Laotian beside me when we have reached whatever altitude is required to cause the steam to clear, "but our government cannot pay the money, and so they do not service the planes. I think this would not happen in your country."

"I think it would not," I say.

"Some of these planes have not been serviced probably for three to five years."

"Hence the duct tape," I say, but I don't think he understands.

"What do the Chinese care about some dead Laotians?" he asks, and there is that off-to-grandmother's-house smile again as the plane lurches suddenly forward, and begins its steep descent.

49. Mallorca, Spain

Everything is green and soft, there are goats in the hills wearing bells around their necks that I hear all night but never see, and two donkeys, one light, one lighter still, who come to the fence for fresh apricots. In Pollença there is a heavenly old square with a place to get strong coffee and liquid chocolate so thick you can stand a spoon in it.

Yesterday we went as a class to one of the world's most perfect beaches and swam far far out—the nice thing about the Mediterranean—and then all the way back and I slept like a rock for the first time in months.

I'd been reading Ethan's most recent *I'm sorry and I want you back* email out loud at breakfast (*I've forgotten how to be who I am without you . . . La Paz was like the first day of seventh grade when the girl I'd been waiting all summer to see (in that case Ellen Sweeny but in this case YOU) hadn't shown up . . . Now in photos you seem nothing short of dreamy —and as we often agreed in luxurious late-night conversations, it's what's exquisite in the world that breaks our hearts*) and all the girls were oohing and aahing and falling for it completely, and then Samantha, who works with military boys in Garmisch, Germany, providing R and R for burned-out soldiers, said, "He sounds like a total narcissist to me."

This afternoon we all pile into Ralph's Land Rover for the Imelda Marcos field trip. Ten women on their way to the Camper shoe outlet: Leah the ultramarathoner who lives on a commune in Santa Cruz where the Master gets to have sex with all the women but the women don't get to have sex with anybody else; Natalie who looks sixteen and is nevertheless battling what Claire calls mole cancer; Claire herself, with her porcelain skin, Botticelli hair, and her BBC voice; Paige, from Ohio, who's only lived in London for six years but has nonetheless acquired an English accent (she keeps referring to Washington and Oregon as the Western Terra-trees . . . and I say, "I know you have been away a long time, Paige, but we call those states now"). Then there is funny Peg who writes for the *Guardian* and calls us all mad as a box of frogs, and Lina, who didn't want to study writing at all but came over because she had read—perhaps erroneously—on Trip Advisor that Ralph has been known to let a woman who's signed up for a course have her way with him, and London Karen and New York Karen, and Sloan, who's written ten cookbooks, and me, all hurtling the wrong way down a one-way because it is a shortcut.

Ralph's a smart sweet guy and a damn good cook with the single glaring exception of the skate wing he served last night, doused liberally in ammonia, and so radically undercooked that you would have had to saw it off the bone.

We had watched the sunset over Cape Formentor and so were late for dinner and already feeling sheepish. Sloan said, "Has there been an accident?" so strong was the chemical smell when we walked into the room, and she took the skate back into the kitchen for a do-over, but even cooked through it was hard to choke down.

After dinner we discovered that seven out of seven of the American women here this week, including myself, have not only been in a sorority but have held a major office in a sorority, in most cases president, though I had been chaplain of Delta Delta Delta— ostensibly in charge of eighty girls' spirituality—when I was just a girl myself.

"In what ways did you advance their spirituality, then?" asked Claire, who had never even thought the word *sorority* one single time in her mind.

"Well," I said, "I blindfolded them and bound their hands with silver, gold, and blue ribbons and told them stories about Poseidon, of course!"

50. Denver, Colorado

I get out of the composer's black-sheeted bed at five-thirty in the morning, get a double latte at Ink! and meet the CEO in the parking lot of the Walmart so he can follow me to the ranch. Tuesday, I have a date in Durango with an ophthalmologist.

The CEO zips over Kenosha Pass behind me in his Porsche and right near the top I hear Henry's ghost say *What the F?* over my shoulder and I think, *This is the summer when my life turns into a reality TV show.*

The CEO gives me an antique book called *Five in One, or How to Make and Save Money*, where all the little pieces of advice are numbered into one thousand mini-chapters, as in #86, "Lice Destroyers," and #349, "Lemon and Its Value," and #760, "Butter Making and Marketing," and #962, "How to Find Out a Girl's Age Without Asking Her."

Long ago, on my thirtieth birthday I took a helicopter ride over Manhattan at sunset. I remember the colored lights of the Chrysler Building, the immovable bulk of the twin towers. I remember feeling like if I wanted to I could reach out and scratch the Statue of Liberty under her chin. I remember the tens of thousands of lighted windows and trying to acknowledge, at least briefly, each life inside that was being illuminated. There were so many individual souls to keep track of, I realized, for anyone who called himself God.

One night a few years before he died, my father and I were out to dinner and I was offering up the résumé of whatever man I had started to date at the time—let's say Peter Sawyer—saying I hoped Peter would see we'd make an interesting fit, and my father said, "What the hell's wrong with you that these guys aren't falling all over themselves trying to convince *you* of something?"

I interpreted him, rightly, I think, as trying to pay me a compliment.

51. Lhasa, Tibet

At Drepung the monks are at morning prayer. Mao's face, ten times bigger than life, is stamped all over the giant stones of the fallen monastery and red writing covers the crumbling walls.

Tsering says the Red Guard knocked the stones over because the Buddha on them was smiling. When no one is within listening distance I ask him if they are forced to leave Mao's picture on the wall and he says, "No, we leave it there to remember."

In the Housewives' Room the lama says, "If you touch this stone you will be a good housewife," and Hailey and I both take huge steps back. There is one temple we are not allowed into and when I ask Tsering why he says, "Because women have a month, you understand what I mean?" and I do.

At the Sera Monastery we get to sit in on the Monks' Debate where a hundred or so monks pair off, and one asks the question over and over and the other answers just as many times, all the while hitting himself in the arm with his own prayer beads, thereby sending good skyward and evil below.

Tsering keeps making eye contact with me like, *Let's go,* and I pretend not to see him because I want to sit in that courtyard for the rest of my life listening to the sounds of their voices that are really more like hyenas or snow geese, imagining all of the things I could be learning that afternoon if only I spoke Tibetan, could be hearing the questions and answers, could be learning what is big, or how is attachment, or why is the path to a valuable life.

Yesterday, on the way into town there was an overturned tractor-trailer (which here means a farm tractor hooked to an uncovered diesel engine with a flatbed on the back that hauls everything from people to animals to rocks to tumbleweeds). There was corn scattered all across the road, one man kneeling over another man who had one shoe on and one shoe off and looked dead. The kneeling man had his hands over the dead man's mouth and I wondered if he was feeling for breath, or holding his face together (literally), or if it was some Buddhist thing, like keeping his soul in there until the proper holy person arrived, and I thought, *What happens now?* and wondered if it was like Lat said it was in Laos, "You know this life? It is nothing."

Later, at the Fill Up the Room with Gold restaurant (for the first half of dinner we think Tsering is saying Fill Up the Room with Goats), eating *momos* and potato soup with cardamom and yak fifteen ways, Denzing asks Hailey to sing the theme song from *Titanic*. We teach them to say, *Go Broncos,* and Tsering says, "I love Michael Jackson until he change his skin."

Denzing runs outside to find an old person who can write our names for us in Tibetan.

I say, "Why are you guys so nice to us?"

Tsering says, "When you do something nice for somebody, it is just like walking around a temple. It is just like saying a prayer."

52. Durango, Colorado

The ophthalmologist, whose name is Victor, says, "I want to say this in a way that makes you think I am a normal person. My daughter Penelope still sleeps with me. She's twelve."

But I already don't think he is a normal person. What he has told me so far is that his half brother is a nonfunctioning borderline schizophrenic married to another nonfunctioning borderline schizophrenic and his little brother committed suicide. His father has children with five different women and those are only the ones he will admit to. His stepfather was so abusive Victor left home at sixteen.

He says he came back home to say goodbye to his mother on the night he was going into the Special Forces, and when the step-father saw him he put a .357 magnum to his own two-year-old's head and said if Victor didn't get out that minute he was going to blow the kid's brains out.

Not that being abnormal is necessarily a bad thing.

I look at my watch. I say the only thing I can think of saying, which is that I used to ride a horse named Penelope. We are exactly thirty minutes into an hour-long lunch date. Then he says, "I must tell you, I am attracted to athletic bodies, not necessarily skinny, but toned." I look at his thinning hair, his stringy ponytail, watch him eat a date wrapped in bacon, watch a drip of grease run down his chin. I want to say, *I'll bet that twelve-year-old you sleep with is very athletic.* I want to say, *I can get toned if I want to but you'll still be short.*

What I do say is, "Excuse me," make myself walk as far as the restroom, turn right instead of left, push through the front door of the restaurant, and break into a run.

The first night the CEO stayed at the ranch—in the guest room— I got an email from Fenton the human that said: *RE: New Dating Plan. I recall your saying, and wisely, about the Rhode Island reverend that good-looking men were at some level all alike. I knew what you said was true, and I proceeded anyway (though, I'm glad to say, with some reservation). We never did the deed, thank God, but in the end, just as he'd led me on for six months or so, he took me out to a restaurant called, no kidding,* The Last Supper, *to confess that he'd met someone else.*

53. New York, New York

In the alley in front of Freeman's, there is a man staring at and praying—prostrating himself, to be more precise—to a life-size graffiti horse. The horse is gray, and looks a lot like the My Little Ponies of my youth, but the words written in fat letters across its back are *Her Glory Always Reinstated.*

Mackenzie and I are staying at the Bowery Hotel, a place so new its rates are going to triple the day after we leave, a place so new that it has been artificially weathered. Both elevators look like people have had chainsaw fights inside of them.

We are here to see Tom Stoppard's play about the Russian Revolution, but we are also being girlfriends on a trip to New York. Mackenzie always knows the best places for everything decadent: double lattes, red velvet cupcakes, Gorgonzola with rhubarb chutney on the cheese board at the Met.

Last night Kevin Bacon stood so close to us, smoking his cigar, I could have tripped him on the way back to the stage. So far today we've seen skinny Kirsten Dunst, and her even skinnier rock-star boyfriend; we have gone to Rice to Riches, the place that has twenty-five flavors of rice pudding such as "Sex Drugs and Rocky Road," or "I'll Take Eggnog for $200, Alex," which they serve in these excellent reusable flying saucers; and Mackenzie bought a pair of white plastic shoes for a hundred dollars and forty-nine cents. We chat with a handsome guy walking two black Danes wearing spiked-out collars (even though they're the sweetest peas) and he turns out to be Janeane Garofalo's dog walker.

Now that's a celebrity sighting I can really get behind.

I grew up in Trenton, New Jersey, and when I was a kid my mother would keep me out of school a day or two a week so I could go into Manhattan with her for her auditions. At the end of the day we would get Italian ices while we waited in the traffic line for the Lincoln Tunnel—she always got lemon, I always got cherry—and we kept the top down on the old Mustang both ways through the tunnel and never even thought about exhaust.

Tucked into our Frette sheets at the Bowery, I report to Mackenzie that handsome Bucky Baxter recently said I was the most interesting woman in Creede, which I realize could fall under the category of damning with faint praise and Mackenzie smiles sweetly, and says, "Bucky wants you to be his next ex-wife."

At the Elks' Fourth of July dance Bucky told me that now that he has turned fifty-two he has decided to only fuck women he really likes. Which was not to make me think he didn't still fuck like an animal, because he could assure me that he did.

I know I am supposed to only think this about outdoor adventures, but there is something about flying down Fifth Avenue in a cab, after dark, barely making lights, you know, like everybody's life depends on it, maybe a fine coating of rain hissing under the tires, the driver screaming in Tigrinya into his cell phone, that makes me feel like I could round a corner and turn my life into just about anything at all.

In Central Park yesterday there were no less than twenty-five birders, ganging up as they do on a three-inch Kentucky warbler, giant lenses jockeying for position between the hippies camped out at Strawberry Fields. Near Belvedere Castle we saw a couple who were walking either to or from their wedding. The man with shock white hair and shock white teeth, the woman in a long white dress carrying a bouquet of white tulips, neither of them a day under seventy, both of them as happy as two people have ever been.

"Congratulations," came tumbling out of my mouth before I knew I was speaking, and they were so grateful, so eager to smile back their gratitude, so humbled by their good fortune.

"Did you see them?" I asked Mackenzie, just to make sure they were real.

54. Creede, Colorado

If there are twenty-nine points of matching, Dr. Carl, Dr. Neil, and Dr. Hans, then why do I keep winding up on coffee dates with men who have just finished reading Ann Coulter?

55. Provincetown, Mass

Class is over and I take a walk out to the breakwater: a million tons of granite in squared-off boulders laid end to end across the bay, from the place where town gives way to marsh out to Long Point, the very very tip of Cape Cod, curled back tight on itself like a fist. When the tide is running in or out it's loud out here, the water rushing under the granite. If you come at night you can see the bioluminescence that gets created when aquatic glowing microorganisms get slammed into something solid like rock.

Now it is slack tide, utterly still. A heron stands in the wide marsh between the nude beach and me. A seal turns lazy circles in the deeper water of the harbor.

The night before I left Davis I stood in front of the old barn, the rabbit patch that will, by the time I get back, be turned into condominiums, and took Orion back from Ethan, gave it to Henry, the one who deserved it, took back the greenbelt and the bats and the whales.

That day at acupuncture Janine had said, "You know, Pam, you *are* supported," and I saw a pair of cupped hands, lined and fleshy, poised to receive, maybe water, maybe something water only stands for, and I said, "I *do* know," because at least in that moment I did.

A barn owl called from the hayloft and I had my toes in the water of feeling-good-without-doing. Also, there is nothing more real about the moments where you are denied love than the moments when it is all right there for you and you are truly in the center of your life.

Now the sun is getting ready to set somewhere west behind Boston, and the sky's gone all soft blues and pinks. "Okay," I say, out loud, which at first feels ridiculous. I'll admit that I don't know who I am praying to. Something somewhere between ocean and God. "I think I am finally ready for love." I can hear the slightest trickle of tide starting up in the rocks below me. "But if you can't do that, if you think I'm not ready, then maybe just a little romance to keep the conversation going." The heron spreads his wings, gives a little hop. "And if you think I'm not even ready for that, then how about just a few more signs I'm on the right path."

Satisfied with my prayer, I train my eyes back on the heron. A dapper little man has been chugging down the breakwater, wearing short shorts covered in pastel fleur-de-lis, walking a westie, who is wearing a sweater, even though the day is warm. He doesn't slow as he approaches—he's got plenty of room to get by. He says, "Lovely place to sit and think, isn't it?"

"Yeah," I say, "it sure is."

He never breaks stride, but smiles wide as he passes. "You're a good person," he tells me. "It's all going to be okay." I watch him retreat over the granite, the tops of the big rocks turning green and gold and purple in the dimming light.

56. Leadville, Colorado

On Friday the thirteenth, after we had dinked around in the cowboy bar; after we had agreed to exchange addresses, and then couldn't find a pen; after we had gone up to Rick's room, nothing salacious but he knew there was a pen there; after he became the fourth man in six months to say, "I want to say this in a way that makes you think I am a normal person"; after he'd told me about the couple who stood at the end of his bed some nights: the woman who had a face and arms but no body, and the man who had no face but was only a suit of clothes; after he pulled out of his briefcase a card with the very same hands I had seen in the sky over Davis; after so many hours had gone by that we couldn't sit up anymore but we didn't want to part; after I said, "Well how about this, we just lie down on the bed, no sex, and no clothing removal . . . It will be just like what we are doing now, except horizontally"; after he told me his favorite song and his favorite color and his favorite fishing hole and I told him my favorite movie and my favorite country and my favorite dog, and it couldn't be more than an hour until the sun started creeping over the horizon, he said, "If you aren't too sleepy can you please keep talking? It doesn't really matter at all what you say."

57. Drigung, Tibet

Tsering and Hailey and I follow an old lama to the top of a bald hill above the monastery in the cool morning air. We have been told there will be three corpses, a man, a woman, and a child, and that they are unrelated, though they appear to us like a little family, laid out on the platform, wrapped in their cotton shrouds.

"We are very lucky," Tsering says. "Many corpses today." When he says *corpse*, it sounds like copse, as in pines.

The man who will prepare the bodies arrives and begins to unwrap the first corpse. A little ways up the hill, roughly a hundred vultures jockey for position against a rope held in place by family members of the deceased. They are wild birds, but Drigung is the most accessible monastery practicing sky burials; the birds know to come at 11 a.m. for their almost daily feed.

Tsering told us the bodies would be quartered, but the word *filleted* is the one that jumps to mind. He explains that the man with the big knife will make four incisions, one around the chin, one down the center of the torso, and two at a diagonal down the shoulder blades. They pull the skin off the bones, he says, because if they don't give the vultures the bones first, they sometimes eat the flesh and leave the bones, and then the whole person doesn't ascend together, and there is more work for the butchers to pound the bones into pulp. He hesitates enough over the word *butcher* that I know he is not quite happy with it, but he doesn't know a better one.

"These men," he says, "that do the cutting. They are not allowed to marry. Their karma is very bad. Same with the men who butcher animals."

"Do you mean this job is punishment for their last life," I ask him, "or that they will be punished for this job in the next life?"

"Yes," he says. "Also jewelers. It is the same."

"Jewelers?" I say. "Why?"

"It is just what we believe," he tells me.

"Is it because they are wealthy?" I ask.

"It is just what we believe," he says again.

All three bodies are cut into pieces, and I miss whatever sign the lama gives to the men who have been holding the rope. When the vultures run in the smell takes up all the air on the mountaintop, and as they rush past me I can see they are huge birds, each of them half the size of a man. There is squawking and shrieking, several birds go after one femur, another makes off with a forearm, the hand, with all the flesh still on it, bouncing along the stones at my feet. No fewer than six birds are pulling in different directions on a skull that is still attached to a spine that is still attached to one leg and the skull is laughing. The old lama plays tug-of-war with a vulture over a leg bone, and when he wins he lifts another vulture, this one nearly featherless, out of the melee and gives him what is left of the bone.

"That is a sick one," Tsering says. Every so often the butcher picks up an especially aggressive vulture by its head and hauls it off to the side.

When there is nothing left but skulls and pelvises the butcher steps back in, and pounds the big bones into pulp with a giant mallet. Bone pulp flies all over the place and a huge wad of it lands on Tsering's arm. In seconds a member of the family of the deceased comes over with a little bottle of alcohol and wipes it clean for him. His preparedness makes me realize this must happen all the time. Tsering smiles at the man out from under his Scooby-Doo hat.

On the walk back down the hill Tsering says, "When I see a sky burial, all desire to have money and get more things goes away, because you see a man, then you see him dead in a ball, then you see him cut to pieces, and in twenty minutes he is nothing, it is like he never existed."

Tsering picks sage so that we can burn it in the little stupa back at the monastery. When we get there he shows me how to stick my whole upper body in so that I won't take the bad dead-people-luck with me back into the world. When I can't see or breathe anymore I pull my head out, but Denzing grabs me by the scruff of the neck and pushes me back in.

"It is very unusual," Tsering says, when Denzing finally turns me loose, "a Westerner, here, at this ceremony. Denzing is afraid that now the car will crash." Denzing holds Hailey in the stupa so long I think she will surely asphyxiate. When he finally lets her out he talks with urgency for several minutes to Tsering in Tibetan and when he's finished we ask what he said. Tsering thinks a long time and says, "Denzing says it is good to be happy all the time."

"Really," Hailey says, "all those words?"

"And," Tsering says, after a pause, "he says it is sometimes also good to be sad."

58. Buena Vista, Colorado

On the phone, Rick says, "I've got something I need to say and I want you to know that it is a considered thought. I know what it means and I know what it means to say it."

I can hear the table saws running behind him. Since that first night in Leadville, Rick has called me once a day from his shop in north Boulder, where, five years ago, when the pine beetles moved into northern Colorado, he and his four employees stopped making custom canoes out of Spanish cedar, and started turning beetle-kill lodgepole into what he calls *the sweetest wood flooring known to man* so lucratively that he's been able to give 50K a year back to reforestation.

I am on my way home from Denver, just past the Gunsmoke truck stop, about to head into the canyon of the Arkansas where I know the reception will get squirrelly, so I pull over near the little airstrip to hear what he has to say.

"I love you already," he says. "I know it to be true. I love you right down to the bone." *This*, I think, *is the difference between an activist and a carpenter.*

A little Cessna is practicing touch-and-goes and I watch it and wait for the *But.*

"But I am forty-nine years old," he continues. "We have gone so far in so quickly. I know what it means to go deep and I can go deep with you. I know I can do it, but I have done it at least once before and it hasn't lasted."

I want to say, *Yeah, but that was with a woman who moved to Boulder and changed her name from Sophie to Sofree.* I want to say, *Six days is not time enough to love me all the way down to the bone.* I want to say, *If I love you, then I will not have the opportunity to fulfill Cinder's prophecy and break furniture with Bucky Baxter.* But on the off chance I already love him back, I, for a change, say nothing at all.

59. Tucson, Arizona

I have not been on the property thirty minutes when I am lying on a massage table in a softly lit, frangipani-scented room with a person named Trevor towering over me.

"I can see," he says, "that you are doing a lot of spiritual work because look how far you are out in your hair." His accent is vaguely South African, and he has the most impressive unibrow I have ever seen. "I do not read poetry," Trevor says, "because I live poetry."

He picks my feet up and lets them fall back to the table. "May I ask you," he says, "why the lower half of your body is perpetually standing in ice cold water?" He means energetically, of course, because the room is warm and my legs are dry. "And what happened here?" he asks, not waiting for an answer. He has his hand on my leg at the exact place where, when I was four years old, my father threw me so hard against a big oak wardrobe that I broke my femur. The bone healed forty years ago—I was casted from the tip of my toes to my armpits for months—but Trevor is not the first healer to be able to "see" what happened.

"My father . . ." I begin.

"I am not afraid of your pain," Trevor says. "I am not afraid of your grief. I am not afraid of your terror. You want to know why I am not afraid of your terror?" I nod. "I am not afraid of your terror because I have gone inside the monster, and inside the monster is pure wonder."

Somewhere in this building my friend Willow, who I have come to Canyon Ranch with, is getting a nice simple lavender scrub and an herbal wrap. Willow looked through the catalog, thought, *Yes, the first night, maybe a nice herbal wrap after all that travel.*

"Pamela," Trevor says, "will you tell me your father's name so that I may ask him to excuse himself from the lower half of your body?"

"Yes," I say, and I do.

"Sebastian," Trevor says, "Sebastian, you must get out of there! Sebastian," he says, "it does not belong to you!" He has his eyes closed and his hands tight around my ankles. "No, Sebastian," he says, more forcefully now, "there are no options!"

We stay like that for an excruciating amount of time. Then he folds my hands across my chest and covers them with his. "If you could have only one thing," he says, "would you choose peace or ecstasy?" Ecstasy, I think, though I'm pretty sure I am supposed to say peace.

"Peace is an illusion," Trevor says. "I am in the ecstasy nearly all the time now, even when I sleep."

I think of the composer's lonely bedroom, the terrible black sheets, the clock radio projecting blood-red digits onto the ceiling, his bald head a glinting cabernet color like someone already dead, the musical he wrote where all the gorillas sang, *Despite what he is, he's alive!*

"Pamela," Trevor says, slapping the bottom of my feet with

his palms. "Yes, sir," I say, out of habit. He's got my wrists now, is stretching them back over my head. No one has ever called me Pamela except my father. "You have two glasses," Trevor says, "one is completely full, and one is completely empty. In which glass is stillness possible?"

"The full one," I say. The questions are getting easier. Trevor now has his powerful thumbs wrapped almost completely around my uppermost vertebrae. "You can get to stillness through ecstasy," he says, "but you can't get to ecstasy through stillness."

I think about all the ways the language of the new age is custom-made for terrorism. I think about when a pink mouth opened in a white sky over Davis, and I saw, for the second time, the cupped waiting hands.

"When one of the doing lines in your life intersects with the circle of your now," Trevor says, "what happens?"

"It has to bend," I say, confident now. "It bends and bends and eventually becomes a circle."

"Precisely," he says, and releases his death grip on my neck.

60. Istanbul, Turkey

At the Sultan's Palace: beautiful long-limbed girl, sexy, but not too sexy, lots of brassy hair, surrounded by seven or eight international travelers her age. To an Australian boy with acne scars, she says, "You are walking through the Topkapi Palace with three beautiful women, what more do you want?" The other young women are not in the same room-of-beautiful as she, but they accept the compliment, don't dare to interrupt.

The boy says, "Maybe if you were all naked." And laughs.

One of the other girls, a Swede, says "No," meaning, *Go fuck your-self, acne face.* The brassy-haired girl holds her fingers to the Swede's lips, says, "My parents taught me never to say no immediately."

"To men?" the Swede asks.

"To anything," she says.

Istanbul is the only major city in the world that is situated on two continents. Since 330 AD it has been the capital of the Roman Empire, the Byzantine Empire, the Latin Empire, and as recently as 1922, the Ottoman Empire. In the hilly streets ruin leans into palace leans into Internet café.

We are in line waiting to get into the harem, miles of tiled, low-lit corridors and rooms so thick with ghosts of women in captivity you can feel their hair on your arm, their jasmine-scented breath on your face.

In contemporary Istanbul, the dervishes have finally invited the women to whirl.

In the Blue Mosque there are two hundred and fifty thousand tiles the color of sky. When the sun comes out, inside is sky and outside is golden. I am forty-six years old and ashamed of the fact that this is the first mosque of my life, but later, when the evening call to prayer catches me in the garden between the Blue Mosque and the Hagia Sophia, call and echo, echo and answer, bouncing off domes and turrets that have stood on this hill for fifteen hundred years; I know faith springs out of doubt like topsoil, and one thing I am is here right now.

Across the Golden Horn where the Bosporus meets the Sea of Marmara, the Asian part of the city glistens in the twilight. As a candidate for the center of everything, Istanbul beats Pueblo,

Colorado, hands down. The gulls are turning cartwheels around the towers of the Blue Mosque and cawing like crazy women. *Byzantium,* I say to them, *Constantinople.*

The circle of my now is wreaking havoc with the lines of my doing. I am learning to say *yes,* if not always immediately. A sweet-faced Turkish boy, maybe nineteen, offers me a Kleenex, puts both hands over his heart when I take it, says I look just like his mother when I cry.

CA #4604

THE STERN-FACED CHINESE GUARD has taken my back-pack behind a partition, and suddenly there is a great deal of shouting. I run through its contents in my head: the two thangkas I bought at the school for the preservation of Tibetan culture; the brass soup pots from the market; the thick cords that resemble curtain pulls that the nomads wrap around their heads to indicate regional loyalties—red for the east, black for the west—the hand-lettered gold-leaf prayer books I bought for pennies out of an old man's satchel—could they count as antiquities? —the long string of jingle bells made for a yak.

Now the shouting has moved itself back out from behind the partition and is directing itself at me. The guard wears a semiautomatic weapon and several clips of ammunition on his belt. The yelling stops and it is my turn to speak.

"I don't understand you," I say.

Another string of angry Chinese spews from the guard's mouth, which I interpret more or less correctly as "Idiot! Tourist! Woman!"

I glance at my watch. My plane is scheduled to leave in thirty-five minutes, my connection in Chengdu tight.

Breathtakingly toxic—even the Tibetans get dysentery there—Chengdu reminds me of the Los Angeles of *Blade Runner*, after the sun has stopped coming out forever. It is not a place I want to get stuck.

"Look," I say, "whatever it is, if it's a problem, keep it."

I'm guessing it is my attitude he objects to, since we cannot understand each other's words. The guard blows his whistle, three short tweets, and two more guards appear on either side of me, grab my arms firmly, but not roughly, escort me to a room down the hall.

They leave me sitting there a long time, long enough for me to miss my plane to Chengdu, long enough for me to miss my plane from Chengdu to Hong Kong, long enough for me to remember every detail of the film *Midnight Express*, the film that kept an entire generation of travelers from carrying drugs across any border including—some of us—between states.

A new guard knocks sharply twice on the door and enters, already yelling. He yells for several minutes, getting so close to my face that I can feel his breath on my eyeballs, but something in me refuses to cry.

"I don't understand you," I say, the next time he pauses, and the next time, and finally, right over top of his voice when it seems like he won't ever shut up.

Startled, he raises his hand, I think, maybe, to hit me. And in that second, I remember the knife. A *woman knife*, the vendor at the market had called it, with its yak-antler handle and its four-inch blade. I had thought it would be a perfect gift for my ultra-butch housesitter Pat.

"The knife!" I say. "I'm sorry! I didn't think . . . To me it was just a souvenir!" But of course the guard can't understand any of that either.

They leave me sitting another long time. I hear planes come in, I hear planes take off. At one point I realize the windows are made of one-way glass. Finally a man wearing a suit comes in. He grunts at me to rise, to follow, so I do. Back in security, he thrusts my backpack at me, and hands me a boarding pass. I go through security again without incident. My woman knife, of course, is gone.

Everything is broken on China Air flight 4402, and the toilet reeks and the four Chinese I am slammed into the middle seats with will not stop spitting onto the carpet, but compared to five years of hard labor at a Tibetan prison, it pretty much rocks. As the plane bumps along the mountainous air currents, I think about my father, about the time I was seventeen and my mother went away for a week and left me in charge of his meals. One day I was racing home from my friend's house on my bike hoping to get there before he did, and he drove his Cadillac right up behind me on the sidewalk and laid on the horn, and even after that it all might have been okay because dinner was only supposed to be assembled cold cuts on rye bread and tomato salad. I dropped my bike on the lawn and ran into the kitchen before he could get out of the car, but he came in just as I was opening a new jar of mayo and grabbed my shirt in the front and pinned me up against the wall and raised his hand in the same exact way the Chinese guard had, and I said, for the first time ever, "If you do this, I'll tell everyone you know," and my father let go of the front of my shirt and went in and turned on the Phillies game.

When we begin to descend the flight attendant comes over the ancient speaker in a demonic whisper and the cabin gets so animated I think we must be about to crash, but then I remember reading that the descent off the Tibetan plateau to Chengdu is the steepest of any commercial flight path, even Cochabamba, Bolivia, where you plummet right past the face of one of the fifteen Christs in South America that claim to be the world's largest, and before I know it we are on the ground.

Miraculously, I have not missed the last flight of the day from Chengdu to Hong Kong, and when I go to the gate a new boarding pass appears.

Stepping onto the Air Hong Kong jet is stepping squarely back into the first world, and when the flight attendant in her stylish purple suit and jaunty tam asks me what I would like to drink, I look at her twice to make sure she isn't kidding. "One country, two systems," the customs official said to me when I left Hong Kong, two weeks ago, and he can say that again.

Just after we land beside the carnival neon of the Hong Kong skyline, the copilot heads down the aisle toward me with a look that tells me he has me in his sights. I suck in my breath as he stops in front of me. "Your knife, madam," he says, bowing, deeply.

"Thank you very much," I say, as I lift it from his hands.

61. Marfa, Texas

When we drive into town the big lights are on and the Marfa Shorthorns (purple and white) are playing the Ozona Tigers (white and purple). The score is 34–0 Tigers, but the Marfa faithful are still present and the marching band sounds peppy as all get out. Down on Main Street, there are two thousand people eating barbecue, most of them art groupies from L.A., and the mariachi band is playing "Más Fuerte Que Yo."

We drive out to the viewing platform to see the Marfa lights and before we even get there, there they are, red, then yellow, then white, blinking on, then splitting in two, then blinking off. Some people say the lights belong to cars on Highway 67 running down toward Presidio, and others say it's a real-life example of Pierre Curie's 1883 theory called the *piezoelectric effect* where quartz heavy rocks expand during the day and contract at night so much they give off a voltage. Some say it's magic or extraterrestrials—even

God—that makes the lights glow and jump, because the closer anybody gets to them the further they jump away.

This is all happening back in the days when I still have hope that Rick might think I'm pretty, so I've bought a silk skirt, two-tone brown with a rose-colored hem and it's rippling softly around my ankles in the warm Marfa wind. Marfa is Rick's favorite place, he says, but even *it* makes him sad because it's where he went all the time to escape from Sofree and the baby.

Over at the Chinati center, the Judd boxes in the old armory make light of their own, different kinds of it from hour to hour, from clouds to sun to twilight to moonlight. A hundred silver boxes, holding and absorbing and reflecting light that, like the surface of a river, goes sometimes flat and sometimes blue and sometimes all the way to gold, shadows stretching out underneath them, light and dark like the world's biggest set of piano keys.

Rick insists the placement of the boxes is random and I argue with him (and the brochure) as if I have something important at stake until I realize my point is that nothing is random, where you are from or who you love or who you think is pretty or don't.

In the afternoon Fenton the dog and I walk out to the place where the railroad tracks make you want to walk forever, and he chases a jackrabbit around and around in circles until he catches sight of the pronghorns, and lights out after them for a while. Eventually they get tired of toying with him and throw it into fourth gear and leave him in the dust.

Rick has spent more than twenty thousand dollars in therapy trying to make sense of his life's last decade, but I've got it down to one sentence: If a thirty-seven-year-old woman swears that the rhythm method has always worked perfectly for her, everybody in the theater knows what happens next. Except Rick, who had made a solemn promise to himself that he would never, under any circumstances, have children, when he was just a child himself. He'd made it past forty without ever having to buy an EPT test, let alone an abortion, but Sofree was pregnant six weeks after the first time they did it. Madison will be eight in September. Once she became an actual child, Rick loved her the way lots of dads love their daughters, helplessly, with a touch of desperation. Madison was barely two when Sofree kicked Rick out.

When I get back to the house Rick has gone out for barbecue so I sit down and make a list of all the ways he is not like a normal person, which includes (1) *He won't put liners into his kitchen trash can, but he is afraid that if he goes to Thailand he will bring something back Madison will catch,* and (3) *Sometimes his face changes into some other guy's face, a guy we think lived in ancient times who speaks with great authority and whom I have nicknamed the Originator,* and (5) *He likes to call me a mighty fine gal.*

If you went to every cafeteria in the country and guessed vegetable beef as the soup of the day you would be right 68 percent of the time. Broccoli cheddar would cover another 20 percent, so what do you do if you are a person who craves Hungarian mushroom?

"Oh sweetie," I say, when Rick comes back with the barbecue, "you weren't ignorant, you were just innocent."

He wraps his freckled Texan hands around me, says, "That's the kindest thing you've said so far."

62. Creede, Colorado

Colt comes by the house to tell me the latest. How Tassie ended things again two weeks ago, so Colt drank a six-pack at home and went to the bar to find someone to hit. He chose the other farrier in town, the one who's famous for having the best ass in Creede.

Colt got kicked out of the bar as he knew he would, and jumped in his truck to drive home. The deputy sheriff had watched the whole thing from *his* truck, pulled Colt over at the town limits and insisted on driving him the twelve miles to my house, where he's been bunking in since the first restraining order, watching things when I am away.

It was in my kitchen that Colt really started to work himself up. First he punched a hole through the dry wall (he shows me the spot and I have to admit his repair job is masterful). It was twenty below out, and he was truckless, so he saddled his palomino and started back to town and Tassie's house. Halfway there he realized he had no feeling in his arms and legs, so he stopped at the veterinarian's, stabled his horse, and sweet-talked Doc into driving him back to his truck. Then he drove to Tassie's house and ripped the front door off the hinges.

"That's how we got to the second restraining order," he says, smiling ruefully. "But things have gotten a little better this week. The restraining order expires Friday, and on Saturday Tassie wants to go shopping for a diamond ring."

"Perfect," I say, and give him a hug.

Colt has done odd jobs for me for two years including painting the house, nursing my dog Mary Ellen back from cancer surgery, and once on Christmas Eve, when I was in Bangkok, keeping a frozen pipe in the mudroom from ruining everything I own. He works on a sliding pay scale, $8 to $20 an hour depending on how much he has to think. If he spends a day ripping old carcinogenic insulation out of the rafters of the barn, that costs $8 an hour, if he makes several calls trying to find the closest thing to a no-longer-manufactured furnace ignition switch, that costs $20. He says the word *deal* four or five times in every sentence the way Jack Here-Here said *On it there,* and he can't ever remember to close a door. *Did you grow up in a barn?* I am always inclined to scream at him, but of course, in his case, the answer would be *yes.*

When Colt doesn't live at Tassie's, he lives in the old homesteader's cabin between my house and the creek and he has it full of all the things you would expect to see in a real cowboy's cabin like a flag and a gun and a hot plate and a Bible, but he also puts little Post-it notes around that say things like *Listen to more classical music,* and tonight there is one stuck right in the middle of his TV screen that says, *I am your enemy.* Last week when I called him on his cell phone he said, "I felt a little vibration near my heart and knew it had to be you."

After the last restraining order expired, Colt said, "Once Tassie allowed me to say I was sorry—the very morning after I was able to apologize—the sun was all of a sudden a color in the sky again and I wasn't living anymore in some black-and-white minimalist painting."

A different day he burst into my living room urgently. "I want to show you something amazing," he said. He held Rick's picture in one hand, and Fenton the dog's in the other. "Look at the hair!

Look at the eyebrows! Pam," he said, "you've fallen in love with your dog!"

63. Boulder, Colorado

In the first email, Sofree@spiritpulsings.com writes, *Rick and I have, over the years, built between us a citadel of the heart, filled with love and understanding, and when a third party tries to scale its walls, it gets our attention.*

Getting attention is only one of the idioms Sofree and Rick overuse in common, another is *field* (which means something like aura) and *tone* (which means something like agenda) and *wank*, which means something I have yet to discern.

Further down the page, Sofree uses the word *honoring* with an article in front of it, as in, *the honoring of it, it,* in this case, being the triad, being Sofree, Rick, and Madison, as if taking and holding power were as simple as turning a verb into a noun.

By the time our lunch at the Boulderado rolls around I know Sofree grew up in Miami, the youngest of four sisters, all of whom graduated from Florida State with a major in communications, her favorite book is *The Da Vinci Code,* she identifies as a flexitarian, and she is about to marry a heart surgeon named Tom.

When I told Rick I couldn't understand why five years hadn't been enough time to get over her, he said, "Because after she found out she was pregnant, it didn't matter to her whether or not I died," and when I still didn't get it, he handed over his therapy journal. As a result I have read hundreds of pages dedicated to Sofree's beauty, sixteen descriptions of the sex act between them, and at least thirty instances of the words *shimmering hair.*

I sit down at the sunny table and Sofree gives me a paperweight in the shape of the goddess Kali. Her hair is in a white-blond pixie, falls in wispy bangs around her eyes and shimmers not at all.

She says, "I know we agreed not to talk about Rick, but can I ask how you broke the news that we were going to be meeting?"

It seems a bad sign that we have gotten here right off the bat. I manage a smile. "I said, 'Rick, I've got something to tell you,' " I say, "and I know you might not like it . . .' "

"You're pregnant!" Sofree practically shouts, and gives me her craziest sexiest smile.

"Very funny," I say, sincerely, fingering the paperweight. Thinking, *What about the triad? What about the love citadel whose walls I've so disrespectfully scaled?*

Three middle-of-the-nights this week Rick has woken himself from a dream screaming "I hate you! I hate you! I hate you!!" but you don't have to have taken Divorce 101 to know this is not the good news.

"I've had a releasing . . ." Sofree says, almost a stage whisper.

"You have?" I say, hearing Cinder's voice in my head: *How could anybody sleep with anybody who so unashamedly cranks out gerunds.*

"After all," she says, "Rick denied me the ultimate expression of my womanhood."

Not hardly, I think, and she takes my hand.

"Now Pam, I know that when I was with Rick I was on a particular life journey, and I don't know about your life journey, but I suspect that one of these days you are going to wake up and realize that you deserve more, and if that happens I'll be here to support you in that fully."

What's impossible to ignore is that she means it. Also that she might be right.

"Thanks," I say, and then we go sit in my car and I play for her Nerissa Nields' new song about asking your enemy to tea, and when it gets to the part that says, *See the criminal in me and smile anyway*, she throws back her head and laughs.

64. Lubbock, Texas

J and B's coffee shop: best coffee in town, crummy couches, Dave Matthews on the stereo, just a few blocks from Tech. Eight in the morning and nine Lubbock city cops are here, drinking lattes and doing Bible study together, praying and holding hands, in uniform.

When I tell Bruce, who has taught here for eighteen years, he says, "So what?" and I say, "Well what if the nine of them were wearing turbans with their uniforms and chanting 'Allah is great'?" and he says, "They wouldn't be," and I say, "That's my point," and he says, "No, I'm pretty sure that it's mine."

My students here blink at me like sweet stubborn calves. I stand in front of the classroom and think, *Don't talk about religion, don't talk about religion*, so every example I come up with has God in it somewhere. I am talking to them about the importance of listening to the sounds of words, how you can hear the sound of a word more clearly when you don't know what it means.

"For example," I say, "I overheard this phrase last night at the barbecue place: 'Fifteen naked Pentecostals from Floydada.' I don't know what those words mean," and Travis says, "Sure you do," and

I say, "No I don't," and he says, "Well, Floydada is a town," and I say, "Okay," and he says, "You know what Pentecostal means," and I say, "No, I honestly don't," and Reagan, the one with straight black bangs that go all the way to her eyelashes, the one who wrote a story about a Muslim named Salim who shot his sister through the breast because he found out she had welcomed Jesus into her heart, says, quietly, and without a hint of irony, "Pentecostal means everything but the snakes."

Driving in on Highway 84, racing the trains from eastern New Mexico, there are silver boxes every quarter mile of track that hold the light long after sunset. One of the things these kids are worried about, I have come to understand in three short weeks, is the Rapture. I knew they were thinking, *She* would *know where Marfa is,* this Christmas Eve Episcopalian, the whole religion invented in the first place just so Henry could cheat.

Ethan called to say that while we were together he thought I wanted something from him, and now that we'd been apart he realized I was a person who considered it her job to bring wonder back into the lives of people who had decided there was no wonder left in the world.

This was overgenerous, if not downright false.

I'm not saying that Sofree isn't pretty, I'm just saying she is pretty like a woman in a minivan commercial. I'm just saying I expected more.

A lot of the time when Rick accuses me of being passive-aggressive I am really being aggressive-aggressive. "I used to be prettier too," he says, "but now I'm losing my hair, now I have a saggy neck."

"I love your saggy neck," I say, thinking, Now *am I being passive-aggressive?*

Bruce says he hopes they turn the burger barn into an exotic dance club, and he's barely said it before I realize the exact translation of those words if you put them in a woman's mouth is, *It's such a beautiful day. I think I'll put on my new leggings and do some stretches in the park.*

65. Powell, Wyoming

Home of the sugar beet; mountains and mountains of them lining the sides of the road. At the Lamplighter Restaurant, one question the waiter asked us was, "Soup or juice?" Here you don't live in Willwood, you live on it.

On the eighteen-seater prop into Cody, there was an enormous nearsighted man who found a way to work the word *buttocks* into the conversation four times before we even took off.

The whole country was talking about change, so I made a list down one side of a piece of paper of all the things I wanted to change, and down the other side I wrote what it would take to make it happen. The left side of the paper said things like: (3) *Let Rick do his own work,* and (6) *Let things fall apart a little,* and (9) *Know that the river is there all the time, even when it's not;* but I really liked reading the right side of the page which said: *Light, Freedom, Time / Heart, Faith, Faith, Courage, Faith, Time, Trust, Self-Forgiveness, Self-Worth,* and *Faith.*

Now I am being shown around by a couple of women engineers from the college, which in Powell means climbing into the front of the half-ton and driving up to the airstrip, then turning back around and driving out to the dam.

The day before I left Boulder, Rick and I took a solemn vow not to fight before departure. Madison and I played leap-frog all afternoon in the yard while Rick grilled burgers and then we watched Scooby-Doo with real people, which we all enjoyed, and we made a strange little family unit, if a somewhat sad one.

I put Madison to bed and she asked me how the earth got made, and while I was taking a deep breath and thinking about my answer she said, "I know all about the big explosion and everything, but I'm betting God was a part of it too."

When her eyes finally drooped shut I went downstairs and Rick and I started the same old conversation again, the one where he says, *How could you possibly love someone like me?* and I say, *This way and this way and after that even more.* But then the washing machine flooded the basement and threw everything off, and after we'd gotten the mess cleaned up he said, "I am experiencing you as very angular right now," and I said, "Well I am quite surprised to hear that because I've never felt so fucking round."

"I'm just trying to connect with you," Rick will say sometimes, like we are in *The Mod Squad* and he is the guy with the Afro, or like the oldest kid from *The Brady Bunch* when his friends got him to try pot that first time. Sometimes he says, "In relational terms, Pam, you are the mountain all of this moves through," which is made somewhat more confusing by the fact that he calls a potholder a *handlin' rag.* He sometimes will use *chat you up* and *might could* in the very same sentence. This he calls being a highbrow hick.

I am still a little traumatized from Saturday's trip to

Roll-O-Rama, where Sofree showed up, even though it was our weekend with Madison. These days my inbox is full of emails from her with subject headings like *Being to Being* that begin, *I'm feeling hurt, apologetic, enthusiastic, sincere.* Sofree didn't stay at Roll-O-Rama long, just long enough to up her winning streak at the limbo contest to ten.

The environmental engineer named Sabrina, mother of three, says, "Yeah, you go to all those birthday parties and see those bitches in their Capri pants, and they're all like, 'Yeah, I may have a Ford Freestar full of kids but you know all the men still want to fuck me.'"

At the Chinese American Restaurant in Cody my fortune cookie says, *You are the reasonable person in your present situation.*

Cinder said, "If I ever told Matthew I was experiencing him as angular, in spite of how much he loves me, he would leave me on the spot." I was safely back at the ocean by then and Fenton the dog was chasing the endangered plovers, making smarter faster plovers, I always reasoned, for the long haul, the winter waves big enough to give even Fenton pause.

"Can't you speak with the Originator?" Cinder asked me. "Tell him to wake up and kick a little ass."

In the narrow neck of the Tomales Bay inlet, harbor seals rode the current, heads high above the riffles, staring hard at Fenton, and Fenton cocked his head at them, considering, I thought, whether or not they were asking him to play.

"Not everything is funny," Cinder said, reaching for an intact sand dollar on the otherwise sea-swept beach, "but an awful lot of things are."

66. Boulder, Colorado

Rick invites me to go downtown for a couple of hours so he can work with his therapist, or more precisely, the woman who used to be his therapist, until she had a nervous breakdown and closed her practice, so now he is her therapist, kind of. What they do mostly is sit in a room and go into trances together, where their faces change colors and even shapes, and sometimes every now and again a bear or a lion shows up. There are two things that make me suspicious of this woman, whose name is Aurora. (I guess that makes three things.)

First, Rick says when they are done working and she goes back to her house, she leaves energetic hunks of herself all around his apartment; and second, she was his therapist when he met Sofree, and she never once suggested he run.

I sit on a bench on Pearl Street and send Practical Karen a text about Aurora and she sends me back the same text she has sent me so many times over the years she probably has it saved for future use: *Pam, really, what are you trying to prove with this guy?* and I text back: *I don't know. I don't know . . . but* something.

I spend an hour in the Boulder Book Store and wind up with a stack of hardcovers so tall I can hardly balance it and just as it is about to topple I get a call from the 610 area code. A chill goes down my spine because the only people who ever call me from the 610 area code are my father, who is now dead, and the man in charge of my father's money, which I can't seem to think of as mine.

It's not all that much money and everyone, including Rick, says I ought to pay off the ranch and make my life easier, but the truth is I love to work and I don't want to make my life easier, and what I like most of all is that every penny that has gone into the ranch has been earned by me.

Sometimes I think I ought to get the money and take all my friends down the Cleopatra Coast of Turkey in a fifty-foot *gulet,* but whenever I call the man who calls himself Uncle Stu (though we are not related) to ask for it, he says something like, "A bet against America is a bad bet, Pam," or "Do you know who went into the factories during the Great War?" and when I say "No" he says, "The women, Pam, the women!" and I don't know what that has to do with the stock market crashing, but I do know it means he wants me to leave the money alone.

But this day the call is from Mary Beth Jenkins, who was my mother's best friend before she died, which seems like a hundred years ago, but was really sixteen. I haven't spoken to Mary Beth since mom's funeral, which I think was before the invention of cell phones, but here she is on mine. I always liked Mary Beth because in the sea of suburban Bethlehem housewives she somehow emerged a painter, and a good one, which maybe wasn't the hardest thing to do since she was married to one of the richest lawyers in town, but likely not the easiest thing either.

What Mary Beth Jenkins has called to tell me is that my mother has visited her twice since her death, once a few days after the funeral, and once just last night. The first time she came she talked about their friendship—hers and Mary Beth's—but on this visit, sixteen years later, the subject was me. She told Mary Beth that I was in trouble, emotional, she thought, rather than physical, and she asked Mary Beth to mother me in any way she could.

Bethlehem is a steel town, and in my eighteen years there I never heard one single person speak of a visitation. So I tell Mary Beth that I might indeed be in some kind of emotional trouble, but if I am I haven't quite realized it yet, and that I'll keep her posted, and that we should talk soon.

When I walk into Rick's apartment he is burning sage, I presume, to encourage the remaining hunks of Aurora to find their way back to her apartment, and when I tell him about Mary Beth Jenkins he says, "I am not surprised in the least, the first thing Aurora said when she got here was that mothers are everywhere today."

67. Denver, Colorado

This morning, at Ruby's house, the kids are playing *Would You Rather . . . ?* and Marla, whose weight is currently at the bottom of her fifty-pound cycle and is therefore all cleavage and ponytails, says, "Pam, would you rather look like you do now forever, or get wise?"

"Get wise," I say, "no-brainer."

"What if you could look like you looked when you were twenty-five forever?"

"Same answer," I say, and Marla narrows her eyes.

Rick always says, "You are so beautiful on the inside," except when he says, "You are so beautiful when I am inside you," which Cinder tells me is even worse.

"Well," says Marla, "what if you could have all the wisdom of a lifetime and still look like you looked when you were twenty-five."

"Or what?" I say.

"What, what," she says.

I say, "I thought we were playing *Would You Rather . . . ?*"

She twists her head like a dog at a foghorn. "Marla," I say, "you *get* the wisdom because you don't anymore look like you did when you were twenty-five."

She says, "You don't understand the rules to this game."

68. Albuquerque, New Mexico

At the entrance to the security line Rick says, "Now you are going to get the story you wanted, that you were broken up with right before your birthday."

But that isn't the story I wanted at all. It's barely sunrise and we left the ranch at three and we haven't had coffee yet. I feel sad beyond measure that we are fighting again, but it seems simpler in the moment to just say, "Fuck you."

Rick walks away from me, back toward the parking lot, and I follow. I grab the part of his sleeve where his arm isn't. "I'm sorry I said that to you," I say, "really, I am."

He says, "If you don't let go of me, I am going to call that man."

What man? I think. "What man?" I say. "What are you talking about?" I am holding his sleeve between two fingers, the way one might hold a feather or a pen.

"What you are doing right now," he says, "is illegal."

"Illegal?" I say, "Illegal? Have you completely lost your mind?"

On the way to the airport this morning, Rick asked me what I do when I am feeling my very worst and I thought, *Uh-oh.*

Make Your Slots Progressive, one billboard said. *A Plutonium Factory,*

Here? said the next. The sun had not quite risen but it was all glowy over there behind the Sandias, and Venus was sparkling like a crazy woman in the west.

"If you don't let go of me," Rick says now, "I am going to call that man." I have to guess that he means some imagined member of the relationship police, though there is no one who fits that description in my line of sight. I release Rick's sleeve, get in line for security.

Last weekend, when we dropped Madison off, I fell on my face right in front of Tom and Sofree's house. Someone had cut down a sign and left four inches of aluminum post behind and I tripped over it and went flying. It is the fifth time this month I have hurled myself to the ground, all the way, spread-eagle. Once in Rick's driveway, once in the arrivals hall of Boise Airport, once over Jude's computer cord, once carrying a dog bed, so at least it broke the fall.

"What you want to ask yourself," Janine said, "is why are you doing it."

"I guess I am trying to make sure the ground is there," I said, and she suggested I try to get down there at least once a day on my own terms.

On the far side of security a woman wearing a fuchsia scarf approaches, asks if she can help. I try to compose my face in a way that says, *Just sad, not crazy,* and thank her, but decline.

"God loves you a whole lot, you know," Scarf Woman says, in a way that sounds not at all generic, but more like she is privy to some top secret information.

"Well yes," I say, "I would like it very much if he did."

69. Austin, Texas

Brenda, as it turns out, is tall and broad-shouldered with big mannish hands and a little bitty Melanie Griffith voice, and she's been chuckling at odd intervals every since we sat down. She is wearing a pumpkin-colored polyester skirt with a zigzag hem and a purple turtleneck, a piece of masking tape over her heart bearing the number of the Iraqi dead.

My old friend Johnny is sitting right between us, so tight to the table that Brenda and I can't quite see each other, a tactic I know is somehow related to the Ostrich Principle, if we can't see each other, maybe it means we are not both really here.

If one more fifty-year-old man tells me he would like to disappear into South America for a while with nothing in his truck but a whole lot of blank paper I think I might kill myself.

"Don't forget your copy of *On the Road*," I say, which gets no response whatsoever.

Howie has ordered three duck appetizers for the table and for the thousandth time is telling the untrue story about my first trip to Austin all those years ago, how I insisted that I was not going to my hotel, insisted that he and I sleep together. Everybody loves this story because we all know and don't say that Howie only has sex with men, and that those men have only gotten younger, so when he tells them that he and I have been sleeping together for twenty years, in hotels and tipis, and several times below the equator, they know he means *sleeping* together, and that part is true. What they don't know is that these days Howie snores like a sailor, so the two nights since I got here, I started out in bed with Howie but wound up retreating to the couch.

I have no idea how much Brenda knows, not that there's much to know, beyond the one kiss in Telluride, and the fact that Cinder, Willow, and Nora have decided that when I get tired of listening to Rick pine over Sofree, Johnny is the one at the end of the road. Practical Karen says I've got at least two more lifetimes to go before I am emotionally healthy enough to attract a man like Johnny. He lost the wife everybody loved best on a dive trip in Australia a couple of years ago.

Wade is staring off into space with the exact look of a man whose wife died in a car one week after he had finally had enough and moved out. I don't know what he'd had enough of. I don't know how much she'd had to drink. I do know that I have made it to an age where two out of three men at any given table might be widowers, that eventually eventually is gonna run out.

Back in Denver, the rocket scientist told me the static on my television is actually the lingering echo of the original Big Bang. He told me you can't get to Pluto without slinging by—like grabbing the post when you are roller-skating—without going to Venus twice and using her gravity as thrust. He was in charge of Mars, he said, more or less, but had recently become interested in the ice plumes on Saturn, was hoping they would send the spaceship whose name is *Cassini*, through the plumes when the mission was done. He said the real reason that Pluto got demoted from planet status was that the anti-Pluto contingent waited till the last day of the conference, when all the pro-Pluto voters had gone home, when what they should have done instead was upgrade Pluto's giant moon, whose name is Charon.

"You are going to tell me that's a slippery slope," the rocket scientist said, "but wouldn't it have made everybody feel more hopeful?"

The rocket scientist was the third blind date in a month, and I thought, *At least this one will be good for some metaphors*, but when he kissed me in the parking garage I felt less than nothing, and I didn't even make it back home before I called Rick.

Rick and I have tried to break up a whole bunch of times, but either he's not ready or I'm not ready and the one time we were both ready I couldn't get the damn dog off the couch.

"Fenton, let's go," I said, three times at some volume, the car loaded and the dog who will not let me out of his sight, who stands sentry at the door at the first sign of suitcases, would not budge.

Howie says, "This duck is so good it would make you think the rest of the food here would be good, but the funny thing is that it's not." When we all look at him blankly he says, "I mean, as opposed to, say, the blooming onion."

"This place has blooming onions?" Wade says.

"No," Howie says. "My point is that if the blooming onion in a place were really good, it would not necessarily make you think the rest of the food would be really good." He rakes his fingers through his wavy hair. "Pam," he says, "do you understand what I am saying?"

Now that there is something actual to laugh at, Brenda has gone silent as a stone.

70. Pagosa Springs, Colorado

Bitter January night in the Amethyst Pool, our hair frozen solid with steam into shapes like helmets and Hailey says I look like Susan Sontag. We all pick out words for the New Year, and Nora's is *guts* and Mackenzie's is *mutuality* and Hailey's is *intention* and I can't think of one right away, so Hailey says it should be *my desires*. Nora points out rightly that that is two words and therefore illegal, and I say, "What about *laughter?*" and Mackenzie says, "What about *limits?*" but in the end I sell even Nora on *spontaneous fun*.

We have all driven down from Creede in two cars to escape the clogged chimney, and we smell just like college students from 1978 who lived in alternative campus housing called the Bandersnatch. When we passed Camp Fun, Rick said, "We just passed a major trauma site."

I glanced in my rearview to see that only a handful of the hundreds of trailers that fill the river bottom in summer are still in Camp Fun this deep into winter. A coyote stood on the surface of the frozen river, waiting for something small and warm to move.

"Camp Fun," I said, "is a major trauma sight for almost everyone." It was my birthday and I was sick sick sick of the subject of Sofree-induced pain.

"I opened up the most fragile version of myself to you," Rick said, "and you tended it so beautifully, and then you lost interest!" and I thought, *Who* wouldn't *lose interest?* But then I thought, *What's wrong with me, anyway, that this is what I do?*

It is well below zero, maybe twenty below, which is my favorite time to come to the springs, when it hurts to run from pool to pool and even the lobster pot at 109 degrees is a possibility, as long as you remember to hydrate. We are just shrouds to each other, four pink female bodies in the frigid dark with ice-colored hair, our voices the most real thing about us.

Earlier tonight Brett Favre lost the first last game of his career to Eli Manning, and Rick gave me what Mackenzie calls *the look* all through sushi, except because of how the chairs were lined up it seemed like he was giving it to her. Just that morning I found the note Mackenzie left for me in the bowels of my Turkish coffeepot: *You are everything you are supposed to be. Don't forget that you give a bunch of really great women several of the best weeks of their lives.*

Now in the hot tub, Hailey makes me tell about the time we pulled up outside Rick's shop on a Sunday and he was all alone in there at his drafting table and then we saw the backs of his bare legs scurrying up the stairs.

"I don't always work with pants on!" he said, when I went up to find him.

"You don't?" I asked.

He said "No!" like, *Who does?* Then I lifted up the bottom of his shirt and he said, "I *am* wearing underwear!" like, *Who doesn't?*

71. Milwaukee, Wisconsin

Driving from Chicago in the minus 6 degree weather, neck craned out the window looking for the lunar eclipse, because the rocket scientist told me to, but the light pollution extends all the way to the Wisconsin border, and I think I am probably facing the wrong direction anyhow.

If I became the rocket scientist's girlfriend, the fortune cookie about me being the reasonable one would never ever ever be true.

In Milwaukee, everything is frozen solid, the river, the stoplights, even my car door, but when I get to my high-rise hotel room, there is the eclipse right out my window, halfway over and looking strange enough to scare a caveman or an ancient Egyptian to death.

Trish comes to meet me for breakfast with her sperm-bank in vitro baby and I have no idea how to respond as she details all the ways her life has become a living hell. She knows I thought she was crazy to do it, at her age, alone, with her eighty-hour-a-week job, and now here she is, as if to prove me wrong, but everything she says makes her life sound about ten times worse than I could have imagined.

The lake is frozen as far out as you can see, blocks of ice heaved up on the shore like wrecked cars, and Cliff Parker, whose law firm is sponsoring my visit, picks me up and takes me to the Milwaukee Country Club for lunch. It is so much like the country club in Bethlehem, Pennsylvania, that my father could just barely afford to belong to it takes my breath away, only it is like it is still 1972 in Milwaukee, Wisconsin, the white wallpaper with little parasol-toting maidens doing tour jetés across it, the four dead gray-haired ladies propped up in the corner as if to look like they are playing bridge.

The place probably seats two-fifty, not even counting the no-women-allowed grill downstairs, and yet other than the dead ladies in the corner, we are the only ones eating today.

The point of this luncheon, I quickly understand, is so that Cliff can show me why he is a lawyer and not a writer, to show me the kind of life he gave up writing for. He has invited eight people to the luncheon besides the two of us and exactly none of them show up. I can't decide if Cliff Parker is a sociopath or just so completely normal that he is incomprehensible to me.

Our waitress is actually named Trudy, she has a beehive hairdo and is at least a hundred and fourteen years old. We both order the Cobb salad, and for some inexplicable reason it takes forty-five minutes to arrive. The room is being heated to a sultry 85 degrees and there is a squirrel hurling himself repeatedly at the floor-to-ceiling window behind Cliff's head.

Over and over he climbs the nearest tree, and then flies—flying squirrel style—and lands splat, with his face against the window, where his paws achieve suction for a little more than one second before he slides, like a cartoon character, down to the bottom of the glass. He does this five or six times before I comment on it, though it makes such a terrible noise every time he hits I can't believe Cliff doesn't turn around.

"Probably rabid," Cliff says with a casual wave of his hand, and I feel my eyebrows go up and he says, "A lot of the squirrels around here are."

72. Bend, Oregon

In my dream, one guy who is in charge a monkey is trying to explain to the other guy how difficult it is to manage the monkey's needs. The monkey has to be placated all the time, he says, the monkey has to be happy, or there is major hell to pay. As he says this, the monkey runs around the room, up to the curtain rod, down to the windowsill, across the floor, and up to the curtain rod again. The other man listens thoughtfully, as a therapist would, offers advice that I understand to be both sage and kind.

Then the session is over, and the first man says, "Okay, let's go," and the monkey reaches up and grabs him around the neck, the way a child would, and wraps his monkey feet around the man's waist and the man cradles him, quite lovingly I think, and closes the door behind him.

The other man sits in the vacated room for a moment, stands and then *he* says, "Let's go," and a big furry rat scurries out from the bathroom, jumps up and grabs him around the neck, just as the monkey grabbed the first man, and they walk out of the office together.

It is Nora's knock on the door that wakes me so fast I remember all of it. She is here to take me to the place that serves Stumptown coffee, and there I am stumbling around in the shirt I wore the day before, my unhooked bra dangling off my right elbow, saying, "You see how it was, don't you, the other guy had a rat!"

The first words Nora ever said to me were, "Robbie Robertson or Rick Danko?" and because there is only one answer to that question I knew we would be friends for life.

When I arrived in Bend yesterday she picked me up at the airport. At four that morning in Boulder, my cell phone had splashed into the toilet while I was drying my hair, but I didn't really roast it until I tried to turn it on before it was all the way dry. At SFO I sent an email to Fenton the human that said I was pretty sure Rick had broken up with me for good this time, but by the time I got to Oregon I told Nora that I knew Rick was difficult but I was too, and you could talk all day, psychology up one side and pheromones down the other, but there was nobody alive who could help who they loved.

Driving up the mountain in Nora's Prius, I borrowed her cell phone to check my messages, but she had forgotten she was hooked up to Bluetooth, and when I hit the 7 key, there was Rick's sad Texas voice filling the car, saying he was sorry, that he wanted more than anything for us to keep trying, that I was a mighty fine gal.

"Welcome to my relationship," I said to Nora, who knew a thing or two about difficult men, and when we got to the hotel and saw the flowers, I said, "I don't think Rick is the kind of guy who really sends flowers," and the lady behind the desk said, "Well, it seems he knew how."

Right before Mavis Staples sang "I'll Take You There," she kicked off her stilettos and said, "I can dance better without these," and I thought about all of us, Cinder and Mackenzie, Nora and Hailey and Practical Karen, dancing around my kitchen with our morning lattes.

I woke this morning with something returned to my chest and made a list of things to be happy about that included (1) *Nora was making bouillabaisse,* because (3) *Seven women were coming from four states to eat it* and (5) *Rick left another message that said he was off to get a clippins (a haircut)* and (7) *Anyone who has no monkey probably has a rat* and (9) *Everybody who said I'd end up bitter turned out to be mistaken (anyway).*

A week after the airport fight, Janine said, "Well, you know I love you, but what I really want to say is that we love you, all of us," and she stretched her arms out wide to include the whole empty room.

"That ferry came in just for you," Fenton the human said last week in Seattle, even though we were standing next to one of the world's busiest ferry terminals. And watching the late sun make mercury on the surface of the water, seeing the clouds lift off the top of the Olympics, smelling Fenton's cologne, mixed with chowder and diesel, sound of the horn, sound of the thrusters, I had to admit he was right.

XE #118

THIS HAS BECOME MY Friday night routine on the week-
ends Rick has Madison: Leave the faculty meeting fifteen
minutes early, race to the Sacramento airport to catch the 6:56
Express Jet which gets into ABQ just before eleven, drive up the
I-25 to Santa Fe, with the methheads on billboards, and the battalions of police cars, sometimes a sobriety-check station, once
past a dead man lying on the side of the road.

If I am feeling too sorry for myself, I stop at Dunkin' Donuts
on St. Francis and get a Vanilla Kreme, white on white, not Boston
Kreme, but the even sweeter kind, the kind that makes your teeth
ache when you first bite in. The sugar powers me most of the way
up 285, across the Colorado state line and on to Creede.

Rick picks up Madison at noon on Fridays and if they get out
of Boulder by twelve-thirty, they've already had hours of ranch fun
and tucked themselves in by the time I get there, but not before

leaving me a *Welcome Home Pam-Pam!* note with a drawing of a horse or a dog or a butterfly.

It is two hours and thirty-six airplane minutes from SMF to ABQ. Tonight is clear, no delays, plus I snagged the upgrade. There are four seats in first class on the little commuter, thirty-two in coach. The African-American woman beside me has on her headphones, listening, she informs me, to Sanskrit prayers. The flight attendant doesn't look twenty.

Fifteen minutes after takeoff and it feels like we hit the side of a barn. *BAM!* one time, the water bladder in the tiny galley explodes on impact and a two-inch river runs down the aisle beside me and then we are falling, falling, falling. The coffeepot is tumbling, weightless, as we have been suddenly freed from gravity, Styrofoam cups are everywhere, and then the plane catches, and shudders, and the pilot pulls the nose back up.

The woman next to me pulls one headphone away from her ear. "Wind shear," she says, "most likely. You want some of this action?" she indicates the headphones. I politely decline and then wish I had not.

I am waiting, I realize, for the pilot to come on and tell us something about what just happened or is about to, but I got a look at him pre-takeoff: very young and cranked hard to one side, most likely just back from Iraq.

I take out my cell phone (over Flagstaff, if the clouds are just right, I can get two bars even at this altitude) and text Cinder saying, *When I talk to myself in that brave ironic voice . . . I don't know, but I think it might be yours.*

Soon after Rick and I met, I was on a plane bound for Philadelphia that had to make an emergency landing at Dulles because of severe thunderstorms. I was reading his therapy journal and in it Sofree was sexily planting tulips, sexily putting Beth Orton on the stereo, sexily lighting candles around her sexily decorated apartment, sexily putting rennet-free cheese and gluten-free crackers on a sexily hand-thrown plate.

When I was safely on the ground in Virginia and waiting for the sky to reopen, I called Rick to check in and he said, "I knew this would happen. I finally have a chance to get my life right, so now you are going to die."

Tonight, when we land in ABQ the pilot thanks us for choosing Express Jet in the most perfunctory manner possible. I drop my seatmate off at the Skyport Holiday Inn Express to save her waiting for the shuttle, and wave at Psychic Mary as I get on the I-25 headed north.

73. Zaafrane, Tunisia

It is already below freezing, an hour before sunset, when we take off on the camels, Rick on Don Quixote, me on Ali Baba, Sasan (which means poet, he tells us, in Arabic, or trickster) on foot. In his Yankees cap and leather jacket, Sasan looks more New Jersey than Tunisia though he speaks French, Spanish, and Arabic, and is, he said, learning English a little at a time.

Sasan tells us repeatedly how tired he is, which comes as a relief after all those smiling guys in Douz who couldn't stop talking right up in our faces, who wanted to sell us a tablecloth their grandmother made, or a camel ride, or a rug. He makes a big deal of telling us how strong Ali Baba is, twice the strength of Don Quixote, and I look appreciatively down at Ali Baba's giant feet, less like hooves and more like bedroom slippers, padding slowly, steadily, and soundlessly across the dunes that are washed golden and deeply shadowed in the waning light.

We haven't gone half a mile when Sasan says the camels need

a rest. I raise one eyebrow at Rick. I thought the whole point of camels was that they could walk hundreds of miles between oases, without a blade of grass or a drink or a nap.

Sasan throws his shoulder into Ali Baba's chest and makes a gurgling noise deep in his throat. Ali Baba drops to his knees, groaning in return.

We sit on the crest of a cold dune to watch the sun—now a ball of hot lava—pour itself onto the desert floor, Sasan between Rick and me. Sasan takes my hand and pours sand into it. "Farina," he purrs, drawing out all the vowels, making gentle circles in my palm. I take my hand back and dig both palms under the sand, but his hand finds mine and continues to draw circles.

Besides a low dune here and there, the Sahara stretches out forever flat in all directions, and Rick asks Sasan how camel drivers keep from getting lost.

"We know the desert like we know the faces of our mothers and fathers," he says. "We sleep in the day and navigate by the stars."

I try not to roll my eyes. What *Sasan* doesn't know is that I used to be a river guide, used to be married to an African safari guide, and this particular brand of guidely bullshit is old news and worldwide. What *I* don't know is that while he is turning circles in my palm with his left hand, he is turning circles in Rick's palm with his right.

Another mile down the camel trail, Ali Baba peels off in one direction, Don Quixote in another. Apparently, Ali Baba is the camel in error.

"Turn him, Pam!" Sasan yells, but I have no reins, and leg pressure has no effect.

We are nearly a mile apart by the time Sasan trots over.

"I ride with you," he says, slinging himself up in the saddle behind me, making a different sort of throaty noise that encourages Ali Baba to trot.

A camel trot is not the world's smoothest gait, and the saddle is not meant for two. First I realize that what I am feeling banging up against my ass is Sasan's little erection, then I realize that his holding on to me right at tit level is no accident. I think, *How old and ugly must one get before this shit stops happening*, grit my teeth, and focus on not falling off.

"Is this how you ride in America?" he shouts, like a guy in a Wind Song commercial.

Then the five-gallon water bottle that has been tied to the saddle falls off, and he jumps down to get it. When he tries to remount I say, "No," and he says, "But I am so tired," and I say, "Okay then, you ride, I walk."

When we catch up to Rick, who has the hood up on his nifty new Obi-Wan Kenobi jacket and has missed the whole thing, I say, "Predicament," and he says, "Klepto?" and I say, "No . . . but egregious."

Minutes later we arrive at a fake Bedouin campsite and meet the French people who will be sharing our camp for the night: the dapper grandfather; his blue-haired wife; his son Eric; Eric's ironic, bookish girlfriend, Madeline; and their four-year-old son Esteban. Immediately we start sticking so tight to them that they probably go home and tell the same kinds of stories we tell about Sasan about us.

Around the campfire, in the icy icy night under a million stars, Rick tells Esteban a story about a camel who comes out of the sky and reaches down to chew the leaves of the trees over Esteban's head. When he is finished Esteban puts his head in my lap in a way that makes me miss Madison and I think, *I wonder if I give off some different kind of scent to all children now.*

When I first smelled the blankets on the cots in our tent I thought, *No way am I getting my face near them,* but then ice started to form in our water bottles and right now I would eat one of these blankets if it would warm me up on the inside, or make me know what to do if Sasan comes in here later looking for a threesome and wielding some big camel jockey knife.

In the morning, the dunes are covered with a thin layer of ice that sparkles in the low sun like water. Rick stands to his full height in front of Sasan as we prepare to remount the camels. "Today," Rick says, and pauses, forcing Sasan to look right at him, "the woman rides alone."

74. Creede, Colorado

The first thing Rick's father wants to know when they arrive is which one is his bathroom.

"That's not," I say, "exactly the way it works around here."

"Well," he says, "then just tell me which one you will be using."

"It all depends, really, on what you want to do," I say. "If you want to take a bath, you use the pretty bathroom, if you are up to something more utilitarian, the ugly one might do."

"But which one should *we* use?" he says, and I sigh, point to the pretty bathroom.

All of a sudden I can see my house through Rick's parents' eyes, Jude's giant painting of the ear of corn with the bright red word *hallelujah* scrawled over the top of it, four $200 organic cotton dog beds taking up most all the space on the living room floor, the set of tiny silver opium weights lovingly carried back from Laos.

We settle in to watch the Texas Rangers play the Tampa Bay Rays and Rick's dad calls the Rangers right fielder a *gentleman* three times before I realize what he means by that is black.

All year long Rick's mother has been sending me email slide shows called things like *Tears of a Woman* and *The Bright Red Hat* which contain a lot of roses and baby's breath and women with strong shoulders and big hearts finally realizing, at sixty, that looks don't matter and they can conquer the world.

The first time I was in her big house in Texas with Rick's dad and all five brothers playing a computer bowling game where you hold a little box in your hand and hurl your upper body at the screen, she crossed the room to give me a hug and said, "It can all be a little overwhelming," and I knew that she knew I didn't want her to ever let go.

Now the whole upper half of her body is inside my oven and she is scrubbing like somebody half her age. "I was afraid we might start a fire," she says to me, under her armpit. This from the mother of a fifty-year-old man who takes all of the spoiled food that is in his refrigerator—rancid salami, deep green cottage cheese, half and half that has gone solid as Play-Doh—and moves it up to his freezer.

"I don't know if you know this," his mother whispered in my ear the night before, "but there are no hand towels in the pretty bathroom." I nodded solemnly and didn't tell her that it would be an accident if there were any hand towels in the entire house.

During the seventh-inning stretch the commentators mention, but do not explain, the team's recent shortening of their name from the Devil Rays to the Rays, the incorporation of a sun into their logo, and their decision to retain the cutout of the sea creature (Mobula Mobular, from the family Myliobatidae) on their sleeves.

I say, "I don't know, but it seems to me that when the biologist or fisherman or maritime explorer made the decision to call that particular ocean-dwelling animal a devil ray, the conversation could have been over at that point."

Rick clears his throat and Rick's mother nods politely.

"It's still the devil," Rick's father says.

75. Boulder, Colorado

At the Flatiron Circus Camp Celebration, I have to sit right behind Sofree and watch her enact good parenting for hours while a whole bunch of little girls warm up on trapezes for careers as Cirque du Soleil performers or worse, while their butch and buff trainers look beatifically on. This is especially trippy after reading Margaret Atwood's latest, a futuristic universe where women only have two choices, to work as strippers *with* embedded fish scales or *without* them, and penises are pretty much blamed for everything wrong with the world.

It is midsummer and Sofree is wearing a sleeveless top that shows off her best feature I have seen so far . . . very prettily shaped shoulders. She looks animated and happy, greeting everyone in the audience, turning around now and then to offer me a trembly smile.

For a little while after the Boulderado lunch date it looked like Sofree and I might be friends. She may have been the subject of every fight Rick and I had, but she was also the only person who understood exactly how it felt to fight him. One time, only seconds after Rick had stormed out of Folsom Street Coffee, Sofree sailed in on his backdraft and bought me a Mexican hot chocolate. When I told her what he'd said, that I'd been responsible for every one of the worst days of his life, she shook tears from her eyes, said, "No, Pam, remember? That was *me*."

We took a few walks together while Rick was in the shop, and on one warm afternoon in Chautauqua Park she said, "Eventually I realized that Rick likes living in that hole of his own making, and the only way I could be in relationship with him was to get down in there too. But it wasn't my hole. It was never my hole. Once I stopped believing when he said I was the cause of his trouble, it was easy as can be to climb right out."

The air around her sentence felt charged with prophecy, like when I'd bring a guy home from college and my mom would say something like, "Any boy who wears a hat at the dinner table will never be faithful," and though I didn't want her to turn out to be right, she somehow already was.

A couple months later Sofree called to wish me a Happy Valentine's Day, because, she said, she knew Rick wouldn't, and when he—in fact—didn't, it started to seem like two trains had left the station and were traveling on a collision course and I was driving at least one of them. When Rick came right out and asked me whose side I was on, the answer could only be, *My own*.

The day after circus camp, Madison and I take the dogs to the playground and she spends several hours flinging herself at the highest bar on what we used to call a jungle gym but is now called a play structure, and flipping all kinds of ways over the top. Then we play freeze tag with the dogs, which is extra fun because the dogs can't figure out the rules, especially Liam.

Even though it is our weekend, Sofree needs Madison for two hours for a special family party and I am in charge of seeing that she gets there. When we get one block from the corner where we are supposed to meet, Madison starts limping badly, and Sofree rushes over and sweeps her up in her arms. When Sofree brings her back to Rick's that night Madison is wearing an Ace bandage and Sofree violates the mediation agreement by carrying her all the way inside.

Madison wants to sleep in the fuzzy brown *Phantom Menace* coat we brought her back from Tunisia. Of course the Berbers were wearing coats like that a thousand years before George Lucas came along.

At the store in Tozeur we haggled over the price in four languages, and Rick finally said, in Spanish, "Amigo, from my heart, I have to make a bargain with you or my woman will think I don't have any balls," and that is when the guy almost started to like him.

The next morning Madison wakes with the coat turned around backwards and goes charging after the dogs again, Ace bandage slapping the asphalt, and Rick gets an email from Sofree that says she is having a crisis in her being.

Where else would she have it, Cinder says, *in her vagina?*

Here's the thing about jealousy: it eats your heart from the inside out and makes you so unlikable even the dogs get skeptical.

"Love is supposed to feel good," Nora always tells me, "at least fifty-one percent of the time."

76. Kairouan, Tunisia

All we want is a fast pass through the fourth-holiest city in Islam, and enough couscous to get us through the day. Few things in life make Rick happier than a Roman ruin, and even though it is 700 kilometers away, I have promised I will get him to Thuburbo Majus by closing time.

We start the day in Tataouine, drive first to Medenne and then to Gabes. It is Eid al-Adha Eve, the Festival of Sacrifice commemorating the willingness of Ibrahim to kill his son Ishmael as an act of obedience to God, but then God lets him off the hook and tells him to slaughter a sheep instead. As a result there are more trucks than usual on the narrow motorways, hundreds of decapitated sheep hanging for sale along the sides of the road, and women, sitting on makeshift tables, selling ristras and olive branches to every third car that passes.

If when I say the driving is aggressive in Tunisia, you think of Boston, or even Rome, you are not even in the ballpark. The roads are single-lane, shoulderless, windy, and poorly engineered, and it is not uncommon, when looking in your rearview mirror, to see a car that is in the process of passing you, being passed by another car. At a stoplight, the instant the light changes, the eighth car deep will honk loudly at the seventh car, and sometimes even grind against it, bumper to bumper. The white piece-of-shit Punto we have rented has significant dents in every single panel, the brights stick on, and the horn doesn't work. But we have come to love the Punto, because in it, moving, is the only place we are safe from being hawked.

It is the low season in Tunisia, and the hawkers outnumber tourists twenty to one. If we stop the car just long enough to take a picture, somebody comes running up the road and tries to sell us a rug. The worst part is that when we try to explain that we just stopped to take a picture of the hilltop village, with the golden Sahara spread out on one side of it, and the blue Mediterranean on the other, and that buying a 16-by-24 Persian rug that weighs 300 pounds and costs—for us, special—$2,500 wasn't on our to-do list for this morning, the rug men get unimaginably angry, as if we have insulted their mother, or carelessly run over their feet.

In Mides, an old Berber town on the Algerian border, there was a hawker who wanted to sell us, not a rug, but himself, as a guide. He said, "You go to the Algerian border, you American, you maybe have a problem, but you go with me, and then nix problem, nix problem."

To Rick, he said, "I like you because you talk seriously to me," and then he asked Rick if Rick liked him, and Rick said, "I am pleased to make your acquaintance," which I thought was a brilliant piece of evasion, but when Rick finally insisted we did not want a guide for any price he leaned over and spit on the ground right next to Rick's foot.

By the time we got to the Algerian border it was late afternoon and there were goats and a goat girl coming down the mountain. There was the call to prayer ringing out of the mosque in the village, and there was a weird border station fortress that looked like a torture chamber in an Xbox game, and little white posts all along the mountaintop marking the boundary. Below was a twisted river canyon, and tables and tables full of a rock called desert rose, which was either a great gift or worthless, depending which way the hawkers were trying to haggle.

Now, in the fourth-holiest city in Islam, I am trying hard not to pause too long at a stop sign, not to miss a light, and we get almost to the wall of the Medina before there is a red light I just can't run, and that is when the guy comes up and bangs on my window, points up ahead to where the Great Mosque is, and says, "*Madame! Madame! S'il vous plaît!*"

I shake my head *no*, and the light changes, and I hit the gas and he follows on his moped. I drive too fast for the cobblestone streets, but he has the moped pegged, gunning for our back window. I hang a left and a left and a left, and then finally a left that turns almost all the way back on itself, and it feels just like *The French Connection* until a man steps out into the street in front of me and I slam on the brakes and the moped man slams hard into my rear bumper. I jump out of the car and so does Rick.

The man is picking himself up off the cobblestones, doesn't appear to be injured or dead.

"Go away!" I shriek, at a volume and intensity that surprises me.

The man walks up to me, gets right in my face, rubbing his arm as if it is hurt, then rubbing the tips of his fingers together for money.

"Leave us alone!" It's me again. Just full-on shrieking.

There are men drinking coffee on porches all around us, watching, impassive. There are always men drinking coffee on porches everywhere in Tunisia. Where the hell, I wonder, are all the women in this country, anyway?

"Get out of here!" I shriek. Rick is watching me now too. He has never heard me make sounds like these. The man is still rubbing the tips of his fingers together. It occurs to me that I am about to strike him. Somewhere, right at this minute, in a land not so far from here, a man has just hurled both of his shoes at George W. Bush.

"Get out of here," Rick says, calmly, from the other side of the Punto, and the man turns and pushes his moped in the other direction.

We get back in the car and turn toward the Medina.

"I've got to get out of this country," I say to Rick.

77. St. Helena, California

In the car, driving down Highway 29 on the way to AKA Bistro. Willow starts telling a story about a 911 call she heard about on TV in which a woman was reporting a drunk driver.

"So the dispatcher said, 'On what highway?' " Willow says, "and the woman said, 'Highway 29,' and the dispatcher said, 'In the direction of St. Helena or in the direction of Calistoga?' and the woman said, 'In the direction of Calistoga,' and the dispatcher said, 'Are you in view of them now?' and the woman paused for a minute and said, 'No, see, them is me.'"

I say, "Was this last night?" because we were driving on Highway 29 last night on the way home from dinner, and Willow says, "No, it was about a week ago," and I say, "Well, what was it, somebody's desperate cry for help or just a prank?" and Willow says, "I guess the woman knew she shouldn't have been on the road," and Nora says, "Is this some kind of amnesty program the wineries have put in place to get more business?" and I say, "Well, why didn't she just pull over and take the keys out of the ignition?" and Willow says, "I just thought it was funny that she said *them is me,*" and Nora says, "Wait, I was driving on Highway 29 last night, and I've been taking Vicodin for my tooth infection," and I say, "Don't worry, it couldn't have been you because you'd remember if you called the police," and she says, "Oh yeah," and I say, "Hold on a minute, this didn't really happen on Highway 29 between St. Helena and Calistoga, did it?" and Willow says, "My God, I suck as a storyteller."

78. Tucson, Arizona

The idea is that you catch, tie, and groom the horses, and the horses reflect back to you your fears, shortcomings, and insecurities, in a loving, nonjudgmental equine way. *Which is fine,* I think, *if you are a wealthy urbanite with an abject fear of any creature larger than a chinchilla.*

Grooming is supposed to take two hours, but Cinder and I get the big gray Percheron looking like a Mercedes-Benz inside of forty minutes, mane and tail all ShowSheened up, hooves painted pretty as a pedicure with Hooflex.

Afterwards, in the group therapy portion of the retreat, after Rachel from Chicago gets teary because it took her so long to figure out the halter and Janice from Westchester flat out bawls as she relives the terror of combing out her Arabian's forelock, eventually Dr. Wyatt Webb turns his attention to Cinder and me and says,

"Looks like you two had a pretty sweet time with Apollo."

We nod in our smug-outdoorsy-Western-women way.

Wyatt says, "Tell me, Pam, what would you have done if you hadn't been able to get Apollo to pick up his feet?"

I think, *But I did get him to pick up his feet.* I say, "I would have walked a few steps away and come in with greater intention, and asked him again," and Wyatt says, "And what if that didn't work," and I say, "I would have untied him, walked him in a circle, come in with better focus, and asked him again," and Wyatt says, "And what if that didn't work?" and I say, "I would have gotten a lunge line, and trotted him first in one direction and then the other, and then I would have tied him up and refocused and asked him again."

We go on like this for several more rounds until finally Wyatt looks around the room and says, "Can anyone tell me what Pam is forgetting?" and Lori from Park Slope raises her hand.

"Asking for help?" she says, and I have to admit it. He could have asked me fifty more times and that would never have been my answer.

If a lesbian has a collection of over four hundred dildos, does that mean she is no longer from West Texas?

On his first day in office the new president said, *We reject as false the choice between our safety and our ideals.*

At the Madison handoff last Friday, we were supposed to collect her at her mother's house, but Sofree, Tom, and Madison had been at a kids' fair down on Pearl Street, and decided at the last minute they wanted to drop her off instead. According to the mediation agreement, Rick is supposed to have his cell phone on thirty minutes before pickup, but his battery was dead so at 4:50 when we were racing out the door to get to Sofree's on time, and they were racing over to Rick's house so we wouldn't miss them, we all but collided cars at the bottom of Rick's driveway.

Sofree flew out of the car shouting about the cell phone and flinging her arms around, and Rick kept backing away from her growling, "Don't touch me, don't you dare touch me!" and eventually backed all the way into the house, Sofree hot on his tail. Madison got out of the car and climbed the apricot tree, and Tom and I exchanged one quick glance through the windshield that might have said, *You and I should really get a beer sometime*, and then Sofree swept back around the corner smiling ferociously, plucked Madison out of the tree, hugged her tight, and said, "Don't worry, darling, this is exactly the kind of thing that happens when feelings run deep," set her down onto the dirt driveway, whirled into the passenger seat, and was gone.

79. Oakland, California

"Come here and talk to me for a minute," Amanda says, after Watsu, bobbing backwards to the part of the pool that is shaded by a fine mesh overhead. "Something happened during our session, and it was pretty unusual, and I think I should tell you about it."

"Yes," I say, "please."

"Well," she says, "we got into the quiet place, you know?"

I nod. So that was where we had been.

"And I was trying to work that spike out of your hip."

I nod again.

"Anyway," she says, "I got that spike out."

I flex my hip under the water, and sure enough, the pain that has been with me since they took the cast off my four-year old femur is at least temporarily gone.

"And then this big . . ." she pauses a moment, "let's call it," she pauses again, "well, let's not call it anything right now." But with her hands she makes the distinct outline of a cage. "It came down with us inside it, and I thought, *Wow, what is this?* And then all of sudden there was this *whoosh!* And this thing pulled every single spike out of your body."

"Like a magnet," I say.

"Exactly," she says. "And they told me to tell you, it's up to you, you know? You can do whatever you want, but as of right now, you are spike-free. You've got a clean slate. It's entirely your call how many of those spikes you want to put back in there."

"None of them!" I say, so I don't have to ask who the *they* is.

"Pretty cool, huh?" she says, and lies back in the water, blowing bubbles like a fish.

80. Portland, Oregon

Rick says, "Pam, if everyone deserved a down pillow, there wouldn't be any more birds."

81. Cheyenne, Wyoming

We have only been in Cheyenne for twenty-four hours, and so far Brad and I have run into a convention of Republican women at the Holiday Inn, the swearing-in of a brigadier general at the community college, and forty Mormon missionaries commandeering the Baskin Robbins.

It has been almost twenty years since Brad and I have seen each other, long enough for me to get married a couple of times, and for Brad to become a dad and then watch his wife go crazy.

All those years ago at Bread Loaf we had walked around together for ten days singing Van Morrison, snapping our fingers to the intro to "Jackie Wilson Says," but we didn't fool around because even then he was so completely in love with Rosemarie.

"This house where we are going has two swimming pools, I hear," says Gloria, who is sitting in the front seat with her stunningly nondescript husband and has tied sparkly ribbons into her hair. Gloria is in charge of driving Brad and me around, even though we both have rented cars because in Cheyenne, Wyoming, you don't want to find yourself stuck somewhere.

What the house turns out to have two of, is not swimming pools, but elaborately landscaped waterfalls. One cascades from the circular driveway around the side of the house to a backyard pond, and the other is entirely inside the dog run. The dog is a black-and-white shih tzu. Of course there is no actual creek.

"Rosemarie's not interested in the kinds of things married people do anymore," Brad says, as we admire the dog run, and I am pretty sure he means sex and not the Home Depot.

Earlier today Trish emailed to say that she saw on *Oprah* that sperm-bank only children feel even more isolated than those with siblings, so she's decided to do the whole thing again, pull another one of her eight fertilized eggs from whatever kind of freezer they are kept in, and shoot it up, so to speak, hoping it will stick.

Brad and I are seated at a table with three sisters from Lamar, Colorado, a small town out east, which is, they tell us, the home of the Savages.

"Still?" Brad asks.

"Russell Means even came to our high school in the seventies to tell us why we ought to change the name," the smartest sister says, "and we had an assembly and listened to him talk for two hours. But then whoever was in charge of these things decided to leave it alone."

After dinner we go to the Holiday Inn bar to watch the Rockies, and it is pretty obvious that Brad is trolling but he won't stoop to the lady Republicans.

The Rockies are beating the Dodgers in the bottom of the eighth inning but Bettancourt, the setup guy, is struggling.

"I can't just leave her, Pam," Brad says, as if I've asked him. "I've loved her all my life."

On the long, silent camel ride with Sasan and Rick out of the desert in the early morning frost, the camels were tied together, and I saw Don Quixote cross too close behind Ali Baba and I knew the rope would get caught under Ali Baba's tail, and then it did, and the two camels started circling and circling each other, and then Ali Baba reached down and took Don Quixote's leg into his mouth and I did a flying dismount, pretty efficiently, I thought, and Sasan said, in French, barely concealing his amusement, "Were you scared?"

I said, "You mean when the camel I was riding twisted around backwards and put the other camel's leg into his mouth?"

Sasan said, in English this time, "It is the marriage of the camels these three months," except he called it mar-ee-age, like découpage—"and Ali Baba tells Don Quixote that he is the man and Don Quixote is the woman, and Don Quixote tells Ali Baba that he is the man and Ali Baba is the woman, and neither of them want to believe."

82. Poncha Springs, Colorado

Exactly halfway home on the five-hour drive between the Denver airport and the ranch I get a phone call from Colt, who says, "What time are you getting in?" and when I tell him he says, "I'll meet you there. I just want to see the look on your face."

Even so, I'm not prepared for what I walk into, every piece of furniture, every piece of art, even kitchen condiments, everything that was not too heavy to move has been. Only the piano, the fridge, and the bookshelves remain in the same spot they were only seventy-two hours before.

My first reaction is classic children-of-alcoholics. "It's not so bad," I tell Colt, "I can live with it." Then I see the gouges in the pine floor, and I notice that she has taken down every single picture of me and my friends to hang up fifteen tchotchkes of almost no value, a wooden fork I bought at a market in Zimbabwe, an Ecuadoran ukulele made from an armadillo—and to hang them she has used four-inch framing nails.

"Who does this?" Colt says.

"Apparently, Harmony," I say. "She's Rick's friend, from Estes Park. I barely met her once for five minutes. He said she needed a weekend away."

Colt shakes his head and goes home to Tassie's. I don't start crying until I pull the first nail out of the wall. I go down to the basement and waste an hour looking for spackling. Finding none, I use toothpaste, which, unfortunately, is no longer white. Then I call Rick, who says he'll call Harmony. I say, "Do you know one single woman who didn't make up her name?"

I can tell by the way Mary Ellen's leg is quivering these days that the cancer is probably back, so I stop moving furniture and sit down and pet her head for an hour. Twenty-five percent of Irish wolfhounds die too young of bone cancer and another 25 percent of heart failure or stomach torsion, which makes most people give up on them after the first or second heartbreak, but for me Mary Ellen, Fenton the dog, and Liam represent wolfhounds number seven, eight, and nine.

In therapy, Patrick always tells me my devotion to the breed is significant, but he has yet to tell me precisely what it signifies.

It takes the better part of a week to get my belongings back where I had them. Several things I like better in their new spots, so I leave them alone. Eventually I get an email from Harmony that says *I'm sorry you didn't appreciate my gift in the way I imaged you would.*

Cliff Parker is paying me to read his novel, which is pretty darn good, although I am having a hard time understanding the character of Julia, who all of the central male characters fall for, including three brothers and two cousins. The love of Julia leads all the boys to lie and cheat and take stupid risks in snowmobiles and kayaks, and two of them even sign up to go to Iraq. The only male character who is not in love with Julia is her brother, who still likes her enough to commit murder in her honor, because she made up a story about being raped.

What can all of these men possibly see in her? I write in big red letters in the margin, knowing as I do that the book is pretty ingenious in its creation of a contemporary woman who can still launch a thousand ships, and what I am really screaming about is Sofree.

Some years ago, when I was agonizing over my second abortion, which anyone will tell you is a whole different category of agonization than the brand which accompanies the first, Nora said, "No, Pam, don't you see? When you look into your baby's eyes, what you see there will become your very own Tibet."

I did not see. I couldn't. Still can't.

83. Davis, California

"You have something on your right side," Janine says. "You are all caved in . . . you are even putting your hair over there to try to fill the hole."

"Is it a blockage," I say, "or a ghost?"

"It's an entity," she says. "But don't get all caught up in that. Just say, *Thank you, thank you, thank you for coming, but I don't need you right now.*"

Getting dressed for bed last night, Madison said, "Daddy, why do I have such a cute little hourglass figure already?"

This morning I had a mass email from Sofree with the subject line *How to Be a Gracious Bitch*, and above the forwarded message Sofree had written, *I love this!* with one of those little yellow winking smiley faces underneath.

The story below the smiley face was about Jennifer, who was determined not to let anything dampen the excitement of her wedding day, including her parents' nasty divorce. It seemed her mother had found the perfect dress to wear, something that would really stick it—visually at least—to her philandering father.

Turned out Jennifer's father's hottie young girlfriend bought the same dress, and even though Jennifer asked the girlfriend nicely to return it, the girlfriend said, "Absolutely not. I look like a million bucks in that dress and I'm wearing it!"

"Who are these people?" I asked Rick, and he said, "These are the characters that populate mass emails, sweetie, don't think too much about it."

So Jennifer was left with little choice but to tell her mother about the dress, and her mother said, "Never mind, dear. I'll get another dress. After all, it's your special day." The two of them went shopping, and indeed found another great dress, but when Jennifer asked her mother if she wanted to return the first dress she said, brightly, "Oh, I don't need to return it, darling, I'm wearing it to the rehearsal dinner!"

Underneath the story, all in caps, someone, possibly Sofree, had written: NOW I ASK YOU—IS THERE A WOMAN OUT THERE, ANY-WHERE IN THE WORLD, WHO WOULDN'T ENJOY THIS STORY?

"Anywhere in the world?" I said to Rick. "Bangladesh?"

I forward a copy of the message to Cinder and she sends me a text that says, *I guess you didn't appreciate the gracious bitch story in the way that Sofree imaged you would.*

On YouTube, you can watch a ten-minute video, set to sad, jangly music, of people committing suicide from the Golden Gate Bridge. Some of them jump down to the cord first, the big orange cable, thicker than an oil drum and pulled tight underneath the motorway. Some climb up on the railing and do a modified swan dive. Others just haul themselves over, unself-consciously, like a kid from a farm vaults over a fence. One guy in the video has at least three feet of straight black hair and at first I think it's a woman, but when he stands on the railing, the wind lifts it to reveal a receding hairline, just before he bends in half and gives in to gravity. It's hard, watching this video, not to wonder about the filmmaker, how he felt setting up the camera, what he told himself as he stood behind it, about the relative value of art.

Janine says, "Are you paying attention to your friends these days?"

I say, "You mean my actual walking-around ones?"

"Yeah," she says, "girlfriends. Mackenzie, Cinder, Practical Karen, whoever."

Later, driving down 19th Street, feeling oddly, solidly inside myself.

In Synesthesia, a color can be a taste or a feeling can be a sound.

Once in Portland, an old man called me *singular*. Then he said, "That must make life very difficult for you."

It was like the time Rick's parents walked into the coffee shop just as I was explaining to Madison why it was important that the president was having a beer with the Harvard professor and the policeman who arrested him for breaking into his own house.

"Well, the first problem," Rick said, "is that you said *beer*."

84. Marshall, California

Walking up the hill with Bob Hass at the Marconi Center, the pleasing way he startles first at the rabbits, then at the humming-bird, then at the explosive obelisk of sparrows, then at the doe and her fawn.

From the top of the hill, looking down and seeing the bay through the trunks of the giant ponderosa, the dissolution of figure and ground, distance shrinking, surface gleam and pattern, all of it in motion, like looking under a microscope at a paper-thin slice of God's brain.

I think of being at the ranch, lying in the tall grass with Mary Ellen, seeing what she saw, blue sky, white clouds, tasseled stalks of seed-heavy prairie grass, framing a magic-eye painting of everything that is not known, dog's cornea bent to see God, but if I got close enough, maybe she could see it for me.

The Rimadyl wasn't working that well anymore and I asked Doc if it was okay to give her the Tramadol at the same time and after a long pause Doc said, "You know, Pam, Sandy's mother lived with us for quite a while before she died. And Sandy's mother really liked ice cream. So Sandy gave her a little bit of ice cream with every meal, you know, along with the meat and green beans or whatever. And Sandy used to always say, 'Now come on, Mom, you need to eat all those green beans before you can have your ice cream . . .' And one day I took Sandy aside in the kitchen and said, 'Sandy, the woman is ninety-two years old, why does she have to eat the goddamned green beans?'"

Which reminds me of going to see that dead body exhibit that traveled all around the world; the German guy who talked all those people into leaving him their bodies so he could make mobiles and whatnot out of them. In a glass case was an entire nervous system, a thousand little pathways of neurons and axons and dendrites and glial cells glowing a kind of fluorescent gold, nothing but black air hanging around it and still making the shape of the body.

Ruby and I stood in front of it for a good long while and studied how many nerve endings there were, how they tangled impossibly in the place where the brain would have been and creeped out in every direction imaginable, down to the pinkie finger, the littlest toe.

"No wonder!" Ruby said, at last, and I leaned over and kissed her on the cheek.

In Hailey's dream she was interviewing a dog trainer to help her with Ripley, and the trainer said the problem was that she said way too many words to Ripley, that dogs like it better when you communicate with them in one- and two-word commands. In the dream Hailey said, "Is that so? Well have you met my friend Mary Ellen? She not only speaks in complete sentences, she also has excellent enunciation."

That was the same night I dreamed I woke up and Rick had gone off somewhere, but he had left his cock and balls in bed with me, they were next to my leg, and I could feel something wet and sticky, which made me afraid they had been severed in some painful manner, but then I examined them and realized it was just a normal amount of moisture (they felt a little like the kidneys you pull out of a chicken), and in fact they had simply been unplugged from the urethra, which worked kind of like an iPhone charger, and he would be back to get them soon.

I gave Mary Ellen a sponge bath every day for two weeks, brushed out her hair in the September sun like Aunt Martha on the lawn of the nursing home. She wasn't ready and then I wasn't ready and then we were finally both ready on the same day. Doc came out to the ranch and gave her the smallest amount of the drug and she put her head down and went to sleep forever.

At the Acoma Pueblo, in 1629, the Spaniards cut the left foot off all of the strongest warriors to make sure they couldn't run away, and then made them haul—one-footed—a hundred giant logs ten miles so they could build a Catholic church right on top of the sacred kiva. Today, at the oldest continuously inhabited community in North America, giant white ladders lean up against each mud-brick dwelling, the tops of the ladders pointed to tear holes in the sky so the prayers can get through.

DL #251

THERE IS A SUDDEN crackling sound and a blue light, like something out of a laser gun, flies down the center aisle of the Airbus, then all the cabin lights go out and the oxygen masks drop from the overhead bins. People reach for them, even though there seems to be nothing wrong with the cabin pressure. The man next to me even secures his before helping his young son, proving that some people actually listen to the security announcement.

Where on the continuum I fall, when this kind of thing happens—between *Oh please not now that things are finally looking up* and *Well this sucks but it will sure solve a great many problems*—has become my mental health measuring stick in this era of exponentially increased sky traffic, airline bankruptcy and accumulating metal fatigue.

This, I understand, is not at all the same as being suicidal.

We enter another cloud, the blackest so far, and the plane rocks heavily side to side. Two rows ahead, a nun says the Rosary. I hear a woman behind me throw up in a bag.

"Summertime in the Rockies!" booms the pilot's jolly voice over the mayhem in the cabin. "Most of you probably realize we were just struck by lightning, but what you may not know is that the blast took out our number two engine!"

"He makes that sound like a good thing," I say to the man next to me who has his eyes closed and is gripping his little boy's hand. The little boy appears calm, staring out into the heart of the cloud, watching it go light and dark as electricity pumps through it.

"But not to worry," the pilot continues, "we land these babies with one engine all the time. I am going to have to ask you now to get in the crash position, and if you are lucky enough not to know what that is, you will find it illustrated on the plastic card in the seat pocket in front of you."

His voice is a ringer for Bob Barker's. The plane does a belly flop through about 1,000 feet of air and that elicits a scream from almost everybody.

"There's the ground!" the little boy shouts, and sure enough, we can now see the Salt Lake, the dry mountains, the weird moonscape of a golf course built on a landfill, the largest open-pit copper mine in the world.

The pilot crabs hard against the wind, bending the plane almost perpendicular to the ground, then straightens her out less than ten seconds before the wheels touch. A roar goes up in the cabin. The little boy's father bursts into tears, two women across the aisle can't stop laughing, the nun has her head flung back, eyes closed tight.

85. Calistoga, California

In the mud bath, there is a rococo-unpainted-ceramics-style bust of a lady coming out of the wall with a garland of flowers and fruit on her head. The woman in charge of burying me alive is named Evalina, she is at least eighty-five years old and no more than four feet tall. She has a long gray and silver braid and the kind of laugh lines anybody would aspire to. When she holds my hand and walks me from the mud bath to the shower and then again to the mineral claw-foot I feel like a big pink giant beside her. When I get too hot in the mineral bath she comes and sprays icy water on my stomach with a sweet little gleam in her eye.

The palm trees at Indian Springs remind me of the oases in the Tunisian Sahara, which remind me of Bugs Bunny cartoons. You drive for hours across the crusted mineral stains and miraged bands of heat of the Chott el Jerid but inside the oasis it is cool and damp and the air smells like fruitcake. Old men riding tiny donkeys look like centaurs and the birdsong is deafening and every date plantation has its own massive hand-carved wooden door.

Last night, the adorable waiter at Mustards said, "Anything else I can do for you ladies?" And Willow and Practical Karen and I laughed and laughed like three old biddies who had been, for a few hours, let out of the home.

Last time I ate at Mustards was almost twenty years ago and I was having a passionate argument with Ron Hansen and Bob Shaccochis about whether epiphany was a language-based moment or if it occurred, essentially, outside of language, and we sat there for hours, amidst the remains of organically raised lamb spareribs and crab chowder and glasses of big gorgeous wine and I thought, *Wow, I am out with the big boys now!*

A week ago at the ranch Madison woke me up at four in the morning. I was so sound asleep that she had to push and push and push on my back to rouse me. She said she couldn't sleep and I know from experience what it is like to be eight and not sleeping.

I got up and we made cinnamon rolls from one of those fancy kits you buy at Williams-Sonoma. I am a good cook but I suck at following directions and I had never used a rolling pin in my life, so it took two and half hours to get them to the point where they could even go in the oven, but that was okay because by the time they were baking, the winter sun was coming over the mountain and we settled in at the kitchen table for a Rat-a-Tat Cat marathon while they baked, and it occurred to me that maybe the real reason I haven't wanted a child all these years is because when you hurt for them when they are hurting it is the hardest hurting of all.

At lunch at Solbar, our waitress says, "I am sorry, we don't have a specific menu that lists our nonalcoholic beverages, but if you would like me to I can verbalize."

After lunch the sun comes out, and Willow and I go for a drive down the Silverado Trail in her rented Mustang convertible. Jackson Browne is singing "The Fuse" and the vines are a month past their prime and backlit. I am thinking about Hass's reading, thinking about how the older we get the more we're inclined to simply name the things of the world: a whole valley that smells of grapes fermenting in oaken barrels, the taste of doughnut holes dipped in coffee-flavored crème anglaise, a great blue heron standing on one foot at the rippling edge of a pond.

I've made a new friend at the University named Quinn and at midnight I get a text from her saying half the English department got arrested for protesting the tuition hikes and the police brought riot gear, helicopters, and dogs, and that she and Pony, her brand-new gorgeous Texas-lawyer girlfriend, were spending the night with them down at the klink. The next text says, *Did you get a mud bath? Is Mackenzie wearing her miniskirt? These things matter too in this complicated world.*

Next to the giant pool at Indian Springs the hot water crashes and crashes up from the ground forever, and during our midnight swim Cinder looks like a beetle on her back with about seventeen water noodles sticking up from underneath her.

"It sounds like a dragon," Cinder says, "like the dragon who lives at the center of the world."

86. Thuburbo Majus, Tunisia

We get there by five-thirty and the guy at the gate says, in French, "We are supposed to close at six, but I am the night watchman, so you can stay as long as you want."

This is how it goes with Roman ruins in Tunisia. Dougga was closed on Tuesdays, but they let us in anyway. In Sbeitla, there was one other couple besides us. Now we walk alone through the Capitolium and the summer baths. The sun is setting and I have to pee so I duck behind a pink marble column that has been rolled off into a hedgerow.

Rick says, "The lack of security is nuts around here. You know there's got to be coins and artifacts all over the place. You could put anything in your pocket and walk with it. Hell, there's no fence! You could drive a pickup out here late at night and cart off a column."

When I was a park ranger at Natural Bridges National Monument, we would get in the mail a couple of small packages a month from people returning the potsherds they had picked up and illegally removed from the park. Some gave specific details about how their lives had spiraled downward since they picked up the potsherds: they lost their job, they lost their woman, their house was swept off the mountainside by a sixteen-foot wall of mud. Sometimes they included a homemade map, asking us to put the potsherds back in the exact place they found them, and I always tried my best to read the map, to get the broken pieces back to the right spot.

At Thuburbo Majus, the night watchman joins us from time

to time, helpful but not intrusive. "This is the Temple of Baal," he says, "the place where they killed all the babies." He is speaking in French and I am translating.

Rick the ex-Baptist says, "Tell him I know all about the Temple of Baal."

The night watchman takes us over the ropes to a section of the winter baths where the two-thousand-year-old tile is in perfect condition, textured like a braid, colored in the traditional patterns of the city of Kairouan. In another room, four delicate fish assembled from hundreds of tiny rectangles of colored tiles face inward, their tails indicating the four directions.

It is almost completely dark now, and the night watchman uses his cell phone to light up a hidden carving of Pegasus, and shows us, in the oversimplified shadows of twilight, how the Temple of Mercury lines up perfectly with the Temple of Peace.

Then he takes a clay lamp out of his pocket and puts it into Rick's hand.

"Roman lamp," the night watchman says, "14 AD."

"Take a picture!" Rick says, holding his hand out to me. "Take a picture!"

My camera doesn't want to take a picture into the pitch dark, but I trick it into working.

"My God!" Rick says. He is as excited as a nine-year-old with a pop gun, so excited he might pee, so excited that I know it hasn't occurred to him what is coming next.

"Twenty dinar," the watchman says, coolly, which equals about eleven American dollars.

Rick's face crumples. He shakes his head, starts saying "No, no, no . . ." under his breath.

Generally speaking, Rick is not a person who cares very much about owning things, but if he were ever going to care about owning a thing, a Roman lamp from 14 AD would be right at the top of the list.

"This is exactly how artifacts leave their country of origin," I say to Rick in English. "Make sure you really don't want it before you say no."

Still shaking his head, Rick hands me the lamp and starts taking big steps toward the exit. The night watchman grabs my arm, imploring in French, *S'il vous plaît, madame; I have five children. S'il vous plaît, madame; you must understand I did not dig this up. The rain, madame, it uncovers this thing and I find it accidentally. S'il vous plaît, madame; it is the holiday, et mes enfants ont faim.*

He shows me how I can shove the lamp deep in my pocket so that it will not be detected by airport security, *Argile! Argile!* he keeps saying, a word I don't recognize, but eventually figure out means clay, as in, *not metal,* as in, *will not make the airport detector shriek.*

I am walking with the watchman and nodding, Rick a hundred yards ahead of me, when I look up and see that there is someone with a flashlight at the gate.

Rick stops dead in his tracks. Because Rick is a person who spends his life waiting to be caught at something he might not exactly have done, I know that he is now vividly imagining the next several years of his life in a Tunisian prison.

The man with the flashlight is approaching. I try to give the lamp back to the night watchman but he will not take it. I shove the lamp deep into my pocket. The guy with the flashlight reaches us, and we all say *Bonsoir.*

We walk in silence back to the gate. I can feel Rick's heart beating across empty space. The man with the flashlight ducks into the gatehouse for a moment and I seize the opportunity.

"Come out to our car for a minute," I say in French to the night watchman, and he follows me through the gate. By some miracle, the man with the flashlight does not follow him.

We sit inside the car with the light on and the door open and hold the Roman lamp in our hands. On it there is a figure of a Roman soldier. There is a hole for the wick, and a hole for the air. It is the essence of simplicity. It is made entirely of clay and it is more than two thousand years old.

"Ready?" I say to Rick, and he nods.

I take twenty dinar out of my wallet, and hand it to the night watchman.

"This," I say, "is for your wonderful guiding. And this," I drop the lamp into his hands, "belongs here. *Merci*," I say. *"Bonne chance,"* I say. *"Bonnes fêtes."*

87. Mount Princeton Hot Springs, Colorado

At Mount Princeton Hot Springs, the master masseuse's name is Luca, and he is from Austria, but the conversation we have on the way to the treatment room is about Che Guevara. I describe the pain to him in strictly sports-medicine terms: severely degenerated L4-5 disk, acute pain in hip joint, referred pain down the left leg, almost constant. Surgery a nonoption.

Luca works on my shoulder for a while, and I say, "Oh yeah, I forgot to tell you, my shoulder is all jicked up too."

He says, "These things have a way of revealing themselves," just before he gets in between my hip and my pelvis with his whole fist in a way that makes me feel, when he is finished, like I have a new hip, and in a way, while he is doing it, that makes forty-seven years of rage fly up to the ceiling in a funnel of black light.

I think of the lesbian performance poet I read with at the Make Out Room last spring, the one who, in two different poems, said the words, "I put my fist all the way up inside you to see if I could actually touch you," which made me feel a little faint at the time, and not in a good way, and now Luca, with his fist in this place that feels to me at least as personal, says, "You okay?" and I say, "Yes," and he says, "But just barely, right?"

I had been avoiding Mount Princeton Hot Springs since I read Rick's therapy journal, in which Rick and Sofree spend a romantic weekend up there and Rick finally gets it up (after a month of debilitating not-yet-ex-wife guilt) and he and Sofree do it for the first time in one of the riverside pools, water droplets sparking off her nipples like diamonds. But walking around Boulder with unmitigated back pain eventually began to seem like just one more way Sofree is winning. My first post-Sofree Mount Princeton massage was from a stringy sixty-year-old woman who introduced herself as a Fish called Wanda and I only cried once. The second time is Luca.

Later that night I get an email from Sofree that says, *Solace now comes in the form of archetypal tales, in the knowing and honoring of what's true: that Rick and I share this glorious girl child who makes us one in her very cells forever . . .*

It is preceded immediately by one from Quinn that says, *Flattery is a bad trap for people like us. Our curse is that we'll do whatever you want us to but then we'll hate you for it. It's a kind of wild passivity, rebellious and compliant. It makes people who need REAL docility and FAKE conflict very confused.*

Later that night, alone in a riverside pool I try to parce out the subtle differences between *paralyzed by jealousy* and *made irrelevant by circumstances*. I think, *No wonder I have back problems, I have been holding my stomach in for forty-seven years,* and even in a hot pool in pitch darkness, letting it out takes tremendous concentration.

88. Denver, Colorado

When the coldest postseason baseball game in history ends, at half past twelve on a Sunday night, and fifty thousand disappointed frozen silent people funnel out into the empty streets of LoDo, giant clouds of breath forming and rising above their heads like empty thought bubbles, it is hard not to think of *Night of the Living Dead.* It is hard not to wonder whether we use the small sadnesses in life to avoid or to access the large sadnesses. We will all be back tomorrow night to watch the Rockies lose for the final time this year.

Meanwhile, over at the Pepsi Center, *my* Colorado Avalanche have changed their mascot from Howler, who was a sort of Abominable Snowman type, a creatured embodiment of an avalanche itself, into Bernie, a cuddly, friendly, Saint Bernard with a little plastic cask around his neck. The change came after Howler allegedly assaulted a female fan wearing a Blackhawks jersey in the parking lot after a game.

Rick said, "I just hope their unsophisticated understanding of metaphor doesn't wind up costing them any games."

When I get out of my postgame shower Rick says, "You mean not drying off is a personal philosophy?"

I say, "I don't mind having the towel near me, or even around me. I just don't like to make the drying motion per se."

He says, "Well what if you are late to go somewhere?" and I show him by shaking all of my limbs around like a dog.

The next night, out at Improv with Ruby, the comic who draws the occupation *plumber*, sings, "And even though my hands smell funny, I'm makin' a shitload of money . . ."

In Tunisia, driving from Thuburbo Majus to Sidi Bou Said, back and forth under the still-standing Roman aqueduct, Rick said, "You know the next German who comes around at closing time is going to wind up with that lamp," and I said, "Sure," and he said, "There was probably a way to get it through security," and I said, "Probably so," and he said, "But the thing is, if you have a Roman lamp on your mantel that you paid a Tunisian night watchman eleven bucks for, you are pretty much an asshole, and if you sell it to some museum in Sweden for ten thousand dollars you are an even bigger asshole than that."

89. Sedona, Arizona

The bottles I pick for my Aura-Soma reading are called *The Puppeteer, Humpty Dumpty, Titania,* and *New Beginnings for Love.* This is out of more than a hundred bottles, with a German woman named Nadira watching, getting ready to tell me what they mean. Nadira is beautiful, tall, slim, fierce and soft at the same time. We sit in a room with the bottles on a table between us. Outside the window, the cottonwood leaves against the canyon walls look like flame.

The Puppeteer is gold on the bottom and purple on top and

means I am both wise and fearful and that I have been put into the fire many times *like an ingot of gold*, Nadira says, in her thick accent, and have come out each time a higher carat. If I buy this bottle for sixty-eight dollars and rub the oil inside it all along my hairline and my abdomen, I will free myself from codependency, overcome emotional naïveté, and ease shoulder problems. It may also allow me to establish access to incarnations in ancient Egypt.

Humpty Dumpty is the problem bottle, orange over orange, and its main theme is shock and all its consequences. I gather from Nadira's expression that picking this bottle is a lot like picking the Death card in Tarot or the Coyote in Medicine Cards, and she tells me that if I buy this bottle for sixty-eight dollars I must apply it in a very specific way: around the entire abdomen; also from the left earlobe to the left shoulder in a small band downward. Then, beginning under the left arm, in a wide band down the whole left side of the trunk to the ankle. Doing this every day until the bottle is empty, Nadira says, will help me recover from disappointment resulting from spiritual deceit (such deceit, after all, she says, puts the soul into a state of shock) and gallstones.

Titania is clear on the bottom and turquoise on the top, and it's all about clarity and artistic expression, which is nice because it is the right-now bottle and the other two are from the past. If I buy the Titania bottle for sixty-eight dollars and rub the oil all over my chest until it is gone it will allow me to release deep blockages, especially if they are related to the inability to speak about spiritual matters, reduce stage fright, and alleviate any problems I am having with implants.

"Implants?" I say to Nadira, thinking I have misheard, and she smiles prettily and draws her hands across her ample chest.

The future bottle is pink on the top and green on the bottom, and just when I am wondering whether *new beginnings for love* means Rick or some person even newer than Rick, Nadira says I should probably try to start with self-love first. If I pay sixty-eight dollars for this bottle it will enable recognition of the love that is already in my life, balance giving and taking in the love area, relieve all heart conditions, especially those of a psychosomatic nature, and help to cope with the impression of being a male in a female body or vice versa.

"I am so happy for you with zis reading," Nadira says, clapping her hands together. "I feel that now you are going to have a really great life!"

90. Creede, Colorado

The doctor isn't taking new patients so I agree to see the doctor's assistant called Chip who is short and wearing hiking boots. When he asks why I am there, I show him the little spot that is flaking repeatedly off my face, and say, "Also, I have been in the sun my whole life."

Chip says, "I don't know you well enough to call you *alligator face.*"

I say, "That's true."

He looks at my face with his big lighted magnifying mirror and says, "There is one thing I have to tell you before we go any further and that is that I don't cut on the face."

I think, *Well, I hope not, since you are not even a real doctor,* but say, "How come?"

And he says, "Because the face is way too precious." Then he says, "Now, if you are a really good friend of Kim's, she might cut on your face."

Kim is the real doctor. I am not her really good friend. I say, "I thought it was supposed to work the other way around." Then I say, "Does that mean you think this thing is something?"

He says, "Oh, it is definitely something. It is definitely something all right. And let me tell you, if it is melanoma, then this is the very worst place to have it." He makes a triangle with his hands on my face. "We call this right here the zone of death. Everything that is happening here is draining straight back to the brain, straight back to the brain, even as we speak."

"Even as we speak," I say.

I leave the office and go back to the ranch and call the Denver Skin Clinic and make an appointment with a real dermatologist. Five hours of driving later, she looks over every inch of my body and gives me a clean bill of health.

Two days later, back at the ranch, I am in the big red claw-footed bathtub and out in the living room I hear Colt talk Rick into opening up his computer so Colt can show him his most recent love connection on eHarmony. Colt has no computer, but he goes in early to use the one at work before anybody else gets there. Tassie has kicked him out again and this time she has moved in with a volunteer fireman.

"Desperate times call for desperate measures," I hear Colt say, over the boot-up sound of Rick's machine. Rick has never seen an Internet dating site, nor a blog, nor a Facebook page—he doesn't even know how to text. I have already been shown the woman Colt calls Oklahoma City. She has posted ten pictures of herself on the site. She is a big girl—a horsewoman, says Colt—with round shoulders and massive, possibly enhanced breasts, and in all ten pictures she is wearing one or another halter top, two of them covered in gold lamé.

When Colt showed me the photos, I said, "Hmm. Wouldn't you think she would have wanted to mix it up a little? One or two shots in her riding gear, or some sort of work attire?" and Colt looked at me as if I was even dumber than he thought.

"So?" he says to Rick, and I hold very still in the tub.

"Gosh," Rick says, "she sure looks like she wants to have sex."

"Well, I hope so," Colt says, some mixture of defensiveness and confusion in his voice.

91. Wupatki, Arizona

There is so much wind coming out of the blowhole it is difficult to stand against it, but I try, for several minutes, up on the little metal grate that covers it, letting it tangle my hair and tear tears from my eyes. The air that is coming out smells cavey and tastes like somebody else's mouth, a little like in college, when your boyfriend would do a bong hit and then breathe it into your mouth, a kind of pot mixed with saliva mixed with Sysco Pizza taste.

Geologists say the earth cracks are tectonic in origin, formed over millions of years as the Colorado Plateau region buckled and stretched in response to plate movements. They got bigger over time because limestone dissolves in water. In the Second Mesa village of Shungopavi, the Hopi believe that the blowholes are openings to the wind god Yaponcha, and frankly their story seems like the better one, because sometimes they blow out and sometimes they suck in and sometimes they just sit there like any other hole in the ground.

Today, though, the Wupatki hole sounds like the Earth is hopping mad and getting ready to do something about it, or like it's releasing one giant breath that goes on forever or at least until the barometric pressure changes, when, according to the brochure, the hole will begin to suck.

The sun is setting on the nine-hundred-year-old pueblo above the blowhole, and I ask Rick what he is thinking about and he says, "How for the people that lived here, woman and earth crack meant the same thing, and how that really just echoes the argument between Plato and Aristotle."

I think, *Hmmmm*, because it would seem to me that if you were inclined to draw some kind of line in the sand you would probably put the Native Americans on one side and Plato and Aristotle together on the other, and I say so, and Rick says, *No*, Plato is on the side of the Native Americans because he locates the ultimate reality inside what we would call a metaphor, and Aristotle thinks the metaphor is just something extra we have added on.

"So for Plato," Rick says, "that tree is only a kind of washed-out copy of the thing that is tree-ness. And a painting of that tree is just a copy of a copy. The people are less important than the tree-ness, which you only get to when you die."

We are back on the road, driving the twenty miles from Wupatki up under the cloud cap to Sunset Crater, where the landscape is gray and burnt. Cinder cones and lava flows line the roadway and the sky is spitting snow. One day between 1040 and 1100 this mountain blew its top, and very shortly after, the ancestors of the

Hopi started building Wupatki. Maybe they were drawn by the volcano, or maybe they knew the ash would be good for crops, or maybe they just liked living on a part of the earth so alive that it breathed and belched and smoked and hurled flaming rocks at them without warning.

Rick's got a master's degree in philosophy and religion and I know very little about Plato and even less about Aristotle, but I am often propelled into arguing with him by something desperate and intuitive, so I say, "But the Native Americans were tree-ness, weren't they? And sky-ness and mountain-ness? Wasn't that the whole point for them, that everything was possible here?"

To my surprise, my nonlogic gives Rick pause, and then, as is often the case, I find out we had really, all along, been talking about Sofree.

"You must understand," he says, "that I trusted the Universe fully. I decided for the first time ever not to watch my back. I jumped in with both feet and the Universe let me down."

I want to say, *I think that only works visa versa.* I want to say, *What self-respecting Universe would ever tell anybody not to watch his back?* I want to say, *None of this would make any sense without suffering.* What I do say is, "It would be a pity if Sofree's enticing you into sticking your dick in her became evidence against the Universe's benevolent nature."

"But what if truth is a woman?" reads a single-line chapter in Cliff Parker's manuscript, and I wrote in the margin, "If it is, it isn't *this* woman."

But sometimes. Sometimes I am seized with a love surge so big and overwhelming for Rick and his sweet round red face and his freckled hands and even more than that his try, a try so big and shot through with so much doubt that it threatens to take him down at the exact same time it propels him forward, it is all I can do not to fall down with the force of it.

"You're the big story here, Pam," Rick says, on the one-mile Lava Flow loop trail. "It is quite possible that you have saved my life."

92. Lucas, Kansas

If you pay ten extra dollars you can see Dinsmoor himself, seventy-five years dead and well on his way to skeleton-hood, his teeth pushing forward like the oldest horse imaginable, his wire-rimmed glasses growing in proportion to his shriveling eyes.

Dinsmoor married his first wife on horseback and his second, who was fifty-nine years his junior, in 1924, just after his eightieth birthday.

Forget the World's Largest Ball of Twine; forget the World's Smallest Versions of the World's Largest Things. Forget every one of Dinsmoor's two hundred larger-than-life concrete sculptures like the one of Adam and Eve where Eve offers Adam an apple of friendship beneath the Devil, five frolicking concrete children, and two love storks. It is the corpse that we will remember, that we will contemplate, on the long haul across Nebraska, or in our dreams, like the one I had the other night, where a woman—some woman—was it Cliff Parker's woman? —was driving.

It was one of those earthquake dreams like I always have, where the ground turns into that ribbon candy you used to see at Christmas, the same pretty colors. What usually happens is that I am in some kind of sweatshop—maybe a garment factory—with all of these women from Africa and South America, and when the floor starts to change into ribbon candy, one of them says, "Don't worry, it's only an earthquake," and I can see that there really is no reason to worry, that the whole point of an earthquake is to learn to ride it out.

But in this dream I couldn't ride it out because this woman, whoever she was, had stolen my car, with me, and maybe even Rick and Madison, inside it, and I had to wrestle her to the floor of the car and pry her hand open, and I remember quite clearly saying, "Give me the keys, you crazy bitch." But when I looked into her face it was Dinsmoor's face, with the skin mostly gone and a shriveled-up apple inside the mouth, which was a nice addition, I thought, on the part of my dream life, because there had been no apple inside of Dinsmoor's actual dead mouth, but you can see how if there were it could have been his idea of a joke, or a metaphor. That maybe, in death, he would finally taste the total apple-ness of an apple, which, as I understand it, is what Plato meant by entering the realm of the forms, or at least what Plato meant according to Rick.

93. Creede, Colorado

It snows so hard I can't see the barn for a while. Twenty-four inches fall in eighteen hours, and then it takes a break for the day and drops another twelve inches overnight. At three in the morning there are wind gusts up to 60 miles an hour, rattling the house so hard it wakes me.

I am imagining the drifts, and the horses unable to get behind the barn, so I get up and spend the hours until daylight on Weather Underground, thinking maybe I can somehow help the horses by following the track of the storm in excruciating detail online, and keeping up on snow depths at unmanned weather stations all over the state.

At first light I brave the blizzard and head for the barn and there they are, all wild-eyed and fuzzed up against the wind, giant icicles hanging from their manes and tales and tiny ones from their eyelashes. I dig out the barn door and double up on the hay, give them some grain too, the low-carb kind on account of Deseo's diabetic condition, make sure Roany hasn't (as he often does) plucked the defroster out of the horse trough with his teeth.

When I get done with the horses, I build a snow kiva before it gets dark in one of the big drifts in front of the house. It is perfect to sit in and look at the mountains. It fits only me and has the exact right slant to be comfortable on my back. Also, it keeps the wind out, and makes me feel like a sled dog when I am inside it.

I realize that I have built the snow kiva, without thinking about it, on the very spot where Mary Ellen spent her last days. Janine would say Mary Ellen is one of the people who are helping me now, and she wouldn't even mean it as a joke.

I take a nap on the couch with Liam and feel considerably better for it. It took him a year to learn to wag his tail and two to learn to lift his third leg into the 4Runner, but what he wants most in every situation is to be told how to be a good boy.

I get an email from Quinn that says, *For whatever reason, someone at 96.9 FM has decided "My Sweet Lord" is a Christmas song and keeps playing it every other hour, in between "Santa Baby" and Mannheim Steamroller, and whoever that person is gets my sincerest thanks.*

Alone here for two weeks I've taken to screaming at commercials, like the one that goes, "What red-blooded American male would walk out on a football game to replace his normal headlights with Bridgestone [or whatever] FogMaster headlights . . ." and the punch line after lots of information about 25 percent more brightness is when the twenty-something daughter comes out of the house and he chucks her the keys it goes, "A man who knows it is easier to replace headlights than it is to replace a daughter."

"Why can't she replace her own goddamned headlights?" I scream at the TV. And, "So his red-blooded American male-ness is suddenly reinstated because he has a daughter who has no mechanical skills?" This is how I can tell I am getting cranky.

Remember Jude? The Division I hockey player whose mother committed suicide four months after his brother died and four months before his father went to jail? His father took his own life just last Tuesday, another airport parking lot fatality, this time DFW. He jumped from the top deck, which is only five stories, lived almost all the way to the hospital, but not quite.

When someone jumps from the Golden Gate Bridge, the official code name for it is a 10-31. When someone throws himself in front of a BART train, they call it a *trespasser incident,* as in *lead us not into temptation.* Of the roughly thirteen hundred people who have tried to commit suicide by jumping from the Golden Gate Bridge, twenty-six have lived. Most of those twenty-six have been willing to talk about it afterwards and they all have said some version of the same thing: *As soon as my hands left the railing, I wanted more than anything to change my mind.*

When Luca finished working the muscles that connect my pel-vic bone to my sternum and wrapped me in the sheet in such a way that he could lift me into a sitting position with one fluid motion and no effort whatsoever on my part, he said, in his heavy Austrian accent, "Pam, have you ever considered there may be an emotional element involved in your back pain too?"

What I want to say on the phone to Rick is, *I can no longer sustain myself if my primary role in your life is witness to the Rick-Sofree War.* I want to say, *I can't bear to watch Madison grow up to limp and vamp and flirt and think of herself as a sweet mossy font of purification.* I want to say, *We don't have sex that much anymore because watching you proofread an email you are going to send to Sofree sixteen or eighteen times doesn't really work on me as foreplay.* I want to say, *The only thing we have between us that isn't fighting about Sofree, strategizing about Sofree, or commiserating about Sofree is baseball, and while we both agree that baseball is wonderful, it is probably not enough.*

What I do say when I actually talk to him is, "I miss my friends," and then I cry so long and so hard you would think that every single one of my friends was dead.

94. Ksar Ouled Soltane, Tunisia

When we first get there, the five o'clock prayer is being sung from the green and white tower of the monastery, and the man who will turn out to be Khalifa Guesmi says, in perfect French, "Where are you from, Colorado? Texas?" That is how we know we are meant to meet.

He says, "I am just closing up for the day . . . but if there are any questions I can answer for you about this place, please do not hesitate to ask . . ."

It is our third ksar of the day, including Hadada, the one that was used in the filming of *The Phantom Menace,* rounded mud structures that rise from the ground and out of each other like swallow's nests, burnt sienna mud against the blue Tunisian sky.

Khalifa Guesmi speaks thirteen languages, in spite of passing every one of his twenty-four years—as he puts it—in Ksar Ouled Soltane. He works in the fields, tending his father's sheep, and here at the ksar, which, he tells us, has recently been declared a World Heritage Site and now will be protected forever. He is as delicate as rain, as different from the men at the camel fair in Douz as the ocean is from the desert.

"The people in this part of Tunisia seem . . ." I say, "gentler," is the word I can finally find in my limited French.

"The people in this part of Tunisia are descendants of the Yemeni people," he says. "They came here hundreds of years ago, but they still live as they did in Yemen. This place, the ksar, is their method of building."

I tell him, truthfully, that friends of mine who have traveled far more extensively than me tell me that the Yemeni people are the finest they have met in all the world, and he beams with unconcealed pride. While he is making us tea he mentions, quietly, that he uses his spare time at the ksar to paint. We say we would love to see his paintings, and when he brings them out we know that the problem of Christmas shopping for all of Rick's family members has been solved.

Khalifa's brother shows up, and he is a painter too, and we drink tea and talk about Yemen and Tunisia, also about America and Barack Obama and hope. We take pictures together in the tiny teahouse, pay for the ten small paintings we have selected for Rick's relatives. Khalifa and his brother give us one painting each as a gift.

It was light when we went into the teahouse; by the time we emerge it is dark dark dark. No moon, no streetlights, Orion and the Pleiades framed together by the ksar's rounded walls.

When we get back to where the Punto is parked I turn my painting over and in the light that hangs over the door of the monastery I read the inscription in French (though he has also printed it in Arabic): *I give as a present to the lady Pam from the USA with my sincere thanks and my wishes to a tranquil Christmas and my best wishes to a happy life with Rick. KG*

Under a million stars and along the weathered alleyway begins the humming and warbling of the seven o'clock call to prayer.

95. Sedona, Arizona

The lady who leads the Zumba class is wearing a hot pink sweat-suit with the words PEACE, LOVE, ZUMBA appliquéd on it in silver sparkly paint. The class is comprised of me, a husband-and-wife sex therapist team, a young black woman whose shirt indicates she teaches at a YWCA camp, a retired rancher and his wife, and two Hassidic sisters from the Bronx. Out in the real world of power yoga Olympics and competitive Namaste, there would not be one of us brave enough to sign up for a class like this, but these classes at the all-inclusive spa are like the Ellis Island of fitness: give me your fat, your nerdy, your clumsy. Zumba Patti loves us all.

Patti herself is not a kid, but you would never know it by her energy level, as she steps us through rumbas, mambas, cumbias, salsas, rap, hip-hop. It is the male sex therapist, and not the old cowboy, who flags first, and the sisters in their kerchiefs and thick glasses who have the most fun. Except for Patti, whose enthusiasm is infectious, and beyond all comprehension.

So far at Mi Amo I have had a Thai massage, an Aura-Soma color reading, reflexology, and something called Shared Soul Seeker with Rick. In Shared Soul Seeker, a woman named Francesca Francesca stood by and made approving noises while Rick and I first interpreted each other's chakras, and then spun healing energy into them.

When Rick put his hand over my fifth chakra he said he saw a deer that turned into a wolf that turned into an owl, so when I got to his sixth chakra I said I saw a purple grizzly bear walking on a clean white glacier, confirming what anyone would have guessed, which is that even in something called Shared Soul Seeker, Rick and I would be inclined to compete.

Twila, the Reiki Master, has the clearest green eyes I have ever seen, but during the healing she closes them and screws her face all up like the Exorcist, especially when she puts her hands near my heart, my knees, or my nether regions. In the picture she draws there is one jaggedy circle inside another jaggedy circle inside my stomach. There is a smooth circle over my heart, one small circle over each knee, and a giant cone coming out of the top of my head.

When she shows me the picture I think the cone is going to turn out to be the good news, but when she goes over it with me it turns out that the cone is about my suicidal tendencies.

"You are so powerful they are trying to pull you back with them," she says. "That's why you have this big strain on your knees." She points to the little circles. She takes my hands. "But you've got to stay here, Pam, because you have very very important work to do."

At this she begins to weep. Not her, exactly, but the thing that comes through her, and I leave the room thinking that suicidal is *not* what I have been feeling lately, even with the days so short, and I'm not as absolutely sure as she is that those jaggedy circles in my stomach are grief over my two abortions, though I have to give her credit for knowing there's been exactly two.

Yesterday Rick and I walked up to one of the eight Sedona vortexes. Rick climbed up on top and when he got down I asked how it felt up there and he said, "Oh, you know, all vortexy."

I sat in the shade of the vortex and contemplated Kachina Woman, a several hundred-foot sandstone tower nearby. Kachina Woman has a boat on her head because after the flood—the big one—she rowed across the water and repopulated the earth single-handedly.

The lady we sit next to at lunch says she went on a hike and there were "sky vaginas" everywhere and Rick says, so quietly he thinks I am the only one who hears him, "Frankly, there seemed to be a lot more cocks."

Rick and I figured out today that the difficulty we are having getting along at the spa we owe to our preexisting expectations. He thought we were coming to a spa together, and I thought I was coming to a spa.

I have my Reiki healing with Twila only a few hours before I have my psychic massage with Nadish, who is also German, and married to Nadira, and we go back to the room with the flaming trees out the window and he asks me what I want to work on. I say a few words about *second chakra* and *self* and before I have even finished my sentence he waves his hand and says, "No, no, zis is just what all the others have told you to say," which I have to admit is true.

"Let me ask you a question," he says, sounding a little like Colonel Klink, "Vy don't you just stop trying to be better?" and I think, *Well there is a suggestion for you.*

"Za problem is that you are trying to achieve an Eastern ideal with Western tools," says the German, who now calls himself Nadish. "Is it possible for you to stop trying to be better?"

"I don't think so," I say.

"And remember," Nadish says, "if you have to try to keep yourself from trying, you are missing the whole point."

"Of course," I say.

"Pam," he says, laying one hand on top of my head like a blessing, "you are a giant tree that many people like to sit under, and you like being that tree very much. Vy not just accept it?" He puts his hands on my cheeks and forces me to look right at him. "You have a thin top layer that is all fear," he says, "but underneath that is a big person, a big mothering presence. You are always so hateful toward your body, but you can't be who you are without zis body."

This must be, I think, why they call it a psychic massage.

"Pamela," he says, "do you know what zis name means?"

I do know what it means—it made me want to die of embarrassment when I was a teenager and absolutely nothing in me wants to tell Nadish the truth. He tells me that Nadish means ocean and Nadira means pinnacle, like *that's* going to up the ante.

"It means *all honey*," I finally mumble.

"Well," he booms, laughing, "that's perfect for you!" He pats my stomach merrily, gives me a wink, and leaves the room.

96. Creede, Colorado

I have the airplane dream again. This time I am with Rick and Madison—we are on our way home from somewhere—and the captain tells us there is such a large and strong low-pressure system over the area the plane cannot stay in the air. We will be making an emergency landing in Melbourne. It is hard to imagine where on earth we could have been that would force an emergency landing in Melbourne on the way *home*, but such is the logic of dreams.

The emergency-landing dreams don't scare me anymore. Partly because I have them so often and partly because the pilot never has trouble putting the plane down softly, usually on a freeway, twice on a major artery, once in a giant lake. I have flown low and slow now through dreamscaped versions of Honolulu, Seoul, London, and oddly, Cleveland, Ohio. It always looks like the wings will scrape the sides of the tall buildings, like we will hit a car, a pedestrian, get tangled in electric lines, but we never do. Sometimes it seems to take forever, from the announcement of distress to wheels down on the tarmac, but we always get there safe and sound.

In the Melbourne dream, we check into a hotel with a giant pool to please Madison and she couldn't be happier with the turn of events. The airline tells us it will be a week before the low-pressure system lifts, and I worry out loud to the chambermaid that Madison's mother will be apoplectic because we'll get all these extra days.

In real life, the lowest low-pressure system in one hundred years dumps another thirty inches on the ranch, on top of the three feet already standing, and the only reliable snowplow guy in the county goes to the hospital with chest pains. Some kind of odd back draft from the garage turns the cars into giant car-shaped snowmen, entirely concealed. It takes all day for Rick and me to dig to the barn, and the horses are glad to see us when we get there. Our range for the next three days is the house, and that skinny little barn trail, and even that blows back in every night when the wind comes up and we have to redig it. We eat through most of the freezer food and never once have the urge to kill each other and that's got to be some measure of progress.

I get an email from Fenton the human who's in Calcutta for a month that says: *Last night as the candles of the pilgrims were floating slowly down the Ganges and the faithful were doing their evening devotions in the vast, wide, polluted, holy river and the hymns were wafting, with the cries of the spider monkeys, over the rooftops, I watched from my hotel balcony and wished you were here with me to see it.*

The snow finally lets up and Madison comes to the ranch for real, and we put on snowshoes and drag three sleds out to the hill where the homesteaders are buried. The little red bullet sled goes the fastest but the old wooden toboggan is the sweetest ride, staying high and light up on the crystalline surface, running fifty yards out into the pasture before it loses enough momentum to sink down in, everything so silent out here with the snowfall that Madison's giggles echo back from the mountains that surround us like a song.

NZ #0015

I HAVE BEEN UP for three straight nights finishing articles and reading student papers, and now a three-hour layover in LAX finds me on the floor in the corner of an unused gate, a year's worth of credit card receipts, bank statements, and bills spread out around me. By the time I get back from New Zealand, April 15 will have come and gone.

Takeoff is on time and uneventful. Once dinner is over I know I can finally go to sleep. A sweet flight attendant who looks like a young Dick Van Dyke offers me champagne and I accept. I eat my dinner with half a glass of bubbles and that's when the cabin begins spinning.

I don't remember getting myself to the aft head, but I must have, because the next thing I know I am being pried out of it. I have passed out with my body against the door, which is making extrication difficult. No one can get in far enough to throw me back against the seat from which I have fallen, until I wake up enough to do it myself.

"You'd been in there nearly twenty minutes when we started to wonder," Dick Van Dyke says, once I have come to, and gotten my pants pulled up, and allowed two of them to help me to my seat. I am breathing comfortably into an oxygen mask attached to a portable tank. The five other people in my row, I notice, are seriously afraid of me.

"Happens to me all the time!" Dick says, flinging his long graceful arms about the cabin. "All the hustle and bustle of getting ready to go, take off, and then *whoops!*"—he executes exactly three quarters of a pratfall—"They find me flat on my back!"

"You are very kind," I say, "but I am sure you are exaggerating."

"Scout's honor!" he says, and his arm comes swinging back up in front of my face, two fingers raised. "You think a body likes to go from sea level to thirty-nine thousand feet in twelve point seven minutes?"

About six times in the next hour Dick tries to take my oxygen mask off, and every time he does blackness rushes in from the outsides of my eyes and he has to snap it right back on. "No sweat," he says, patting the silver-bullet-shaped tank and wiggling his eyebrows, "I got a case of these babies in the back."

The pilot comes over the loudspeaker and tells us there are ten hours and fifteen minutes left in our trip. I wonder about their policy, if they will try to land somewhere like Rarotonga if all of a sudden I start to die for real.

Somewhere over the equator I finally fall asleep. I am on my third oxygen canister by the time the wheels touch down in Auckland.

"You'll want to stay in your seat while the others deplane," Dick says. "They'll be coming for you. They'll need to check you out before they let you in the country."

Because everything Dick says is kind of a joke, I don't realize he's serious until I find myself in an ambulance on my way to international quarantine where a nurse takes about seventeen vials of my blood and puts me in a sunny room with clean white sheets and a sweet breeze coming in through the curtains, where I sleep like a baby for fifteen hours.

What I don't find out till the next morning, when they release me with a sheaf of papers that proclaim me healthy beyond all reason (but possibly allergic to champagne), is that New Zealand, at this time, is free of many diseases, and still has a very low occurrence of HIV.

A kind orderly with an accent so thick I can barely understand him drives me from the hospital to the Hertz office. I get my car one day late and head north to Cape Reinga where I've been told the blue-green Tasman Sea meets the midnight-blue Pacific in great crashing waves, and the spirits of the dead leap off the eight-hundred-year-old kahika tree into the place the waters come together. The kelp divides to reveal the way to Hawaiki, their mythical hereafter home, and the spirits, it is said, turn back briefly at Three Kings Island for one more look toward land.

97. Gunnison, Colorado

New Year's Day up the Taylor Fork. The fortuitously named Becky Barkman sits comfortably in the sled while I drive her ten-dog team through the six inches of new snow that sit on top of the two feet they got in December.

"I've decided to get rid of the horses," she says, legs stretched in front of her, Tessa, a blue heeler, who does not pull, sitting on her lap. "I've had them for twenty years and decided they're pushy, insolent, greedy. Even the good ones, when it comes down to it, are all about the food."

By my best calculations I have not seen Becky Barkman for seventeen years, although technically, with her down and Mylar all-in-one suit, her fur-rimmed hood, and her wraparound glasses, I am not exactly seeing her now. We have picked up a conversation we must have been having seventeen years ago. Disappointing men, overachieving dogs, cutting your own wood and hauling your own hay and living a life held together with paper and string, but how many people, how many people get to do *this* today?

"It's not that there's anything wrong with horses," Becky says, "they simply don't give back." She is talking herself into this, I suspect, because in this recession something's got to go and if it's not the horses it's some or all of the twenty-five dogs, who are giving back and giving back with all their little hearts even as we have this conversation. "You might say, come on, how *can* you ask a horse to give back, but if we are talking energetically, I think you know what I mean."

"Uh-huh," I say, because I do, more or less, and as far as I am concerned, Becky can talk about anything she wants to all day, as long as she lets me drive, because driving a dog team, whipping down a snowy path at 15 miles per hour through the silent woods behind ten joyful, hardworking canines, I re-remember, each time I get to do it, is the thing that makes me happier than anything else on earth.

Driving the other sled, the one where Rick and Madison are riding, is a crazy-handsome, soft-spoken, and kind man named Matt, who works for Becky, and who is taking a lot of care teaching Madison the names of the dogs, letting her stand in front of him on the runners, giving her the feel of what it's like to drive the sled.

Madison has the best intuitive sense of how to be around animals of any child I have ever known. I bought her this trip for Christmas, to encourage her toward her interest in animals and away from both her parents' dream of being a singing star, for which she also shows a lot of talent. It's none of my business, as I am finding out daily. When you are a stepparent nothing that really matters is any of your business, but when I look down the road of her future to the fork I prefer Joy Adamson to Janis Joplin, Dian Fossey to Britney Spears.

Now Becky is talking about the Age of Aquarius and Mercury, dropping down into alignment at last, and I am watching the ice crystals fall from the trees, and shifting my weight from rudder to rudder to stay in the middle of the narrow trail, and smiling back at the dogs who turn now and then to smile at me (*How we doin'? How we doin'?* they seem to say), and hearing the whisper of the runners in the new snow, and easing my weight onto the drag break for the steep downhills, and jumping off and trotting beside the sled on the uphills, and thinking if the Age of Aquarius has made it all the way to Gunnison, that's the best evidence I've heard that it's really real.

98. Davis, California

For my birthday, Quinn makes me a playlist with one song from each year I have been alive, and it starts with "The Wanderer" and ends with a Bright Eyes pre-release download called "Heavy Love" which, she says, gives me a head start on living at least another few months. We are listening to it and playing our third game of Cranium in which Rick is the best at factoids and Quinn is the best at solving word puzzles and Pony is the best at drawing with her eyes closed. I think we're on 1983 ("Radio Free Europe") now but every time somebody has to hum or spell backwards we turn it down and sometimes we forget to turn it back up.

Quinn also got me a Ben & Jerry's ice cream cake made out of peanut butter cookie dough ice cream, the flavor I didn't know I had been waiting my whole life for them to invent, and the frosting is a blue sky with white puffy clouds. Pony made her famous brussels sprouts, and it's hard to believe that they are precisely as good as a cookie dough ice cream cake, only in a different way, but it's true.

According to one of her ex-girlfriends who went on to study something called the Michael teachings, Quinn is a seventh-cycle sage, which at least is some explanation for how she knows so much at thirty. We don't really know who Michael is or was, but we do know he said that before taking a body each lifetime, every essence determines for itself, perhaps carefully, perhaps not, the culture, sex, personality, and body type in which it will be housed. "Essences generally try to set themselves up in the vicinity of their entitymates," Quinn reports, and then we have to take turns saying *entitymate* a whole lot of times out loud.

It doesn't matter how many times I say *Come up and see me sometime!* Rick cannot get Mae West, but then I save the day with my charades rendition of "gravity," where I hold an imaginary golf tee in my hand and collapse repeatedly to the floor.

At the queer-cluster symposium this afternoon, all of the snacks were vegan. If there is a God, why would he waste all his time making hell?

Later, the Dean's Office called to see if I was willing to become the chairman of the committee on committees. For some of us, faith has to be a chaotic, ungovernable thing.

At the faculty meeting Sadie said, "Well, we certainly don't want to send the dean the message that we are the kind of department who cares if one of their writers wins a National Book Award!"

It's like the way the expression on the Pakistani owner of the Davis Dairy Queen's face when he turns the Peppermint Patty Blizzard upside down to impress us with its thickness makes it indisputably clear that back in Islamabad he was a neurosurgeon or something even more important than that.

In her latest email Sofree said, "Lest Rick forget, I am the manager of Madison's life-rhythms."

To paraphrase Quinn, paraphrasing Michael Jackson, some people are always throwing stones to hide their hands.

99. Waitomo, New Zealand

In the language of the Maori, Waitomo means water hole. In this North Island region the rivers flow underground in deep limestone caves, and I have come here to go *black*water rafting. The fog is thick and the air is chilly as we struggle into our wet suits, which, because at 9:30 a.m. this is already the third trip of the day, are as their name implies. There are twelve of us from seven countries and four continents, though we look almost identical in our black outfits and metal miner's helmets, crammed in the minibus as it rattles toward the cave.

So far the guides haven't told us much of anything and the guy next to me, Bryan, from Tasmania, who likes boats but can't swim a stroke, is getting a little nervous. I hear him quietly tell the guide that he can't swim and she says, too loudly, "That's great, neither can I. We'll stick together," and I can't tell if it's true or if she's kidding or if she thinks he's kidding too.

We pile out of the van next to the river which is, at this moment, aboveground, and they tell us to choose an inner tube that fits us and then they teach us how to *eel up*. To eel up is to form a twelve-man chain, and we do it this first time sitting in the dirt parking lot, our inner tubes around our middles, our feet up under the next guy's armpits, someone else's feet under our own.

"You'll have to eel up right after we jump off the waterfall," the guide says, and Bryan shoots me a look and I shrug. Then they make us jump off a ten-foot platform into the deepest part of the river, to build our confidence, and Bryan has to take three runs at it, but when he bursts back up through the silvery surface, his grin stretches ear to ear.

We turn our helmet lights on and wade down to the place where one river channel enters Ruakuri Cave. At first the water is shallow, ankle, then knee deep, but as we get farther into the cave one stream joins another and we are forced to float through the passages, the cave floor rising up to touch our feet momentarily, and then disappearing under the black water again.

There are drops, slides, and whirlpools to negotiate, and in some places the ceiling comes right to the top of the water and we have to put our heads under and yank down on our tubes to make it through, trusting that the ceiling will rise again a few seconds later when we get to the other side.

In the echo of the cave the waterfall sounds gigantic—even from a long way off—and when we get there, our headlamps aren't strong enough for us to see beyond it to the bottom.

"Jump way out," the guide says, "there are big rocks below you," and so we do, one at a time, far out into blackness, not knowing if we'll hit the water after fifteen feet or fifty, the force of the jump plunging us through our inner tubes and underwater, almost impossible, in all that darkness, to tell whether we've come back to the surface or not.

"Okay, eel up, eel up!" the guide yells, and we do, just in time, before we reach the end of the plunge pool and the current, which is fast and strong now, sweeps us away. Under my armpits are the feet of Albi, a windsurfing instructor from Berlin; my feet are in the armpits of Haruki, on his honeymoon from Osaka. The walls of the cave move past in the glow of our headlamps and we bump along the sides like a giant caterpillar gone blind.

"Turn off your headlamps," the guide shouts, and though this seems illogical no one hesitates because she hasn't steered us wrong so far.

The cave goes dark and above our heads thousands of glow-worms hang like constellations, tiny globes of light dangling on invisible strings of their own making. We are struck dumb by the sight; the only sound for many minutes is the water slosh-ing against the sides of the cave. The depth of the cave ceiling changes, from as little as six feet to as much as sixty, and when we pass under one of those tall chambers it's like we have turned in to face the center of the galaxy, the lights are so dense, so thick and deep.

100. Tabernash, Colorado

Through the snowflakes, the shape of a giant white pelican becomes apparent. We are at 10,000 feet, it is 21 degrees, and though we try to call it a snow goose, try to call it a trumpeter swan, even try, in the mind's tireless attempt to make sense of non sequitur, to call it an albatross, nothing has a beak like a pelican, and when it lands on the little pond behind the Tabernash post office, dunks its head under the icy water and pulls up a fish, there is no more denying what it is.

In a few minutes I've got the whole story in my mind. Some developer in West Vail or Breckenridge, a big guy with a perpetually unlit cigar in his mouth building a condo-slash-single-family ski home extravaganza with a moat and a name like Xanadu, on the phone, saying, "Get me some of those giant white pelicans from Sumbawa . . . We'll install little heaters for the winter months, bring in minnows by the truckload" . . . but this pelican, *my* pelican, during the requisite wing clipping, tucked his feathers tight tight to his body and retained just enough wing length to fly. Now he is bound for a happy reunion with his pelican brothers and sisters in the bright Indonesian sunshine, and would get there, too, if he hadn't been foiled, as we all have been, by the can't-make-its-mind-up weather, and now he will starve, shiver, his little webbed feet freezing to the surface of the Tabernash pond most likely that very night.

"Do you think I should call Fish and Game?" I ask Rick, and he says that kind of decision is usually my department.

The postmistress of Tabernash assures me that *of course* she knows there is a pelican out her window, that there are only 153 residents of Tabernash, who pick up their mail on average twice a week, and she has very little to do all day but stare out at the pelicans who come through with some regularity at this time of year up the flyway from some lake or another down south.

"But we're so far from the ocean," I say, and she looks me up and down and says, "I guess the pelican's got that figured out."

"See?" Rick says, when I get back in the car, by which I know he means, *Things are often not as dire as you think they are,* and *Maybe there is more to our life together than baseball after all,* and *The story you tell yourself about how you are just a witness to my war with Sofree might have been true at the beginning but it is not true anymore because look, here we are in Tabernash, for instance, not to mention Scotland and Tunisia,* and *While it used to be you all the time talking me into this relationship, now it is the other way around, and I don't mind, because it is probably my turn, but it would be really nice if you could at least try to hear me.*

"You make some really good points," I say into the silence, and he smiles at me like a man who has never had a bad day in his life.

101. Woody Creek, Colorado

Steak Fajitas Special Night with Art, Allison, and the kids. It's been twelve years since the boulder fell from the wall of Glenwood Canyon, crushing the car Art was driving, killing his wife and two little boys, Tanner and Shea, and leaving him entirely untouched. Now his new boys, Rider and Burke, play their Game Boys at the table while Allison, their mother, asks Johnny how far along he is in his grief.

I have brought Johnny to meet Art and Allison shortly after the three-year anniversary of his wife Sue's death. They were diving on the Ningaloo Reef north of Perth, a trip to celebrate ten years of marriage, when Sue reached for a shell and was bitten by a blue-ringed octopus which, though tiny, carries enough venom to kill twenty-six adult humans in minutes and there is no antivenom, even if you know right away.

Johnny looks better than he did this time last year, his eyes less shocky, his spine held slightly less erect. It took ten minutes of pleasantries for both men to start weeping, and now they are deep into all of it: Ram Dass and Joseph Campbell, Eckhart Tolle and the Dalai Lama, *temenos* and vision quests, sacred datura and peyote back in the seventies and the one question that won't ever go away: Was this all part of some indecipherable plan?

Art and Allison got together after Art's dead son Tanner came to Allison in a vision as she was backpacking in the Grand Canyon—on the Tanner Trail. He told her where the turns in the trail would be, what the approaching campsites would look like, and eventually, where she'd accidentally dropped her car keys at the trailhead several days before. Then he asked her to go back to Aspen and tell his dad that he and his brother and mother were doing all right. He told Allison his favorite toys, the number of his hockey jersey, the color of his favorite fleece—yellow—so that when she told Art he had come to her in a vision, Art would not doubt it was true.

Now, Allison turns to Rider, her soul child, a kid who is surrounded by ghosts every evening and can talk to them, not only the ones that belong to his family, but countless others, who, according to Allison, recognize him as a portal, a chance to get through.

"Rider, honey," she says, "put the Game Boy down for a minute," and he does.

"Johnny's wife died in the ocean, honey," she says. "Can you take a moment and see if she's got anything to say to him; can you maybe tell him if she's okay?" Rider sighs a little sigh and closes his eyes to try to see Sue. He is ten years old, a left winger

on the Aspen Leaf's hockey team and he is a bit tired of this gift
the Universe has bestowed upon him.

"Mom," he says, "I think you are going to have to ask God
those questions." He pauses for a minute like there might be more.
"But she did come to my room last night. She has a thin face and
glasses, right? And brown hair that she keeps in a ponytail most
of the time. She seemed okay to me."

Rider shrugs, picks up his Game Boy, and turns back to his
brother. The look on Johnny's face confirms that his description
is right on and I can't tell which I love more, Rider's gift or his
boundaries. Around us the Woody Creek Tavern sighs content-
edly, like an old dog returned to the porch after a long day hunting, and the ghost of Hunter Thompson, who is surely somewhere
here among us, orders one more drink at the bar.

102. Freestone, California

Cinder and I go to a Zen spa in west Sonoma County to get what
is called a Cedar Enzyme bath. We change into our robes and sit
on meditation pillows and look out the floor-to-ceiling windows
at a man-made waterfall tumbling down rounded rocks beside a
little slate pathway, the whole scene looking suspiciously like a
life-size version of one of those Rolling Rock beer signs in bars
where the water pretends to move.

After a while a young woman with badly shaking hands pours
us some enzyme tea, and then we are shown to the baths themselves, which are really more like horse stalls, if you cut the walls

off a horse stall about three feet up. Picture side-by-side cut-off horse stalls, piled high with steaming cedar shavings. The shavings, the woman tells us, have not been heated using any outside source. They were mixed with the enzymes twenty-four hours ago, and have generated this heat entirely on their own, like compost.

She takes our robes and we climb naked, awkwardly, over the walls and into our individual horse stalls. The heat is overwhelming. She buries us, one at a time, in the steaming shavings, leaving our heads exposed. It is impossible not to think of childhood, all the years I spent cleaning stalls in exchange for getting to take a three-year-old thoroughbred fast over a set of jump standards, or slowly along an oak-lined path.

After about three minutes of sweating, I say to Cinder, "This is like being buried in horseshit." After twenty minutes, after I've pulled first one arm, then the other, then both legs out of the shavings to get some relief from the heat, and I look like a stinkbug rolled up onto its back, I say, "No, no, that's not right. We *are* the horseshit."

"Anything is possible," Cinder says, "and I mean that in the very best way."

103. Saguache, Colorado

Slept very well pulled over in a pig farmer's field. The heater kept the car toasty all night even though now, an hour after sunrise, on the far side of Saguache, it is still 19 below.

The darkest hour may be just before the dawn, but the coldest one is right after it, at least up here. It's like the night holds on to every scrap of heat it can until sunrise and only then lets go, the thermometer dropping a handful of degrees before it starts to rise again—a kindness the night pays all the cold and hungry cows and horses, elk and coyote who are probably starting to wonder if this winter is ever going to end.

I slept in the back of the 4Runner, no wolfhound to cuddle up with but plenty of other stuff including two cardboard boxes of books, a 64-quart stainless steel Coleman cooler, the largest rolling suitcase that can fit in the overhead bin, and two weeks' worth of groceries.

The pig farmer woke me at dawn, checking to see if I was dead in there. The sky was all pink over Great Sand Dunes National Park and the Sangre de Cristo. I heard the farmer's tires on the snow and popped up among the boxes and clothes I had pulled over me for warmth. He jumped out of his truck in his insulated coveralls just as I lowered my window.

I was immeasurably cheered up by the conversation under our conversation, that he wasn't there to rape me, that I wasn't there to rob him. I said I'd be heading down the road now that it was daylight and he said, *No, you go on and rest as long as you want.*

The main reason I slept in the pig farmer's field is that I was really tired. Also, I didn't want to have to carry the heavy cooler in by myself when it was 25 below, which it would have been had I arrived home at 2 a.m., *and* I didn't want to have to empty it, one bag at a time while my earlobes froze. Not to mention everything else in my car—toiletries, laptop, camera—that would have been frozen solid by morning. There would have been no thought of Rick getting up to help me unload the car, because he is still trying to make up for all the sleep he lost those years when his soul was shattered.

You *might* say I had avoided going home all day, missing my Sacramento-Denver flight on purpose and standing by for the next one, spending a long time at a Denver Office Depot trying to decide between a 4-gig and an 8-gig memory chip for my phone.

Wednesday is Communication Day and I will do just about anything to miss it. According to the agreement, Rick and Sofree are supposed to quit by midnight and are limited to subject lines of emails until the next Wednesday rolls around. This Communication Day promised to be a particularly gnarly one because both the summer schedule and the chicken pox vaccination debate were on tap.

Quinn sends me a text that says, *The biggest problem with Communication Day is that it's boring. You slept on the side of the road because we are prone to dramatic acts of desperation, in which we find great beauty, because we are insane. Our insanity is far more interesting than anything that happens on Communication Day.*

I send a text back that says, *Plus, the day after Communication Day is Philosophy Day, where Rick decides that he can't fight with Sofree anymore because he is a gentle person who needs to let the flow come through him. He is the tree, and it is the sap . . . but he doesn't make the sap, the sap makes him, etc.*

Quinn texts me back a link to a ladies' baby doll T-shirt, which is available in five colors, and says in black letters, *I saw your sad, and your sadness is very sexy, strong fragile man, you know what I mean? Because this is love, maybe.*

By the time I get to Del Norte, which is not pronounced *Del Nor-te*, the Peace of Art Cafe is open for business and the buffalo in the field behind the railroad tracks still have thick frost on their backs.

104. Rotorua, New Zealand

It looks a little like Yellowstone, this geothermally active region full of geysers and hot pots sacred to the Maori people, but the busloads of tourists who come here each day come mainly to see the Maori living "traditionally," washing their clothes in one steaming pool, cooking their vegetables in another.

Today there is a Maori woman, in traditional dress, cooking ears of sweet corn and selling them in Ziplocs, with a pinch of salt and a pat of butter, to the tourists for fifty NZ cents.

The man who shoves to the front of the corn line is Japanese, but clearly taking his wardrobe cues from American movies, *The Outlaw Josey Wales* meets *Saturday Night Fever*. His cowboy boots have toes so pointy his feet look reptilian, and gold chains hang in layers under his unbuttoned yoked shirt.

He offers the corn lady a single American dollar. She shakes her head and turns away.

"Wait a minute," the man says, in heavily accented English. "You not take this?"

The woman shakes her head again, doesn't speak.

"But this is the almighty American dollar!" the man says, "the most powerful currency in the world."

The corn woman moves out of the man's proximity to serve customers in another part of the line. Another Maori woman, one pool away, has stopped washing her sheets to watch.

The man turns back to his fat billfold and pulls out an American five.

"Madam," he shouts, "I offer you five American dollars for one ear of corn. With the current exchange rate, that is twenty times your asking price."

The corn woman holds her arms over her head in a gesture of refusal and protection. This is not the first time something like this has happened to her, since her homeland got turned into a theme park, but as with many things in life there is little to be done.

The Japanese man pulls out a twenty. "I'm offering you twenty American dollars for one ear of corn!" He is shouting now, and has the entire crowd's attention, but the corn woman ignores him. The man throws up his hands and climbs back on the bus. The second Maori woman puts her arm around the corn woman's shoulders, says something low into her ear.

The Japanese man emerges from the bus waving a U.S. hundred-dollar bill.

"In exchange for one ear of corn I am offering you one hundr—"

"Okay," the woman says, before he has a chance to finish, and plucks the stiff bill from his hand.

105. Boulder, Colorado

"You are not being very useful to me right now," Sofree says, seven hours into mediation, leaping out of her chair and putting one knee up on the table as though she might come at me across it. And while Tom invites her out into the hall for the fifth time today to calm her down, I think, *Well, there you have it.*

Three days ago I got an email saying Sofree wanted very much for Tom and me to come to the annual mediation so we could *bear witness, sustain and corroborate,* and so here we are with our little Styrofoam cups of tea. Sofree has lost a bunch of weight, and looks—I have to admit it—pretty darn sexy, though Rick's eyes have hardly left the floor all day.

I'd been thinking I might get through the day without crying, but an hour ago I came back from a bathroom break and Sofree said to the mediator, "While Pam was gone, the three of us were having a very amiable conversation, but now that she is back I am experiencing the field in here as very toxic," and I opened my mouth three times to defend myself, but all that finally came out was a series of hiccuppy sobs. I wanted to say, *I'm sorry,* or *It hurts,* or *I never got one chance to be the shiny thing with Rick, and you of all people ought to understand that.* What I did say was, "I'm just trying my best to be a decent stepparent," and Sofree made her hands into pep-rally fists, held them out in front of her, and said, "Thank you, Pam, thank you, Pam, thank you for that."

"Of course you would be her target," Cinder says on the phone when it's finally over and I'm alone in my car, driving up to Mount Princeton, where I have rented Rick and me a cabin for the weekend. "She had three whole years to make Rick feel worthless and she can heap rectitude onto Tom any night of the week." There's a special room in heaven, I think, for the girlfriend who always takes your side.

Just before the canyon swallows the cell reception, half a text comes in from Quinn: *What I keep saying to myself is, Quinn, what you know is that the world keeps opening up. You never know how or when it is going to happen but it always does. You . . .*

Once we are soaking in one of the creekside pools, Rick asks if I want to process what happened in mediation and I say, yes, I do, but I think it might be better to wait about a week.

It is an uncharacteristically prudent suggestion coming from me, but a good one because if anyone asked me right now what I would give up to never have to see/hear/think about Sofree again I would say, anything. *Anything.*

The next morning I tell Gyana that mediation was like a wreck where all the cars were totaled but everyone walked away. After he has worked on my pubic bone for twenty minutes and it's all I can do to keep from doing a backflip off the table, he says, in his thick Austrian accent, "Do you have a scar here?" Which I do, of course, because of all of the shenanigans my father got up to when I was a very small girl and the subsequent surgery I had at sixteen, performed (hush hush) by his urologist to remove some percentage of the damaged tissue that was so large it was creating infections down there and has caused—even since its removal—more than one gynecologist to blanch, and then want to *talk* about it; which I'm perfectly willing to and have done, at length, in therapy with Patrick and others (though, as Quinn says, *in this new millennium, who really wants to?*). But what I *think* Gyana has said is, "Do you have a car here?"

So I say, "Sure I do." And when he doesn't say anything I say, "Was I supposed to take some kind of a bus?"

"One day, Pammerz," Quinn is fond of saying, "you are going to stop being so sorry for everything." Down the hill and back in cell reception the second half of her text shows up: . . . *are so much more than a witness to anything. You are my friend, and I will be wherever you need me to be.*

106. Narbonne, France

The SNCF woman says, in French, that the train does not exist. Rick, who speaks Spanish and is generally shy around the French, says, in English, "I suppose you are going to tell me that the ticket I am holding in my hand for the train that does not exist, does not exist either."

The woman slams her office door on him, and we are pretty sure that is going to be the end of our lesson in postmodernism until ten minutes later when the biggest bus in the world appears at the curb in front of the station. There are four of us going to Barcelona. The bus holds roughly seventy-nine. The Catalan driver looks like he has been up for a week, between the unpronounceable volcano and the SNCF strike, and to keep himself awake he whistles Beethoven's Sixth, then "Bye Bye Blackbird," followed by the entire score of *Cats*.

At the Cave of Pech Merle, near Cahors, the twenty-six-thousand-year-old drawings of the spotted horse and the bear and especially the woolly mammoth on the wall looked like the work of a fine art grad student—a pretty good one at that. But it was the female handprints with little ochre spots around them that brought tears to my eyes.

Standing with Rick on the stone balcony of Château de la Treyne overlooking the Dordogne River, the air full of the smell of lilacs in bloom, I felt my life do cartwheels back on itself. It turns out people die one day and then they keep on dying, and Henry kept dying around every corner in the southwest of France. Every time I ordered a bottle of Badoit, every time I saw a sign that said *Centre Ville* (we used to shout it together in the rent-a-Citroën on our way into any town), every time I saw red poppies blooming in a spring-green field.

I said, "Why does anybody ever stay with anybody anyway?" and Rick laughed and put his arms around me, but in that moment I really wanted to know.

In Forest Grove, David St. John said time has only one message and it is that it continues and we do not and it is our job to learn how to trick it. The lastest addition to my suicide list is David Foster Wallace. Maybe faith is really more about surrender with a little self-directed mercy thrown in.

In 2001, after one of those glorious lazy Henry-inspired France extravaganzas, I had to fly home from Paris the day after the shoe bomber, twenty-four hours later on the very same flight. My favorite part about the shoe bomber story was the way they kept referring to the flight attendant who spotted him, who sicced those beefy businessmen on him, as *mature*.

107. Davis, California

After acupuncture, Janine says, "We've talked about the whole . . . what you really are thing, right?" But I'm not sure that we have.

"See, the problem is," she says, "I can't really get it for you, but I can tell you about my experience with it, okay?"

I nod and try to listen with my whole body.

"Well, the question I asked," she says, "was, *What do I see?* And I looked right out there in front of me and I saw a crystal obelisk—I think that is the word, just a big crystal obelisk—and they said, *That's you,* and I said, *Really? Me?* and that's how I knew what I was."

Last week in therapy, I told Patrick that in that awful mediation, it was actually Tom who repeatedly stood up for me, but that I wasn't mad at Rick about it, because if anybody ought to have been taking care of anybody that day, it ought to have been me—of him.

Patrick said, "Can we sub out the word *mad* here?"

I said "Sure, for what?"

He said, "*Abandoned, demoralized, crushed like a grape.*"

I meet Fenton the human in the city for dinner at Greens and we eat Padrón peppers with olive oil and salt just like the ones in Barcelona, and while we are waiting for the main course he asks me my philosophical stance on suicide, but it comes out more like a statement in one of those rolling-hills-of-Kentucky constructions of his: "I am interested in finding out your opinion on this matter though I would assume you feel as I do that suicide ought not to be thought of as a tragedy but rather as one of the few unalienable rights left to people in a time of vanishing liberties . . ."

I wait while he talks on, an *oh-no* trying to get purchase around the edges of my eyes, but the next day I get an email from him that says: *Not very good Buddhist that I am . . . I want to hold on for a moment to sitting with you discussing matters great and small at that lovely table with the seal lazing in the tide and the sun sinking beyond the Golden Gate. If I weren't so perennially pessimistic, I might believe I was leading the life that, forty years ago, I could only dimly imagine . . .*

One time, long ago, when I got stuck in Hamilton, Ontario, with a bunch of people who wanted me to feel inconsequential, Henry sent a limo to pick me up, all the way from Detroit.

108. San Francisco, California

Driving down the tight curves of Lombard Street, with Madison standing on the center console, head out the moon roof in the bright winter sun.

Rick says, "Outings like this are so much better now that I am a whole person again," and Madison says, "What do you mean?" and he says, "Oh back there a-ways in time I wasn't so happy," and Madison says, "I know that, but me and Pam-Pam got you going again."

She gives me my favorite Madison smile and I think, the only reason Rick and I made it through the first year is that I wouldn't have been able to handle losing both of them at once.

Icelandic artist Olafur Eliasson says space is process, and I think it's true. When Rick and I went to see Eliasson's 360° *Room for All Colours* at SF MOMA when he came to visit that first fall we were dating, it was the only thing we did that made him anywhere close to happy.

We stayed at the Hotel Rex, which is supposed to be literary in some way, and when we walked, holding hands, downhill to the Ferry Building and our dinner reservation at the Slanted Door, thirty high school girls stuffed into a cable car started chanting, "Kiss her!" "Kiss her!" "Kiss her!" and even though Rick couldn't understand what they were saying, I thought it was some kind of miracle sign.

I remember the English acrobats on Pier 39: the skinnier, less charismatic, possibly drug-addled brother, perpetually falling from the waist off his towering unicycle as if onto the crowd, the older brother's muscles, which did not go at all with his high-pitched and infectious giggles.

I remember the cats at the museum in Bend, the sleepy sleepy lynx with the white ring around his eye. And the poet in the wheelchair and the woman he called his *one true love* who picked him up and carried him everywhere.

I remember riding in the convertible with Willow, listening to the Jayhawks singing "All the Right Reasons," thinking: *Maybe, finally. Finally, maybe.*

After treatment, Janine said, "Just as I suspected, you have jumped a whole level of vibration, but you have left your body behind. No wonder your back hurts so much!"

It was Marianne Williamson who said, *Our deepest fear is not that we are inadequate. Our deepest fear is that we are powerful beyond all measure,* but it is often misattributed to Nelson Mandela.

Surely it counts for something that Rick and I worked really hard and then it got better. The last time I saw the rocket scientist, he told me that Mars is only twenty light-minutes away.

DL #55

THE PLANE IS GRADUALLY but perceptibly descending. It is barely light outside, and we aren't due at Orly until nearly noon. There is an odd ticking noise coming from the wing outside my window. I come fully awake and realize we are listing strenuously to the right.

I glance at my seatmate on the aisle. Her name is Rebecca. She is a twenty-six-year-old bank teller from Cincinnati who has never flown before, who has saved for five years to take her dream trip to Paris. I spent most of dinner telling her how much safer airplanes are than car travel, how the 777 has a minimum of three fail-safes on each of its major systems, how even if one of the engines fell clean off the fuselage it is designed to tumble backwards, up and over the wing, so it doesn't tear the wing from the plane. Now, in spite of all my reassurances, we seem to be heading shoulder-first into the North Atlantic.

"Ladies and Gentlemen," the pilot says, "as many of you are

probably aware, we are descending, preparing to make an unscheduled landing into Reykjavik, Iceland. Approximately thirty-five minutes ago, we experienced an explosion in our number two engine and that engine is now inoperable. The ticking sound you hear is the wind running through it, spinning the blades backwards much like a household fan. You can probably also tell that we are tacking toward Iceland—much as we would in a sailboat—as our current engine configuration will not give us full power in a straight line."

Now Rebecca is awake and looking at me wild-eyed. "The man likes a metaphor," I say, and offer a small smile.

The light out the window has strengthened and I can see white caps on an angry gray sea.

"I always kind of wanted to go to Iceland," I say, but by now Rebecca is no longer looking at me. She has her eyes closed tightly, has given herself, I imagine, to prayer.

"We will be landing in approximately fifteen minutes," the captain says. "Please give your undivided attention to the flight attendants as they instruct you in landing in the brace position."

I like that he did not say *crash*. I like that he is a language guy. The ocean is getting quite a bit closer, no sign of Iceland out my window, and I hope that Reykjavik Airport does not turn out to be a metaphor for *fucked*.

Just when it seems that our wheels have to be skimming the water, land and runway lights appear, and then more of them, so many lights it is hard to count them, a sea of spinning red and blue, every ambulance and fire truck in Iceland seems to have come out to greet us.

"Holy shit!" I say, just before the wheels hit the foam and the foam splashes up and covers all the windows, throwing the cabin in a half-light exactly like waking up in a tent after a snowstorm, and then everyone is cheering, as the plane glides to a jerky, sticky stop.

Much later, in an upstairs blank space of terminal, as we are being fed rice with some kind of yellow chickeny goo all over it by something resembling the Icelandic Red Cross, the crew tells us the reason for the emergency equipment. When the number two engine exploded, it spit jet fuel all over the fuselage. We were a Molotov cocktail hurtling through space, is the way the literary copilot puts it, there was no way to be certain that the friction of the tires on the runway wouldn't make a spark and ignite us, turn us into a 90-mile-per-hour ball of flame.

109. Knoydart Peninsula, Scotland

From Euston Station, you take the Caledonian Sleeper to Glasgow, and then the local all the way to Mallaig. If you are lucky you talk a boatman into taking you from Mallaig across to Inverie, and today we are lucky, sharing the boat's tiny wheelhouse with a Catholic family, three beautiful and frivolous teenage girls, and a Stephen Dedalus of an older brother who hates them all so entirely we can taste the venom dripping out of his ears.

Our first sight of Inverie is the tiny line of whitewashed buildings strung out along the shore of the bay; almost insignificant under the towering bulk of Sgurr Coire Choinnichean. Claire and Emma are waiting for us on the dock, two heads of brilliant red blowing in the substantial wind. It is six miles from Inverie to Airor, over the hills that are so green you think they have got to be kidding, on a tiny farm lane barely wide enough for the tires of the jeep that came with the vacation home, around the west end of the peninsula and past the Plastic Mary.

There is only one bar on the peninsula, the Old Forge, rec-
ognized by the Guinness Book as the remotest pub in Britain.
There are guitars and banjos on the wall and Arran Sunset and
Red Squirrel on tap, Talisker behind the bar, haggis, tatties, and
neeps on the menu.

Jonathan, the caretaker of the Airor house got kicked out of the
bar five years ago for starting a fight—"out in the lane," he is quick
to emphasize, "not even inside the bloody bar." The owner told
Jonathan he had to stay away for five years, and only a month ago the
five years was up so he went back in and the owner said he'd changed
his mind, that Jonathan couldn't come back in the bar forever. "So
as I've got nothing to wait for, I guess I'll be going back Glasgow
way," he says. "Now my father's dead I have naught to be afraid of."

It rains most of most days here, great clouds rolling in over the
Isle of Skye, but then the sun comes out and it is granite and green
jewels everywhere. If I sit in the big chair by the window for even
a minute, I can see sea lions, dolphins—once even a whale—pop
its head above the surface of the silvery bay.

Everything was quiet around here the first few days until Claire's
boyfriend Kent showed up, trying so hard to prove himself it hurts.
Charging up and back and around us like a border collie when we
climbed Roinna Bheinn, nearly drowning himself trying to swim
to a tidal island, taking so long for his turn at Scrabble the games
don't end till 2 a.m.

Claire believes in using something called *sow pods*, two-letter
words like *ee* that nobody has ever heard of, and they change the
game entirely. "That's fine," Rick says, meaning it isn't, "but if we
are going all professional-grade, shouldn't we at least use an egg
timer?" Rick is ultra competitive at board games, so much so I

have learned that when I win I lose and when I lose I lose; the best case being to call the game somewhere in the middle.

Each morning, with a good strong cup of Monmouth Street coffee, I read to Rick and Emma from a book of old Scottish tales which were told way back when to actual people on this very peninsula. They are full of blood and mayhem, and someone usually gets tricked into killing their mother for a gag, and selling sexual favors with her dead body for a hell of a profit, and it is always the trickiest and the meanest people who get all the money and cows in the end.

Rick gets melancholy about the ways Americans are disconnected from their heritage and keeps insisting to Claire that hers surrounds her. "Look around! Look around!" he says, so we do, but all there is to see are the green green hills, and occasionally a lazy sea otter, and way down the beach the flash of the lighthouse that marks the place where *Ring of Bright Water* was written, and a group of what Claire calls *wild campers* across the channel on Skye.

What she means by *wild* is *in a tent,* just like when she says *Red Indian* she means Sioux, or Navajo or Hopi or Ute. What she means when she says *Darling!* to Kent is *Disappointment!* and everything she says to Emma means, *If I were ever not your mother, I would surely die.*

110. Seaside, Oregon

When the wind blows through the aging Best Western in the middle of the night it sounds exactly like a crying baby. It is unaccountable, how much rain the sky above the Oregon coast can hold. In ten days here, we have seen the sun for exactly seventeen minutes one late afternoon, just before it set, when it turned the gray beach golden, and made the hundred plovers that stood together, braced against the shoreline, illuminate magically, like a string of bird shaped Christmas lights, advancing, and receding with the waves.

At the Crab Shack the owner called both Tayari and me *sis*, repeatedly, as in, "How's that chowder working for you, sis?" or, "Need a hand, sis, cracking those claws?" He wanted Tayari to know that he was glad she'd come in, that he had no problem with a black president, that he'd lived some places in his life and knew a few things about the destructive power of hate.

In the stranger-than-truth department, one of the 150 students at this residency is a guy named Steve who I lived on a commune with back in Fraser, Colorado, when we were barely out of college. In the bar tonight, we get to talking, and I remember that not long after I left the commune I was living in Utah, and Steve, who had, in the interim, fallen from a helicopter while doing Search and Rescue work and broken so many bones they would still be finding fractures years later, the same Steve who would soon become addicted and then unaddicted to Advil, who would eventually move to Houston and come out of the closet and entirely remake his life . . . Anyway, after the helicopter, but before the Advil and Houston, Steve came to visit me in Park City.

It was early fall, and we climbed to the top of a hill and ate mushrooms which made the late summer grasses beautiful beyond measure, and then we came back down to the tilted little Victorian I lived in and got the munchies, and all I had in the fridge were green and red bell peppers, and we ate them raw, like apples. Steve said, "Whenever I'm tripping, fruits and vegetables really come alive for me," and I said, "That must be really scary," and then we realized what we thought the other meant—you know, like Mr.

Potato Head?— and we laughed till we peed. Remembering it all, of course, I had to tell it, so now everybody around here is calling him Mushroom Steve.

When another student named Jenny, one of the best writers in the bunch, hopped onstage mid-poem during Pete's banquet reading because she was moved to convey her gratitude to each of us, students and faculty alike, I heard the phrase *manic episode* fly around the room, but after it was over I noticed everybody wanted a chance to talk to her; touched in that moment, however she was, by whatever hand it might have been, as if she were the crack in the universe we'd been hell-bent these ten days to step through.

Jenny's eyes were so bright that day. She had come to my room before the banquet and asked me two questions . . . "How do you slow down?" and "What about gratitude?" which seemed like excellent questions for any aspiring writer to ask. I said I thought that when art took trauma and turned it into form, maybe it was the marriage of innocence to intention that mitigated our terror, that helped us love the world when the world was least lovable. And maybe what she did at the banquet wasn't crazy at all, but simply a way to answer back to the answer I had given her.

In Tomales, Dorothy said, "We want the sex, the sexy, the catastrophic." It is times like these when I understand precisely why the Acoma built those ladders to tear holes in the sky.

111. Trenton, New Jersey

Let's say, for the sake of argument, that my back hurts so much because when I was four and in my three-quarter body cast, my mother found it easiest to carry me around upside down like a monkey, using the plaster bar the doctors had fashioned between my knees to keep them, for three and a half months, the correct distance apart. And let's say she did just that, until my second to last appointment when the orthopedic surgeon said, "You haven't been carrying her around by this bar have you?" and my mother shot one quick glance at my father and said, "Of course not, no," and it became a funny story the two of them liked to tell together to friends over a couple of drinks. And let's say that when their friends asked, as of course they would, how in the name of heaven a four-year-old breaks her femur, they said that I had somehow managed to pull the giant wardrobe over onto myself, except instead of *wardrobe* they would have said *credenza*, because it would have made us sound richer than we were.

I *still* don't see how it would make me feel any better to think of the pain in my hip and spine as anything *other* than my most loyal and valuable companion, the continuous nonvoice in my ear that says, *You got out alive and you still get to go.*

No two people who have ever lived, loved to travel more than my mother and father. They gave that love, in their fashion, to me.

112. Taylor Fork, Colorado

Becky's old lead dog died this morning. Becky knew it was coming; the dog stopped eating a week ago. "I was all prepared and everything," she says, "but still."

We are in the sleds on our way to Crystal Lake, and even though it's Matt's birthday he is letting me drive. If I soften my eyes I can see all forty paws at once rising and falling in front of me, like the world's happiest meditation.

A long slow climb from Tin Cup, lots of running behind the sled, over a fin and then two hundred yards down, fast and furious to the surface of the lake where we do doughnuts and let the dogs eat snow and try to get Roja to eat some turkey.

Roja is one of the smaller dogs, and hypoglycemic, but nobody pulls harder. She is the only dog who will not stop to rest with the others, who will not even grab a mouthful of snow on the run. When we are stopped, standing full on the brake, anchor set, the dogs cooling their bellies or rolling on their backs, Roja will tug, and tug, as if it is the only thing in the world she knows how to do, as if it is the only thing she will ever do again, as if she can move the weight of the anchored sled, two humans, and all nine of her teammates single-handedly.

Roja has died in the traces twice, Matt tells me. Becky had to bring her back with mouth-to-mouth. Now, on the flat surface of Crystal Lake, Matt offers her ham and chicken, morsels the other dogs would take his arm off at the elbow for, and she looks up at him like he is crazy, gives another smart tug on the rig.

Matt tells me about the last dog death in his family, a dog who truly belonged to his wife, a dog he would have said he didn't like that much, because he was headstrong and misbehaved.

"One day Max came walking into the living room and just looked at us," Matt said, "and we knew what he was saying, so we loaded him up and took him to the vet, and I thought, *No big deal, no big deal,* but when it was all over I started crying and couldn't stop and it got so bad I started hemorrhaging from my nose, and finally the vet told my wife to take me to the hospital."

For many years Matt ran a successful construction company in Aspen, building homes for the rich and famous, negotiating what he calls *the antics of excess* with architects and interior designers and some new thing called a *space expert*, until he decided to quit and move to Vulcan and work as Becky Barkman's hired man.

We are on our way down from Crystal Lake in four inches of new snow, a gentle descent that lasts forever, and I only have to touch the brake now and then to keep the sled off the wheel dogs—mostly it is perfect velocity on the brink of out-of-control—even Roja is smiling, and I say, "Counting a prizewinning thoroughbred, counting Back Bowls at Vail in eight inches of powder, counting coming home across the Gulf Stream in front of a following sea in a 57-foot catamaran, surfing down the rollers, this is the very best way to move through space on the planet."

"Correct!" Matt says, and spreads his arms out of the sled bag and up to the sky.

113. Sacramento, California

Rick comes to California for a whole month and I take him to dinner at the Waterboy, my favorite California restaurant east of the Carquinez Bridge, where you can get white anchovies as a little pre-appetizer appetizer, and the bottled water they serve is Badoit.

We don't have a reservation, so we have to wait on the patio for a table, and because putting actual miles between ourselves and Sofree has started to make us feel all in love and grand about ourselves, Rick tells the waiter to ask the bartender to make us something interesting, one with rum and one with tequila, and he comes back with elderflower this and Vat #54 that and even though we know they are going to cost twenty dollars apiece it is nice to see Rick be spontaneous.

Before we have time to finish our drinks we are tucked into a corner, and at the four-top next to us there are two couples who seem to have made their money in something like Ski-Doos. They spend a good fifteen minutes reading the wine list out loud, saying *succulent, ripe,* and *juicy.* There are jokes on the subject of boob jobs, hand jobs, hose jobs, and blow jobs.

When they look guiltily over at us we smile, magnanimous in love.

When Rick orders the sweetbreads I am pretty sure he is thinking, like, *accompanied by some kind of danish,* but I don't say anything, because, let's face it, I can be a know-it-all bitch. He is a good sport when they come, not afraid to ask the waiter what he is about to put into his mouth, and the waiter is pleased to tell him. By the time the waiter comes back to ask about dessert we are stuffed, and the foursome next door has jollied their way out of the restaurant.

We agree to look at the menu, perhaps split one dessert just to prolong the evening, when the waiter says, "Just so you know, the gentleman at the table next to you has picked up your entire dinner. He felt that you were trying to have a romantic evening and that it might have been compromised in some way by their rowdiness."

"In fact, it wasn't," I say, and then I say, "That's unbelievable."

"They've left more than enough for dessert and gratuity," he says, grinning. "How wonderful," he says, "that there are a few people who remain conscious in the world."

114. Ashland, Oregon

In the soup and sandwich shop called Pangaea, over a bowl of smoking curried yam soup, I point out to Quinn a painting called *Undaunted, They Face the Future Together.*

We've been singing along to Jim Croce all morning in the Prius, eating red licorice Scotties and drinking IBC root beer. Another thing Quinn and I have in common is that we've always liked the dude-ish songs better: "Don't Fall Apart on Me Tonight" and "The Long Way Home" and even "No Regrets, Coyote." Quinn always calls friendship *the better kind of romance.*

I tell Quinn that Rick says his biggest problem with our relationship these days is that I have taken away the cone of tenderness in which I used to envelop him, so we are brainstorming about ways I might find to redeploy it.

Last night we stayed in Quinn's little sister's apartment which could have been my apartment, if I had ever had an apartment, when I was her age, which is twenty-eight. There were giant eucalyptus leaves hanging all over the bathroom, a bottle of Dr. Bronner's soap the size of a car, lots of pictures tacked to the walls of outdoorsy girls kissing their dogs, a painting that incorporated the words of Khalil Gibran, a lithograph of three monks looking over their shoulders and several B. Andreas posters—those little colorful stick figures who sit on bridges and the man-stick waits for the woman-stick to say something magical and then she does—every item in the apartment chosen and carefully arranged to say one thing: *You're okay . . .* really.

Two nights ago on the phone, Trish said she had used up all her frozen fertilized eggs: four attempts, none of them viable. So even though she is broke from the implantations, even though she doesn't have one spot on her body that is not black and blue from shooting herself up with hormones that made her suicidal, she wrote to a lesbian couple who used the same sperm donor she used the last time, and is negotiating the purchase of one of their fertilized eggs.

Way back when I lived in the commune, in the sheepherder's trailer called the African Queen, we sat around the campfire every night and sang "Will the Circle Be Unbroken," and "Fido Is a Hot Dog Now," and one night we called Dr. Bronner because after all the number was right there on the bottle and why not? And he answered, as the bottle promised he would, and talked to us for a little while about God.

In those days my mother would send me letters that I remember mostly for her odd habit of putting a few words per sentence into quotation marks. Sometimes it seemed like there was a secrect code I was supposed to break, as in: Your *"father"* has gone to play *"tennis."* More often I couldn't make sense of her choices, as in: *This "morning" I cooked an "egg" for the "cat."*

The first title for this book was *Suicide Note, or 144 Good Reasons Not to Kill Yourself,* but I changed it, because the contradiction felt dishonest, and also because I realized if I ever did kill myself it would simply be a preemptive strike to keep my father from getting to do it first, which, turns out, is something I've been worrying about forever, or at least since I was four.

Patrick told me it would only get worse after my father died, and boy, he wasn't kidding. Dead, my father can live in the airplane engine, in the black ice on the highway, in the water bottle that is not BPA-free. If you are wondering why 144 reasons, and not 100 or 150, I can only tell you that I have always thought in 12's, which I hope has something to do with moons or months, and nothing to do with the apostles.

Last time I went to Santa Rita Springs to see Amanda for Watsu she said, "I don't think it is so much about the story anymore. I think it's about what kinds of possibilities are out there when you can finally stop telling the story."

The single most incontrovertible fact revealed in that terrible day of mediation is that Tom truly loves Sofree. He wants her to let him help her be better than she is.

Back in Pangaea, a real couple sits beneath the couple in the painting. They are fiftyish, in brand-new love. The man says to the woman: "I already miss the dogs we haven't gotten yet."

115. Tucson, Arizona

At the Rockies–Angels spring training game, war planes of every vintage do loop-de-loops in the sky and in the end the scoreboard, which must be the last one in America that only shows balls, strikes, hits, runs, and errors, reads *Rockies 11, Angels 10.* When I ask Clint Barmes for his autograph, he looks at my hat, the one I've brought to every spring training, and just like the boy he seems on TV, says, "Man, you got Matt Holliday! That's a really cool one to have."

The King of Hearts is playing for free at the Loft Cinema, and I tell Rick it is terrific and then get consumed with worry that it might seem sillier now than it did in 1979, but by halfway through I can't stop smiling, and every time Poppy says *Coquelicot,* I feel it down in my bones.

The next day Rick and I plan to hike up Ventana Canyon four miles to the Maiden Pools, but we can't agree about lunch. He wants to buy some sandwiches and bananas to eat at the pools, I want to hike hard up and back for four hours and then go to the In-N-Out Burger. There are points to be made on both sides, beyond the customary: his plan is more sensible, mine is more fun, but then he says, "Can't you see that this is an example of how you need to control everything?" So I swerve into the Safeway parking lot and pull up to the door without speaking.

We manage not to speak on the rest of the drive and a quarter mile up the trail and he finally says, "We ought not to spend the entire hike at this absurd emotional distance."

I say, "My feelings are hurt."

He says, "I have some hurt feelings of my own."

I roll my eyes, say, "You go first."

He says, "I don't have to go first, but we have to start somewhere."

"Do we, really?" I say, watching a water skimmer on the surface of a slickrock pool, "Because I was just thinking, I might be able to suck up all of my hurt feelings, if it meant I didn't have to listen to yours."

116. Corrales, New Mexico

Walking in the Bosque with Hailey and Ripley, sandhill cranes in every farmer's field. Last night we took the train with the roadrunner on its nose up to Ristra, and had one of those dinners where it all was so good and kept getting better—tuna tartar and butternut squash soup—and we talked and laughed like people on the Löwenbräu commercials I used to see when I was a kid in my angry little family and wonder *who were these people who got to have a life like that?*

Hailey left her scarf, which has major sentimental value, at the restaurant, so she made a run for it, only nine minutes before the last train. When Practical Karen told the conductor Hailey would be back in a flash, he said, "I sure don't like to be late," but then a transvestite who was just getting off work at World Imports picked Hailey up at the far end of the parking lot and drove her back to the train platform with two minutes to spare. Which is just one of many reasons it comes as a shock to us this morning when Hailey tells us she voted for John McCain.

"Sarah Palin?" Rick says, caught, as he often is, between the urge toward politeness and disbelief.

"Does she hate transvestites," Hailey says, "I mean, specifically?"

When the girls all came to the ranch last summer, Mackenzie and Cinder both wore tight black turtlenecks and tight single ponytails and big gold hoop earrings. Mackenzie wore her mini-skirt and cowboy boots even though there were no boys there to see her, and she always sat on the piano bench butt to butt with Cinder, and finally Willow took me aside and said, "Are those two sleeping together or what?"

Rick says now that I finally really have him I don't so much really want him, and if that is true I am the simplest kind of person on earth and the worst. In my twenties I pretended I wanted a long-term relationship but just kept picking wolfmen by mistake. In my thirties I thought my marriage phobia was something chronic I needed to get cured of, like back pain or herpes, but now that I'm almost fifty I suspect freedom is the secret pleasure girls born in the sixties won't fess up to. What if Janis was wrong, and it's actually a whole lot better to be free?

Driving over Slumgullion pass at dawn, listening to *Ashes of American Flags* at volume 50, watching two hundred elk gallop chest deep through the new snow. *All my lies are only wishes.*

When Madison shouts *Pam-Pam!* and leaps off the stage into my arms in her lion cub costume, her face all painted with a button nose and whiskers, I think, *I cannot save her from her suffering.* Nor is it true that nothing I do will make any difference in the end.

117. Barcelona, Spain

Here is the city and across the street here is the beach full of sand sculpture. Giant sand dogs and giant sand cats, peace signs, entire adobe villages with water fountains and tiny fires inside of hogans, even a to-scale Sagrada Familia.

Only the men here seem to want to be naked, strutting back and forth on the sand, dangling, and stretched out on their backs spread-eagle.

"Whoops!" Rick says, because a guy is getting a hand job from his girlfriend out here among the masses, her hand so white it's almost ghostly against his radically more colorful cock.

Seeing the real Sagrada Familia for the first time, from the Olympic port, backlit and through several windless days worth of carbon monoxide, makes it waver like some holy mirage. When we get up close we see that all of the stone is carved to look like living things: sheaves of wheat, bowls of grapes, and a giant canopy of trees to lie beneath when you talk to God.

Before Sagrada Familia, Gaudí built a house called *Casa Batlló* that can breathe and cool off and shed water all on its own like an animal. We say *gaudy*, but we might also say *functional*, we might say *constructed in serious conversation with the world*.

Across town, at the Barcelona Cathedral, there is a big hole, with stone steps that descend to the crypt, which contains the alabaster sarcophagus of Saint Eulalia, who was martyred for her beliefs by the Romans. The cathedral is dark, the steps down to the crypt even darker, the sarcophagus illuminated by a creepy red light.

We are standing at the bottom of the steps with a handful of others, looking through ancient iron bars, when a woman starts descending, much too quickly, toward us. She tries to catch herself, but her weight is already too far forward. First it looks like she is falling and then it looks like she is tap-dancing, and then it looks like she is trying to fly, and she does fly, for a moment, with only eight or ten steps still to go. But gravity prevails, and she bounces, headfirst, and then skids to a stop against the gate, her arms twisted awkwardly around her. After a terrible moment where it seems we might all be paralyzed, she gathers her limbs and rolls up to a sitting position, and several of us help her back up the stairs and out of the church.

It's easy to see what Miró loved: women, birds, stars, and almost anything strongly backlit. At his *Fundación* on the flank of Montjuïc, it is hard not to fall in love with the names of the paintings even more than the paintings themselves. *Women Encircled by the Flight of a Bird in the Night. The Half-Open Sky Gives Us Hope. The Smile of a Tear. The Gold of the Azure. The Lark's Wing, Encircled with Golden Blue, Rejoins the Heart of the Poppy Sleeping on a Diamond-Studded Meadow.*

Out of crushed Venetian glass on the roof of the apartment building he named *La Pedrera* (the quarry) because of its cave-like walls, its curves and concavities, Gaudí has formed fragments of the angel Gabriel's greeting to Mary.

If Karl Rove's book can be called *Courage and Consequence*, what on earth does it matter what my book is called.

118. Jackson Hole, Wyoming

Snake River at sunset, gray glacier water, shiny steel. A pair of trumpeter swans flying north. It is reaching 50 degrees in the heat of the day and the snow beneath our skis keeps getting soupier. Hailey says she doesn't mind bringing up the rear, but I keep thinking if I were a grizzly bear, I might be about to wake up hungry.

If Rick were here he'd say, "Do you think we are going to get a peek at Mr. Nipper?"

Willow and Practical Karen are waving their poles at Hailey, Nora, and me, and we can't figure out what they mean until we are right on top of the she-moose, three of them, agitated and not ten feet off the trail, but we just ski on by like idiot tourists while the locals hide in the trees gripping the collars of their dogs.

On Saturday morning, the whole of eastern Wyoming was closed, so Nora and I drove up the Poudre and stopped for lunch in Saratoga Springs at a place that opened exclusively on the first Saturday of every month. It was only chicken salad but we felt pretty special anyway.

Nora had never been to Wyoming so I insisted we go the Moran Junction way, where you come over the pass and get the first view of the Tetons, side-on, and I don't know who you would have to be not to gasp. The sun was setting in an orange smudge behind them, making them all backlit with Cecil B. DeMille rays and Nora said, "I knew they were big but I didn't think they would be like this."

The marble sinks in my room are decidedly seventies and look like something right out of *Willy Wonka and the Chocolate Factory.* Hailey bakes bread and I make beef bourguignon and while it cooks we all get in the hot tub together. Nora and Willow are discussing whether *helicopter parenting* is a neutral or a derogatory term and Practical Karen says, "What I want to know is whatever happened to benign neglect?"

At dinner everyone is talking about Santiago, and Haiti before that, and Willow says that thing you always hear: *If Yellowstone goes, it will take the whole U.S. with it,* and Hailey says, "Do you think we should worry about being this close?" and Nora says, "I think if Yellowstone goes, close will turn out to be the good news."

I get an email from Quinn that says: *If freedom is a quantity, or is exchangeable like money, then what if love is, too, such that the love you feel for Rick is measured by the freedom you give him* not *to get over Sofree and the freedom he gives you to live your come one, come all frequent-flyer life. This might be one way of keeping track of what's "real," what's exchangeable and what's unspendable, where it turns out that the real reason you won't spend your father's money is that you don't want it to be true that he'll never give you anything again."*

Nora hasn't seen *Shut Up and Sing,* and even if it means driving all the way to Idaho Falls we are determined to rent it. My favorite part is where Natalie says, "Well, now that we have completely fucked ourselves, I feel like we have a responsibility to continue to fuck ourselves." There, as Quinn would say, is a woman after my own heart.

119. Goosenecks of the San Juan, Utah

Dawn breaks over camp, rose-colored and cool on the San Juan River in southeastern Utah, twenty miles downstream from the town of Mexican Hat. Yesterday Rick and I parked my boat outside the San Juan Friendship Inn and went inside for Navajo tacos and vanilla milkshakes, bought another bag of ice for the cooler, reclaimed our raft and headed down into the deepest, most labyrinthine part of the canyon. We camped below the notch of the Mendenhall Loop, an oxbow in the making where the river turns so hard back on itself that I let Rick off to hike up and over the crumbling canyon wall and he got to the other side faster than my boat could float around the five-mile bend.

Today we'll load up the raft and glide through the Goosenecks, traveling five river miles for every air mile we accomplish, passing through the Tabernacle and the Second Narrows, the river 3,000 feet below the Grand Gulch Plateau. We'll have plenty of time to stop and hike the trail built for Henry Honaker's horse, who fell from it to his death in 1892, and if we are really lucky, somewhere between mile thirty-six and John's Canyon, the river will give us some sand waves.

The result of a perfect combination of streambed gradient (steep), suspended silt load (heavy), and water velocity (fast), sand waves develop along stretches of the San Juan where the gradient flattens somewhat, allowing the coarser particles to settle out of suspension. The sand grains accumulate and build ripples on the streambed which migrate upstream, and as those dunes build, waves form on the surface of the water that can grow to ten feet before they wash themselves out, the entire cycle taking less than ten minutes.

Now it's midmorning, and the canyon air is heating up in earnest, the water as flat as a short-order grill as far as the eye can see. It's a good day for dozing on the raft's big rubber tubes, limbs dangling in the water, and Rick has fallen asleep with an unfinished sandwich clutched in his hand.

All of a sudden they rise around us, like something out of the Twilight Zone and in about ten seconds the perfectly flat river on all sides of us has grown seven-foot waves. I point the nose of my boat straight into them, and gear is flying everywhere, some onto the floor of the boat, some along with Rick, into the river with a splash.

I want to tell Rick to tighten his life jacket, to point his feet downstream, to pull himself back into the boat with the lifeline, but I can't because I'm laughing so hard; the canyon so deep and grand, the sand waves so decidedly silly. They make me want to do cartwheels, to give indiscriminate kisses, to hit somebody in the face with a pie. The waves are so big now I can't see beyond them until the nose of my boat rolls over each crest. The motion is blissful, like skiing bottomless powder, like sailing over a woodpile on the back of a horse you trust.

But the look on Rick's face is the opposite of blissful and my brain registers alarm. "There's nothing in these waves that can hurt you," I shout between giggles, and there isn't, no rocks, no stumps, no sharp-edged falls. Just perfectly round, perfectly symmetrical, ridiculously large, entirely temporary waves. "Sit back and enjoy," I choke out, "it will be over in a minute."

The words are scarcely out of my mouth when, just as miraculously as they appeared, the sand waves shrink and fade, and there we are again, in the Goosenecks, the river as flat as Grampa's new haircut, and I throw the lifeline to Rick, stow my oars, and haul him in.

120. Point Reyes, California

Redwing blackbird sitting on a wire. White horse, green field, gray barn after a wet winter in California. No place on earth more beautiful.

At Ad Hoc you always have what they are serving: English pea salad, lamb sirloin with sunchokes, peanut butter ice cream over banana bread. Cinder rents the Jasmine Cottage for the weekend and brings some seeds to put in our yogurt that were the miracle food of the Aztecs. On the Internet she shows me a company called Eternal Earth-Bound Pets who will ensure that when the rapture comes, your left-behind animal companions will have good homes with caring atheists: $110 for a ten-year contract, $15 for each additional pet.

When I invite Janine, for the third time, to go to Moloka'i she says, "You don't know . . ." and pauses, and says, "I'm not really . . ." and pauses, and then points at the room where she does acupuncture and says, "I am my best self in there."

I say, "I know who you are," and am pretty sure I mean it.

She says, "I'm just trying to figure out how to be here."

"Davis?" I say, and she says, "Davis . . . California . . . the world . . . this vibration."

It hardly needs saying, but if I didn't have any back pain, I never would have met Janine.

The last time I visited the commune where we sang "Will the Circle Be Unbroken," Gloria, fifty-one, was pouring hot home-made soap into egg cartons and Bella, fifty-two, said, "Come here, Pam, I want to show you something," and she took me over to her nightstand and put a medium Pace picante jar into my hand with something that was not Pace picante inside it.

"What is it?" I asked her, and she said, "My uterus. When I had my hysterectomy, I said to the doctor, *You can't have that, it's mine.*"

On the way to the airport, Rick says, "Little yoder running down the road. He'd put a nippins on you, but it wouldn't hurt that much." This kind of talk, I know, means Rick is happy.

Sign on the back of a park bench in Tucson: *A career with a future! Are you being called to be a Catholic priest?*

Being born in New Jersey probably rules out Buddhism, and anyhow, for me, this life, it is something.

When I told Ruby what Sofree said about climbing out of Rick's hole she said, "Oh, Pam, Sofree lives in a hole. You . . . me . . . everybody lives in a hole. But what's great is if you go over and tap on the wall of your hole, you find out we're all connected."

"We can only do what we can do," Rick says, about Madison, and I expect he's right about it.

When I tell Quinn he calls Amarillo *the Riller Diller,* it makes her like him even more.

UA #368

AFTER FOUR DAYS AT the Four Seasons Sydney, the
Novotel where United puts us up feels not so great. Still
we are all in it together, all four hundred and eleven of us, and
the pilots and the copilots; a little cheer goes up every time they
walk through the lobby.

The next day, Terminal A is back to business as usual and we
reassemble at Gate 44. I have bought my greyhoundesque flight
attendant friend candy and flowers. Looking at the faces around
me, I'd say more than one of us was freaked out enough to have
considered an alternative means of transportation back to San
Francisco. Looking into steamships on the Novotel Internet was
the first time I truly understood exactly how far from home I am.

They board the premiers and premier executives first. Sister's
Wedding Guy and I settle in for another conversation. There are
about a hundred of us on the plane scattered through first class
and business class and economy plus. Then there is a lull and

after a while it starts to seem odd that no one else is getting on the plane.

My friendly flight attendant crooks his finger at me and I meet him behind the partition in the galley. "You're not going to believe this," he says, "but a Qantas luggage handler just backed a cart into our number two engine. Nobody's gonna take this baby out of here today."

It is only a few minutes later when the announcement comes over the loudspeaker. "One of our colleagues at Qantas . . ." is how they began. By the time we have all shuffled back out to the gate there is another announcement. Since our group has been inconvenienced already, United is going to give us SFO passengers the plane bound for LAX, and make the LAX people stay overnight tonight while the engine on the SFO jet is repaired.

Most people are glad to be rid of the jinxed plane, and I can see that logic, but any bookie would tell you our odds have to be worse on the heretofore-untroubled Los Angeles plane.

An hour and a half out of Sydney, the pilot's voice comes over the loudspeaker just as we start to feel the first bumps. "Ladies and Gentlemen," he says, "I know I am the last person you want to hear from right now, but we are getting reports of extremely severe turbulence over the equator. Planes a few hours ahead of us are reporting turbulence so severe that two flight attendants have been injured. One plane is making an emergency landing in Guam. I am going to have to ask the flight attendants to take their seats for the next several hours, in-flight service stops now, and will resume only when conditions allow. In five minutes I will turn the seat belt sign back on, and from that point forward you are on the honor system to remain seated, with your seat belt securely fastened. Your safety and the safety of those around you depend on it."

There is the predictable rush to the bathrooms. "Honor system," Sister's Wedding Guy mumbles, closing his eyes, and letting his head fall to the window.

It gets turbulent. I would even say it gets very turbulent. A few overhead bins rattle open, a couple of teenage girls find it difficult to hold back a scream. But after sixty full minutes of hurtling through the air in double time, contemplating the phrase *fuel system failure*, a little equatorial roller coaster doesn't seem like that big a deal.

When the meal finally comes it has the consistency of rubber, so I go for the salad, take a bite, look down, and see half a fat earthworm wriggling between the cucumber slice and the carrot.

"Look at that," I say, to Sister's Wedding Guy. "That worm had to have been cut in half in some airport kitchen like ten hours ago, and it is still wriggling."

Sister's Wedding Guy looks at me with pity in his eyes.

"Unless . . ." I say, but it is too late. I have already swallowed.

When Mr. Greyhound comes back I say, "I know this would make me queen in some countries . . ." and show him the half earthworm, and that is enough to get us free drinks for the rest of the flight.

When we land at SFO, only twenty-four plus four hours late, the purser has something resembling joy in her voice when she welcomes us to San Francisco. "I probably don't need to tell you all to open those overhead bins with caution," she says. "If your contents haven't shifted, you must be carrying lead weights."

Our crew of tall, blond, and blue-eyed pilots strides past us in customs, the sixty-something captain, the fortyish copilot, the thirty-something third officer, and this time the ovation is unanimous and loud.

"Nice work," I say, to the aging captain when we wind up in line side by side.

"Oh," he says, "I didn't do anything except turn a plane around."

"I think," I say, "you did a bit more than that."

"That is one hell of a smart airplane," he says, and I hear his voice catch. "It's going to be a sad day for everybody when they take those big birds out of the sky."

121. Quirpon Island, Newfoundland

In the eighteenth century, it was the last safe harbor for leaky, overweighted schooners to snug into, if the Labrador Straits were choked with ice. You could try for Little Quirpon Harbour at the southern end of the island, and if you missed it (most of the fishing boats even into the twentieth century were powered by sail alone) you could try for Ron Galet's Bay. Your last chance was the tickle at Colombier Cove. After that you were on your way to Labrador.

We've been told in an email to meet the ferry in the minuscule mainland town of Quirpon, and when we get there it is 35 degrees with 50-mile-per-hour winds from the east and the rain is coming in sheets, sideways. A rugged little man in wool pants and a green slicker comes to our car window and speaks in the heaviest Newfoundlandese so far, a beautiful song-of-a-paragraph that sounds less like words and more like a turkey gobbling. When he repeats himself the third time we get the gist of it. The open sea is too rough for the ferry to take us to the lighthouse side of the island. The skipper will drop us off in Cod Cove, a forty-minute walk along a cliffside to the inn, if he can make the landing. Our luggage will go to some other, more distant landing, where this man has parked a quad. Dress warm, pack light, be ready to go in five minutes.

We have driven a day and a half through this storm past out-ports with names like St. Jones Within and Come By Chance, speculating about the size of the ferry. The marquee at the Miracle Temple in Gambo said simply, *Why Burn?* But the rain came down so hard all day burning seemed impossible. Near the Happy Gang 50+ Club, a dozen lobstermen were checking their traps in boats that looked so tiny against the giant waves it seemed like lunacy. "Little boat," I said, "Great Big Sea," because of course we'd been listening to them on the car stereo, mermaid's tails and whale bones and fifteen children to every house, drinking screech and dinking Molly two times daily.

We repack and layer and when the ferry pulls up it is half the size of the lobster boats, fifteen feet of shiny aluminum, already loaded and listing with groceries. Then we are over the edge of the dock and bouncing the bottom hard and fast off the glassy rollers and the wind is in my face and I finally feel like I am somewhere. The fog is so thick we can't see five feet off the bow, but the skipper points out the islands as if we can: Salt, Nobles, and Grandmother.

"There's icebergs all around ya's, right?" he says, slowing his elocution markedly. "Shame you can't sees 'em."

Quirpon is officially in Iceberg Alley. After a berg breaks off the Greenland Ice Shield it takes two years for it to get this far. Bergs are classified as large, medium, and small, bergy bits and growlers. The largest berg ever recorded off this coast was 208 miles long and 61 miles wide, making it slightly bigger than Belgium. The farthest south one ever got before melting was Bermuda, meaning it traveled a distance of 2,500 miles.

When we get to Cod Cove, the urgent talk between the Skipper and Mr. Green Slicker about which boulders to nose the boat against has the quality of an African language, clicks included, and we understand not one word. The sea heaves the little boat and at the skipper's signal we scramble onto the wet rocks and he says, "Mind your fingers or you'll lose 'em."

"Give us a wave when you're to the top that you've seen the pegs 'n' can follow 'em," Green Slicker says, though it takes me the whole hill climb to turn the sounds he made into actual words that might apply to this situation. At the top, wooden stakes slashed with red head off across the tundra between tarns, bogs, and fins of upthrust granite. The fog, if possible, is thicker now, the rain harder, the storm so low and close it feels like dusk. I wave and the skipper twirls the little boat back into the breakers and down the coast, and we take off after the pegs.

"It's a cold wind," Rick shouts, "but at least it's wet."

Long before we can see the lighthouse, we hear the foghorn, every fifteen seconds it moans out into the gray. The trail follows the high spine on the west side of the island. Far below us the sea crashes and thunks into cracks and inlets, every now and then we get a glimpse through the fog of foam or wave. We are soaked through three layers of what passes in the Rockies for waterproof gear. The air smells clean and tastes good in my lungs.

We crest a hill, and the greenish white beam from the lighthouse burns one ghostly flash through the fog, and then the house itself emerges. Freshly painted red and white, it has stood on this hill in unimaginable weather since 1920.

Inside is a woman named, of all things, Madonna, who shows us to our rooms while a woman named Doris makes us tea and dries our clothes and calls us *my dears* and *my darlings*. Madonna and Doris whip up pan-fried cod and potatoes for dinner. Doris puts a hunk of ice from a growler into the pitcher of drinking water, says, "My darlings, this is as close as ye are going to get to seeing an iceberg tonight."

The foghorn calls all night and at five I am awakened by its sudden absence. I get up and go outside in my fleece and flip-flops to see the sun rising over the Sea of Labrador, the wind howling now from the north, dozens of icebergs in every direction as far as the eye can see.

" 'Tis a lazy wind," Doris calls from the porch behind me. "It won't go around you, it would rather go through you." At the sound of her voice, a shaggy fox with serious black eyes springs up the path, rolls in the grass, and runs in circles like it wants to play. This must be another of Doris's darlings. The wind dies for a moment, and just that fast the fog is back, swallowing the bergs, the sea, the top of the lighthouse, and finally the fox. I wait to hear the first call of the foghorn before I go inside.

122. Barcelona, Spain

Rick and I are charging through the massive subway station at Catalunya Place on our way to Montjuïc, on our last full day in Barcelona. In the round room near the La Ramblas exit there is a young man, skinny, big hunk of dark hair hanging over his eyes, playing the first chords of "With or Without You," and however we might feel about U2 intellectually, there is something about hearing those chords, played in that perfectly shaped space, that makes us stop to listen.

He is a fantastic musician—CD quality—says Rick. He has a very heavy Catalan accent, so heavy sometimes it seems he might not even know exactly what words he is saying, but it doesn't matter, the music is so sweet and true, the acoustics so fine in the circular room, tiled with pictures of trains and trees, birds and planes, dirigibles and sailing ships, this soulful young man knocking off Bono as well as he can be knocked off for the commuters.

We have seen plenty of street musicians in Barcelona, all of them good. The Afro-Cuban combo making everybody happy in Port Vell with the lead singer in the white hat who had the world's highest dose of charisma per cubic centimeter; the gypsy woman on acoustic guitar and the giantess on stand-up bass; the trio near the cathedral on clarinet, kora, and hang.

Rick says, "Nobody's paying attention," but he's wrong. All around us body language is changing, some people sing along, some smile and pick up their step. A few walk all the way into the tunnel toward the L1 or the L3 before realizing exactly how good the guy is and then they come back—a middle aged nurse, a tall woman in sweats, a smart-dressed business man—to lean against the wall and listen.

Three years before he killed himself, David Foster Wallace said the next twenty years would be the very best time to be alive on this planet.

The first time I saw Janine after the terrible mediation, she took both my hands, said, "Pam, really, what made you think you had to stay in that room?"

The boy in the subway plays "Where the Streets Have No Name," and "Still Haven't Found What I'm Looking For" and "One." When Rick reaches for his wallet the singer grabs his arm, tells him kindly to watch out for pickpockets. As the boy plays the first chords of "Running to Stand Still," a seventy-five-year-old Catalan woman with perfect posture, beehive hair, and an Armani suit retraces her steps across the vestibule to throw a handful of euros into his open case.

123. Taylor Fork, Colorado

When I get in the car just before daylight, the outside temp says 33 degrees, as sure a sign as any that this will be the last mushing trip of the year. One of Hinsdale County's finest lets me off with a warning ten miles south of Lake City, 48 in a 40, a stretch where the speed limit changes so many times even a local can't keep track.

We take off in Becky's smallest sled, across slush that is getting ready to thaw but hasn't yet, Becky all bundled up in the sled bag, rattling on about oatmeal cookies and astrological forecasts, and *man* the sled is squirrelly. Every time I touch the soft brake with my foot the nose of it wobbles thirty degrees to the left or right. The dogs are more het up than usual, more in shape and getting used less often. It takes less than a mile for me to dump the sled, the first time all year, though we had a near miss last week at the hard right turn in Tin Cup. That time I went down hard but managed to hold on, my shin grinding into the metal brake as I made the corner, and righted myself again. I've got a hematoma the size of a lemon to prove it.

This time, though, I get pitched clear of the sled, hit the downhill side of an ice bank nose-first, and Becky goes sailing too, though her knee catches in the sled bag, just long enough to tweak it. I knock the snow off my sunglasses and posthole over to her.

"You okay?" I say.

"I'm upside down," she says, and it's true, and she's making no attempt to right herself. It is the first time I've seen her look less than invincible, this Annie Lennox of dog mushing, and I reach out and let her use me as an anchor to spin herself around.

The dogs run on, of course, after Matt's sled, and while I help Becky hobble along the growing distance between them and us, we watch them close in on Matt at the top of the next hill. "He doesn't know yet," I say, "he doesn't know yet," as Pisces and Bella begin to nudge the back of his knees. "Now," I say, "he knows."

From our distance of more than a mile it looks effortless, though it can't be. Matt, straddling two sleds, trying to get on both hard brakes simultaneously like some kind of mad charioteer, twenty well-seasoned four-legged athletes pulling for all they are worth.

He leaves his passenger, whose name is Irene, in charge of one team and comes charging back to get us with the other. "Our hero," Becky says. Then Shredder knocks Becky over and her knee starts to hurt for real.

I don't want hurt Becky in the small sled I can't control, so Matt and I trade. The trail has been so hammered by spring snowmobilers hundred-yard stretches of it are solid speed bumps. Deep ruts alternate with ice slicks so that even in Matt's big sled I never feel far enough from the edge. Irene and I tip over once, but nothing serious, and then the runner on Becky's sled cracks and Matt has to go one-footed, and the sky gets all steely and the predicted

45-mile-per-hour winds start and that is when we decide that for three people who pride themselves on being able to read the signs, we've waited pretty long to turn around.

On the way back we go around the big hill, and I keep Matt in my virtual rearview mirror to make sure the broken runner hasn't snapped off entirely.

Back at the truck I have Irene stand on the hard brake so I can attach the gang line to the truck's bumper, and I am just snugging it down and giving Pema and Angelina pets for being such smart lead dogs when Irene says, "What's with Roja?"

I turn to see her in mid-seizure, on her side, tongue out, gasping for breath, getting none. I drop my gloves and leap over six dogs to get to her just in time to see the life fall right out of her eyes as if somebody has turned a switch. I unhook her neckline and tug line, and her head lolls to the side. I can see Matt's lead dogs rounding the last corner.

"Matt," I scream, "Roja's coding!"

"CPR!" Matt yells.

I flip her over and thump on her heart with both hands. Wait a half second, thump again.

"Harder!" Becky screams, one foot already rising from Matt's sled. Two more hard thumps and I feel a tiny half breath. All of a sudden she is back behind her eyes. It is like on a cartoon, the change is so dramatic and complete.

"Again!" Becky shouts, and I thump twice more. Then Matt is there, covering Roja's whole snout with his mouth, breathing for her. He pulls back and she takes another small breath on her own.

"I love you, Roja," he says. "I love you, Roja, come on back." She breathes again. Her tongue is still hanging out of her mouth like a dead dog, but she is here now, when a minute ago she was not.

Becky limps to the truck and Matt sits in the snow with Roja on his lap while Irene and I feed, water, and unharness both teams. After a while he sticks her tongue back into her mouth for her. He squeezes a packet of honey between her lips and she obediently swallows. By the time we have all the equipment put away, he has convinced her to eat some chicken.

124. South Berwick, Maine

There are eighteen live lobsters in Sloan's refrigerator, and our task is to make five cookbook-worthy recipes using them. She's the boss and I am happy to sit at her big butcher-block counter in her state-of-the-art kitchen and do what I am told: peel mango, slice avocado, dice onion, shuck corn.

Earlier today I threw the ball for her lab Chloe into their environmentally friendly saline pool at least fifty-five times, just for the pleasure of watching Chloe launch herself off the insurance-approved diving rock (no boards allowed) with all four legs tucked tight tight to her body, watching her hit the water and grab the ball in one motion, and then snort and fuss over to the cement stairs where she would rise, and shake, and bring the ball back to my hand.

Last week, in Provincetown, Sloan and I walked the length of the breakwater, and then swam all the way around Long Point just in time to catch the last water taxi of the day, which arrived like magic as the current swept us into the harbor, no planning on our part, no knowledge of the schedule, nowhere near enough daylight to make the five-mile walk back. A seal had popped his head up to look at us every so often while we were swimming, and the next morning, out on the *Dolphin V,* an adolescent humpback exhibited every behavior of an adolescent humpback, breeching, fin flaps, tail flaps, barrel rolls, as if he believed he was the star of his own National Geographic video, though there was no one there to watch him but us.

Last year, on that same long walk across the breakwater, Willow left behind first her sweatshirt, then her shoes and eventually even her giant purse, which contained six hundred dollars cash and her brand-new VAIO computer, which is the exact effect P-town is designed to have on anybody who is willing to let it.

Sloan asks if I think a Bahamian goat pepper would work in the lobster, avocado, and corn salad. Watching her use her knives on vegetables is like watching an aficionado play a complicated string instrument, a harp or a hammer dulcimer. Even the way she lays the chopped pepper into the bowl is less like cooking and more like dance.

My oldest and most chronic recurring dream is about a lobster, dating all the way back to grade school. My class is going on a field trip to some kind of factory lodged among the oil refineries off the New Jersey Turnpike. I get separated from the group somehow and think I can hear them above me, so I get into an industrial elevator and push the higher of the two unmarked buttons. As the doors to the elevator begin to close, a man-sized lobster squeezes through, cocks his head at me, and snaps his pincers. I know this is somehow about revenge—lobster was my favorite food even as a kid, and though I wasn't allowed it very often, though I never had to drop it into the pot myself, I had been in the kitchen more than once to hear the scream.

In the dream, though, I am something other than scared of this lobster. We stare hard at each other as the elevator travels up and up and finally bursts out the top of the warehouse, hurtling upward into the white of the New Jersey sky.

125. Mallorca, Spain

Gina is elegant as the rain in Spain and was raised on a farm in Africa. At breakfast, she cuts her eyes at me when I roll my little round of goat cheese up in the Parma ham, which I assume means she thinks I am a barbarian, until minutes later I see her do the exact same thing.

When I tell her what I thought she thought, she says, "It's the only way to eat it," and then she says, "What do you care what other people think, anyway?" It turns out we also both put strawberry jam on our white cheese slices, and that we both have had crocodiles jump into our canoes (though technically mine was a Grand Cayman), mine in Ecuador, hers in Botswana.

The volcano turned this year's Mallorca class upside down: half the writers couldn't get in and all the wine tasters couldn't get out, so the foodies are learning how to write pantoums and the writers are learning about varietals. Claire's stuck in London, which she says is heaven without any planes in the air. This morning she and Emma rode their bikes to Windsor Castle just to lie on the grass and gaze up at the wide empty sky.

Jen flew direct from the States to Madrid, and Gigi took the bus all the way to Barcelona from Frankfurt, and Freya Coquet, personal assistant to Fat Boy Slim and his wife, had a train reservation to begin with because she hates to fly. Back home in Sussex, Freya is getting a PhD in Writing for Therapeutic Purposes, and looks forward to being able to answer the phone: "Fat Boy Slim, Dr. Coquet speaking."

Every day at lunch either Rick or I steal an apple to take to the lonely donkey in the hilly pasture at the end of the lane and when we whistle to him softly we can hear him clip-clopping on his sharp little feet over the ridges of slate to meet us.

In our room with the giant square bathtub Rick asks me if I think Pony and Quinn are entitymates and I say, "I think the way it works is that Quinn and Pony are two bodies that the essences of Quinn and Pony are currently inhabiting and those essences are the entitymates."

Rick messes up the hair on the top of my head. Says, "Well, that's you and me, pardner."

126. St. John's, Newfoundland

The first night in St. John's we go to Trapper John's to get screeched in. We eat baloney, get on our knees in front of the bar, kiss a frozen cod, and learn to say, when asked if we are a screecher, " 'Deed I is, me ole cock. Long may your big jib draw."

It's an hour and a half later in St. John's than it is in Manhattan. The Newfoundlanders are the only people in the world on this time zone and they like it that way. In 1948 they voted narrowly for confederation and they say some people voted from the cemeteries. They are Newfoundlanders first, Irish (or Basque or Portuguese) second, and Canadian third—maybe—depending on how drunk they are when you ask them.

We were supposed to go to Namibia, but Rick, let's face it, is afraid of Africa, so then we were supposed to go to Greenland, but the volcano erupted and closed the airport in Reykjavík, so we wound up in Newfoundland, not unlike the sixty-five hundred people on thirty-eight planes when 9/11 closed U.S. airspace, except those people landed in Gander, and we landed in St. John's.

In 1912, it was the Marconi wireless receiver in the Cape Race Lighthouse that picked up the *Titanic*'s distress signal. All I think of when I think of the *Titanic* is Celine Dion thumping on her chest, and I didn't even see the movie, but in real life at Cape Race that night Jack Goodwin said the most famous words in shipwreck history to his stationmate: "My God, Grey, the *Titanic* has hit a berg."

Now, hiking out to Cape Race, I think, *I didn't save Rick's life any more than Sofree ruined it*, but without romantic hyperbole, how would we ever move ourselves along?

If I, for instance, go to YouTube and type in *Newfoundland* and see a series of commercials so staggeringly beautiful it becomes impossible *not* to go there; even though I know all along I'm being had by a bunch of twenty-eight-year-old hipsters living in a converted low-rise in Toronto; and when I get to the real Newfoundland it is bleak and cold and rugged—in the sense that rugged is one part wild and two parts ugly—and the people are surly and a lot of them subnormal, and I think, *In Alaska at least there would have been glaciers and grizzly bears and the midnight sun*, mightn't I also be capable of understanding that the Newfoundland I create in my mind isn't necessarily bound to either the YouTube version or the all-too-real end of a four-hundred-year-old cod fishery and the invention of all weather siding, and therefore, what would it really cost me to love Newfoundland anyway? Why not, for example, love the puffin, that stripey-beaked bird that flies like a bowling pin, because the whales, the fishermen say, are still twenty miles offshore and being slow about approaching. And when Rick says he loves Newfoundland because it is one of the few places we get to discover together, maybe that right there is reason enough.

What I'm trying to say is that some of the drivers behind my bottomless wanderlust might not be so insistent anymore. What I'm trying to say is that when you are in the good company of a man who loves Don DeLillo and the NHL, of a girl who needs you to teach her to dive and to laugh at herself, of two dogs who sing for their supper and two sweet ancient horses who lie down every morning to soak up the sun, staying home becomes more of an option.

Maybe.

Regardless, I send a whiny email to Quinn and get one back that says: *So you travel a long way to spend a few weeks in a place that resembles Buffalo, New York, where Rick is happy but you are confused, where the people are impenetrable precisely because they are not exotic. Perhaps this was always the ending you were looking for. I hope you see a whale, or if not, that is poetic in its way too. Newfoundland as the poetry of absence. Isn't that what the New Age says it wants?*

127. Fallon, Nevada

The house is full to the brim with death art, a cleaver about to pierce the skin of a concrete duck, a dead horse on its side with actual horse leg bones sticking out, a Day of the Deadesque skeleton sitting on every flat surface from side table to end table to bookshelf to fridge, tiny lighted shadow boxes full of artistic inside jokes and a bathroom painted deep purple. It is the kind of house where you think maybe after dinner the hostess will say, "And now that we have eaten, we'd like everybody to draw straws for the human sacrifice."

The hostess looks mostly sexy and only a little desperate in her red red lipstick and her flowy halter top and it's clear she can cook like a house on fire. Outside, in the yard filled with lilacs and agonized Christs, a peacock screams without ceasing.

It was always Rori, at the ranch this winter, house-sitting, when the dogs brought home some part of a dead animal. A horse leg with the shoe still on it, an entire hide of elk, three quarters of a freeze-dried coyote—so it was perfect that it was also Rori who had picked us up from the train in Reno and driven us to this house in Fallon.

The Amtrak from Denver was full of 2012 types who thought the volcano portended the end of air travel. There was a couple calling themselves *newlyweds* (after nine years, wink wink) who kissed between every sip of orange juice. There was Dartanian the musician, who used to play for a jazz band called Chase, and there was the Reno High School Band at the station, featuring the shy girl with purple hair who ripped a startlingly good version of Hendrix's national anthem.

I drive through Fallon often, on the way from Creede to Davis or back, but it is usually late and I've never stopped for anything besides gas. A few miles east of town on the way to the mines and Utah, but before you get to the giant cottonwood that people seem bent on killing with shoes, there used to be a whorehouse called Salt Wells that had a sign that terrified me about as much as anything I've seen in my life. Three little stick-figure go-go dancers that moved somehow, twisted their black and white bodies in some 1960s special effect.

I would pass Salt Wells a few times a year and shudder, say something like a prayer for whoever was inside. And then one year the sign had been shot out with a rifle, and the next year a chain-link fence went up around the place, and the next year someone must have torched it, and now the whole thing has kind of folded in on itself.

Eventually the desert will reclaim Salt Wells, will suck it right back into the earth, which proves that it is not always the bad things that last forever, and the good things that always die.

128. Creede, Colorado

It takes till May 1st but the ice finally melts. Even Deseo comes back to life.

After this winter I would amend the old saying thusly: You can lead a horse to water, you can carry a bucket of water to a horse and stick it right under his nose, you can float carrot bits on the surface of the trough, you can lie down on the ice in front of the trough and pretend to slurp up water yourself, but you cannot . . .

In March, Deseo was so dehydrated you could have pushed him over with two hands, both his back tendons were bowed and his face looked like that guru they put in the hospital in India to try to catch him in a lie. Now he gallops a quarter mile across the pasture to take a carrot from me; his coat is shiny and even his tail is growing back.

When the ranch turns green after a long cold winter the air is so clear and clean it feels like I might be hallucinating. Madison and Rick and I play Frisbee behind the hill when the wind blows and the dogs follow us out there and lie under the pine trees to watch.

In a bold innovation in coparenting, Tom and I have taken over Communication Day from Rick and Sofree, though we're allowed to contact each other any day of the week. Madison comes to the ranch for the whole month of July this year, the longest stint ever. She and Rick are building a fort down by the creek and sometimes I stand at the window and watch, impersonating a woman standing at a window and watching, thinking, *This is my family, really, it's mine.*

Hiking a roadless coastline in Newfoundland, Rick and I came upon a sign that said: *Kerley's Harbour, Resettled, 1963.* The harbor was still there, of course, heaps of rotting pine and the ghost of a fish trap curving out to the silver smile of the sea. It was only the people who were resettled, their houses famously floated on oil drums to a government-sanctioned road-accessible insta-town called New Bonaventure, a few miles up the coast. Everyone had to agree to go or nobody got the subsidies, and the jobs they were promised never came through.

Nowadays tourists come to New Bonaventure by the busload to see the former set of the popular Canadian miniseries *Random Passage,* a Hollywood re-creation of an outport that looks better than the real thing ever did, built on a site where an outpost never was. The tourists are greeted by people dressed to resemble nothing so much as extras in the now-canceled show.

When it gets dark in Newfoundland, traveling turns into a video game made by the Far Side. So many moose in so many positions, waiting to hurl themselves at your vehicle. In 1878 somebody imported two moose to Newfoundland to see what would happen and now there are 120,000 of them, poised to inherit the island when the fishermen give it up for good.

When I tell Rick's dad that it was Rick's idea to get screeched in in St. John's he says, with only a touch of derision, "See how you've loosened that old boy up?"

Among the cracked plates and copper pipes and fallen chimneys of Kerley's Harbour, Rick and I found a grave. Anna Cody (Miller) died in 2005 and was returned to the harbor by her family, the words *home at last* etched in stone.

129. Tucson, Arizona

On the hike up Pima Canyon, Fenton the human pulls out a tiny clothbound book of Shakespearean sonnets, and reads #29 and #30, while three anorexic hikers tromp by chatting about fitness classes.

We are surrounded by the radiant green of the new ocotillo, the Martian green of the palo verde. In the intermittent creek bottom, which at this moment is holding enough water to hide prizewinning trout, a single cottonwood is leafing out a green so vibrant it almost hurts to look at it. Greener still is the watercress that lines the creek bed, and desert jasmine is filling the air with its syrupy perfume.

Tucked into Fenton's Shakespeare is the printed announcement for Larry Rose's memorial, and I recognize Fenton's prose style . . . *Larry Rose was cremated in Père Lachaise crematorium and interred in the columbarium, in the city and country of his dreams, in the company of the writers he loved.*

"You wrote this," I say.

"I'm sure I did," he says.

Also tucked into the pages is an index card, with notes in Fenton's delicate hand, the ink still sharp after twenty years: *Remember to thank L's parents. Ask five students to say something about L as a teacher. Describe: L marching in SF parade, L in the Dordogne, final days in Paris.*

An hour earlier, there was an army of women coming down the trail we were going up, wielding those expensive hiking poles that take away all of one's natural balance and talking at a volume that made me think *academics*. Fenton, Rick, and I stepped off the trail to let them pass on a rather steep downhill, and one lady, perhaps the oldest in the group, paused at the bottom, and for no discernible reason toppled backwards into what in Tucson passes for a large soft bush. Five or six of the other women were on her instantly, tugging her up, which she resisted.

I was thinking, *Maybe let her get her bearings for a sec,* when one of the tuggers, a fit, fifty-year-old no-nonsense woman of Italian descent with bullet-gray hair and black eyes gestured toward the three of us and said to her group, "Can you believe that these people are just standing there gawking and not helping? Can you believe how rude they are?"

Fenton stepped forward, to apologize, I thought, but said to the woman, "Are you serious?"

"No, I was kidding," said the woman, meaning she was not.

That night we marinated ahi steaks in ginger, soy, sesame oil, garlic, and lemon in Fenton's tiny kitchen. I said I didn't think "Why I Live at the P.O." ought to be Eudora Welty's most anthologized story just so Fenton would tell me all the reasons I was wrong. Now that twenty years have gone by there will be no way to say for sure whether Fenton and I got to know each other so well in a former life or this one. The grapefruits on the tree in his side yard are the sweetest in the world.

130. Forest Grove, Oregon

In my dorm room, there is a sign over the toilet that says *Harvested Rainwater, Please Do Not Drink*, and the whole phrase is in quotation marks.

When I get up to the residency, Madison calls to tell me she set my place at the ranch kitchen table and made a silhouette of me to put in my chair while they ate.

The first day I ever met Madison, she took me up to her room and told me we were going to put on a play. I was to puppet half of her stuffed toys including a bunny, a horse, and an extra large, hideously ugly human doll called Sister, and she would puppet two dogs and an elephant dressed as a bumblebee. The plot was based roughly on *SpongeBob SquarePants*, a show I had heard of but never seen. I would make each of my toys order either a crabby patty or a hamburger, and her toys would serve me. Each character was to have at least three different names and voices so it seemed like lots of people were ordering. After two dress rehearsals we performed it for Rick. I was so far outside of my comfort zone that day it still makes my stomach turn over three years later. But I ordered and reordered crabby patties, before I had any idea what they were.

"I would lie down in front of a car for her," I tell Dorianne, over the college cafeteria lunch which generally sucks but always includes cake: red velvet, angel food, German chocolate; and Dorianne says, about her own daughter, "I would live on one saltine and a thimbleful of water for a month if it would take away her pain."

If I were a young poet, I would have woken up this morning and written a poem called "Barry Lopez, Full Moon, Dairy Queen." When we popped out from under the campus redwoods on the way to get Peanut Buster Parfaits and saw it, huge and yellow, rising over fields of strawberry and mustard, Deborah said, "Look Barry," even though I was driving and Rachel was in the backseat too, and it begged the question, could we even see the moon as he did, and the answer is probably not.

At the reading last night, Kwame said, "Whenever people say to me, 'I can't imagine what you are going through,' I say, 'Well, work on it.'"

I didn't trust it at first, the way Madison and I fell for each other. "You don't even like kids," she likes to say now, flirtatious as hell.

131. Quebec City, Quebec

There are two boxcars, one on top of the other. You enter halfway up via a sheet-metal staircase on the outside. The young woman tells us in French that we may close the door but we must not touch the walls and we must not jump up and down. At least I think that is what she said. She may have said we can't close the door, and we ought to jump up and down, but I don't think so. *C'est une expérience,* she says about six times, to make sure we don't think we have just paid her eighteen dollars expecting to climb the stairs into a rusty boxcar and see some recently discovered Monets.

The walls are covered with broken pieces of mirror, in a kind of mosaic arrangement, and where the floor of one boxcar should meet the ceiling of the other there is only steel cable stretched across what looks, because of the mirrors on the floor of the lower boxcar, like infinity. The cables run vertically and horizontally, leave squares of space just too small for our feet to fall through. The cables give a little when we step onto them and Rick takes my hand. When we look up our faces are multiplied into infinity. On both sides of us there are an infinity of Ricks and an infinity of Pams holding hands, taking careful steps across broken glass.

132. Davis, California

Back on the greenbelt, this time with Fenton the dog and Liam, big brother showing little brother the ropes. If you have spent every day of your life, as Liam has, on a ranch in Colorado, the tiniest things can impress you. Streetlights, water sprinklers, fire trucks, bicycles, roller blades. Everywhere he looks, so many people, each one of them the keeper of a potential pet.

In my undergrad nonfiction class a kid named Zachary reads an essay about his mother whipping him with a belt, cursing at him, leaving marks, and when he's finished I say, "How many of you actually got beaten as a kid?" When at least twelve of the eighteen students raise their hands, I say, "Huh. That's not the impression we have of your generation at all. We think you have parents who spent their whole days driving you to clay class and judo and start-your-own-business camp and wrote your term papers for you and never even once raised their voice."

When I went around the room on the first day of class and asked everyone what song they would take to the desert island, a kid named Daniel Liu, who went to a high school so rough all the kids called him Yao Ming even though he is only five foot one, said "Stella Was a Diver and She Was Always Down," so right at the end of class Monday I said, "I've got two tickets to Interpol tonight in San Francisco, and if Daniel wants them he can have them but if not they are up for grabs."

Daniel started furiously texting the one guy he knew with a car on campus and when his friend didn't respond I said, "Just take the tickets anyway, if you can't reach your friend come back this afternoon and I'll give you money for the train," and he smiled really big and said, "Professor, are you telling me to have an adventure?"

I love when the whole world does an end around itself, like the way all the boys in my class are writing about their broken hearts, and all the girls' stories have sentences in them like, *I fucked him with my eyes.*

When I am walking with the wolfhounds on the greenbelt,

everybody wants to remind me of their super-short lifespan, as if I wouldn't already know about it, as if I was enjoying their company in too carefree a manner, as if the value of a life ought to be measured in months and years instead of moments: Liam bounding after a wild turkey, Fenton running between two rows of durum wheat, his coat the same rich blond as the quivering sheaves, his head just tall enough to be seen above them, a giant smile on his thin black lips.

In the room with the periodic tables on the wall, Barry Lopez said we are pattern makers, and if our patterns are beautiful and full of grace they will be able to bring a person for whom the world has become broken and disorganized up off his knees and back to life. He also said discipline is the highest form of self-respect.

Back at Indian Springs with Cinder, someone has set two hundred yellow rubber ducks aswim in the giant blue pool, and you might not think rubber ducks could make you gasp at their beauty but in the late afternoon sun I assure you they can.

Last night Cinder read *The New Yorker* while I fell asleep next to her in the comfy spa bed. Of all the things I love to do with Cinder, this is the thing I love most: going to sleep being watched over by her because I know she can kick the shit out of anybody. What Cinder loves most of all is being able to read long into the night without keeping somebody awake. This is why we say we might get married to each other, after the men are dead.

Anybody trained in close reading knows there's no real difference between bravado and bravery. If we were playing *Would You Rather . . . ?* and you said, "Would you rather continue to circle the globe prophylactically collecting suicide prevention nuggets," I wouldn't even hear the second half of the question. Would it therefore be wrong to admit that part of me wants to be Rick's special girl?

For a long time I thought the object of the game was identifying the question, love versus freedom, Mandela versus Buthelezi, *leave or stay* forever ghosted under a thick curtain of oil. Nora said, *Maybe a choice isn't the right way to think of it,* by which she might have meant, *A question loses its power when there is only one answer,* as in, yes to Bhutan *and* Barstow. Yes to chanterelles *and* portobellos. A temple. *Yes.* A mosque. *Yes.* The changeable heart of a child.

Turns out after all that Truth *is* a woman. She's an Apple technician working at the Mac store, Corte Madera, her hair doesn't shimmer and she's not very nice.

On Thursday night, in front of the Baskin-Robbins, the president of the Fire University filled his mouth with kerosene, set his breath on fire, and roared like a dragon.

How did I ever think I'd get to freedom, without my arms swung open wide?

Janine said, "Swimming is a great idea, but you're also probably going to have to drown a little."

It staggers the imagination to contemplate what *Harvested Rainwater, Please Do Not Drink* might really mean.

TG #944

ONCE UPON A TIME, I decided to take Ethan around the world. It was probably an ill-advised decision. Let's just say that when I saw the email to his third most important other girlfriend two weeks before we left, the one that said, *Pam is dangling this round-the-world trip like the proverbial carrot at the end of the fishing pole,* I wished I had my $14,700 back.

We went to Paris, Bangkok, Bhutan, Perth, Alice Springs, and Sydney and I suspect that in reality, it was a pretty wretched trip, the betrayals revealed, the breakup imminent. There was likely some screaming and crying, no doubt tensions were high.

But here is what I remember: the little boy pouring himself a shower from a bucket in the labyrinthine canals of Bangkok; the sign in a café window in Geraldton that said, *Lost: Kangaroo. Beloved pet and dog's best friend,* and a number to call should the kangaroo be discovered; the middle-aged Italians singing Happy Birthday to me on the airport bus at Uluru; Ethan's smile, backlit by the sun coming through hundreds of white prayer flags on top of the Dochu La in Bhutan.

Also this pleasure: flying over the part of the globe I had not flown over before. I had flown west to Asia, east to Europe and Africa, but everything east of Germany, everything west of India, was in my imagination a big blank space.

The Thai Air 747 from Frankfurt to Bangkok traveled mostly at night, but there was a nearly full moon, and snow in the mountains. According to the computerized route map we would fly over Moldavia, Ukraine, Russia, Uzbekistan, Turkmenistan, Afghanistan, and Pakistan. I stayed up all night while Ethan slept, knowing that though life is long, and every time I get ten bucks ahead I go somewhere, this was still the best view I would ever get of many of these countries.

Afghanistan was mostly snow-covered treeless mountain ranges dotted with occasional flashes of red, possibly infrared light. I am 39,000 feet above a war, I thought, the closest I have been in my lifetime.

These days Rick wonders (aloud) if I will ever grow up enough to realize that everything I'm searching for on the other side of the world I could find just as well at my own kitchen table.

"Maybe someday," I say, cheerfully, "except that I can't."

Sofree told Madison she doesn't like to fly, the *she*, of course, being Madison, and when Madison reports the conversation to me I say "do too," and she says "do not" and I say "do too," and she says "do not" and I say "do too" and then we tickle each other. Last week she said, "I don't know what all I got from my mother, but what I got from you is not to be grossed out by things."

Madison will be nine years old next Saturday, which means I have known her for exactly one-third of her life. We get her from Sofree for twenty-four hours at five o'clock and we are taking the Amtrak up to Winter Park to play mini golf and ride the Alpine Slide, which I realize is not exactly the Orient Express but it's something.

I think about the places left to go: Mongolia, Namibia, Sri Lanka, Yemen, and have grown up enough to realize it will be good not to get to all of them. Also to recognize the two long straws I drew in the psyche lottery: I have no memory for the really bad stuff, and I've never quite understood shame.

The first time I saw the Earth get made, cool from lava, to black glass to something called Hawai'i, I didn't think I would cry but I was mistaken.

Eventually, on that long night over the parts of the globe I'll never see, the sun rose over Myanmar, and in Rangoon, where the Yangon River meets the Andaman Sea, the turrets and domes of the temples lit up as soft and gold in the early light as a fairy tale.

Acknowledgments

In the Kingdom of Bhutan, it is not enough to simply say thank you. In the language of Dzonka, a direct translation of the words used to express gratitude is, *Thank you beyond the sky and the earth.*

To the writers who gave me artistic permission for this book including but not limited to: Richard Bausch, Tim O'Brien, Fenton Johnson, Mike McNally, Mark Doty, Nick Flynn, Larry Levis, Carl Phillips, Lucy Corin, David Shields, and Toni Morrison.

To the writers who each read this manuscript at a critical time: Tami Anderson, Shannon Pufahl, Tina Watson, and Cindy Martin; and Karen Nelson, my human safety deposit box.

To the healers: Denise Platt Lichtig, Irit Schaffer, Chris Trujillo, Gyana Freund, Gerhardt Dietrich, Pam Kafer, and John Howard. Also Bhadra, Bahkta, Daryl, Aaron, Michael, Damien, and the awesome Thai masseuse at Mi Amo.

To Alane Salierno Mason for her unfailing ear, her abounding insight, and her knack for saying just the right thing at just the right time.

To Liz Darhansoff for hanging in there, Denise Scarfi for a million little things I will never even know about, Amy Robbins for her keen eye, and Matt Crosby for his optimism.

To Linda Russell, Sarah Schoentgen, Dex Decker, and others who cared for my animals while I was gone.

To the friends and students whose wisdom has touched these pages in one way or another.

To Greg and Kaeliegh Glazner for being exactly who they are and for loving me.

Thank you beyond the sky and the earth.

The author also wishes to thank the editors of the following magazines where excerpts of this book appeared in a slightly (or in some cases radically) altered form:

Ploughshares
Hayden's Ferry Review
The Iowa Review
The Idaho Review
Iron Horse Literary Review
Orion